Highland Hearts Holiday Bookshop

Tricia O'Malley

Lovewrite Publishing

"Once she knows how to read there's only one thing you can teach her to believe in and that is herself." ~Virginia Woolf

Glossary of Scottish Words/Slang

- Bit o' banter – Scots love to tease each other; banter is highly cherished
- Bloody – a word used to add emphasis; expletive
- Bonnie – pretty
- Brekkie – breakfast
- Braw – beautiful, good
- Burn – river, small stream
- Clarty – dirty
- Crabbit – cranky, moody
- Eejit – idiot
- Get the messages – running errands, going to the shops/market
- Give it laldy/laldie – do something with vigor or enthusiasm
- Hen – woman, female
- "It's a dreich day" – cold; damp; miserable
- Neeps – turnips

- Och – used to express many emotions, typically surprise, regret, or disbelief
- On you go then – be on your way; get on with it
- Scran – food
- Tatties – potatoes
- Tetchy – crabby, cranky, moody
- Tea – in Scotland, having tea is often used to refer to the dinnertime meal
- Wee – small, little
- Wheesht (haud your wheesht) – be quiet, hush, shut up

Chapter One

Rosie

"You're going to have a riot on your hands."

I eyed the line outside, where a group of determined women crowded by the door, a few going so far as to bang on the store windows. My shoulders tensed. These women were out for blood. This was a "take no prisoners" situation. I could see it in their eyes. The thrill of the hunt ran through them, and they would eat me for breakfast.

This was my worst nightmare.

I hadn't signed up for this.

I mean, I worked here, so *technically* I had. If you can call my employment via emotional manipulation from my boyfriend's family a choice. I only worked at Davidson's Discount Store because I was dating the owner's son and somehow hadn't put up a fight when they had insisted I join the family retail business after losing my job as a tech writer for a medical systems company. It was a toss-up which job had bored me more, but at least the tech writing gig had been virtual, and I had *actually* used my degree. Alas, the higher-ups had frowned on my comparing the sound of snoring to a dragon's roar to describe the benefits of a sleep apnea device. Apparently, I had a history of sprinkling in references to magickal elements far more than I'd been aware of, and I'd been quietly asked to leave with the suggestion that I stick to creative writing.

When John's family had immediately insisted I join them at Davidson's Discount—*because that's what family does, Rose*—I hadn't had the energy to say no. Frankly, I hadn't had the energy to do much, of late, and it had just been easier to go along with it when they gave me an apron and a key to the shop.

That being said, taking the easy way out was starting to look a lot like I was about to get mauled for the latest trending color of a forty-ounce water bottle. Apparently, TikTok had kicked off the need for a mustard-colored water bottle with neon pink writing on it, and for some unknown reason we were the only store in the metro area to get a shipment of them.

What had my life become?

When had I stopped caring enough to voice my opinion? To stand up for myself? Lately I felt it was just easier to say nothing because everyone else's voices had grown so much louder.

And what I really craved was the quiet.

A lovely quiet life.

Without fluorescent lighting and neon discount price stickers.

Without my bland boyfriend who I held on to because I was afraid of change. Of rocking the boat. Of doing ... anything, really. Nothing had lit me up, excited me, got my juices running, so to speak, in ages. I could feel, down to the very marrow of my bones, that I needed to make a change. But I just hadn't been able to bring myself to do it. Not yet. Maybe if I had some direction or found a passion that excited me, then I'd finally work up the courage to walk away from Davidson's Discount Store and the tedium of selling products I cared little for. *They didn't even have a book section.*

Everyone said you needed to take the bull by the horns, but have you seen bulls? They're terrifying. I was so *not* the type to wave a red flag at my future. Couldn't courage come in the form of a thousand tiny steps neatly written out on a checklist in my color-coded and indexed notebook?

I eyed the feral women outside.

Where did they get their energy? Maybe I could bottle some of it and it would make me become bold and fearsome, ready to take on the world and *Do Exciting Things* with my life. Yes, I saw that in all caps, like when I scrolled Instagram and saw everyone out *Living Their Big Lives*. Maybe I didn't need a big life, but I definitely needed a different one.

A buzzer sounded and I choked, taking a step back.

"Now, Rose, you'll want to stand here to greet everyone."

Still, he called me Rose. No matter how many times I'd asked him to call me Rosie. Even my mother had deemed me bland as an infant and had graced me with the deplorable name of Rose Withers. Getting people to call me Rosie had been a lifelong battle, but it was my small attempt at growth—like a flower reaching for sunshine instead of withering into sadness like my name suggested.

John's hand came up and squeezed the back of my neck, and I looked up at him in disbelief.

"*Greet?* John, there's no greeting. They're going to run us over and beat us over the head with their purses until they get every one of these cups. The smartest thing we can do is move out of the way and let them at it."

"But we need to tell them about our early Black Friday deals."

They don't care about your crappy deals on your crappy mass-produced crap, I wanted to shout at him. Instead, I pasted a fake customer service smile on my face and gripped my hands behind my back, digging my nails into my sweaty palms.

John's father unlocked the doors.

Crappity crap.

"Ladies, welcome to—"

Before he could finish the sentence, he was knocked to his knees by an overzealous woman sporting three totes and the single-minded determination that only a quad espresso from Starbucks could give you.

4

"Dad!" It was too late. John pushed against the crowd, but it was like trying to swim against a Tsunami. When he took a shopping basket to the crotch, I winced as he went down, a long keening noise escaping his mouth. The women behind him leapt over him, mirroring Olympic hurdlers, and thundered toward the display of water bottles.

"Right this way, ladies," I said, stepping way back and sweeping an arm out to point in the direction of the water bottle display. The idiots had placed the display at the back of the store, seeming to think that buyers would wander the shop and check out the other deals on their way to their destination. Instead, the crowd blasted past racks of Christmas decorations, Thanksgiving knick-knacks, and boxes of wrapping paper. When a display of ornaments went flying, I sighed and stepped farther back and away from the pandemonium.

I couldn't find it in myself to care about the chaos that was currently unraveling the store like someone had tossed a bouncy ball into a crystal shop. I'd quietly voiced my opinions at the staff meeting, pointing out that a ticketing system, or even just a table directly at the front of the store, would be the most seamless route to sell these bottles, but my thoughts had been immediately dismissed. As usual. It had been easier to bury my nose back in a book, nodding at the right times, than to point out how stupid they were being with their planning. Now, as John hobbled across the store to help his father off the floor, I shrugged.

I should feel bad for them. And in a loose sort of

human way, I did. I never liked to see people get hurt. But since they were both up and walking, it didn't seem like too much damage had been done, so I wouldn't waste more energy caring. Just the right amount to not make me a sociopath, I decided, and slipped further out of their sight, not wanting to hear what they'd order me to do next. Instead, I walked down a long aisle full of kitchenware and household goods, trying to ignore how the screams from the crowd sent the hair on the back of my neck standing.

I liked people.

I swear I liked people.

I just liked them in small doses.

Small *quiet* doses.

Preferably when talking about books, playing board games, or in online forums that required little face-to-face interaction. It wasn't that I was shy, necessarily, I'd just always found solace with a book in front of my face, and somehow along the way that had become a wall of sorts between me and the outside world. One which I dearly wished I could put up now, as I gingerly crept toward the shouts in the back of the store. Should I even try to do anything to help? What could I possibly say to break up a fight? I'd never even *seen* a fight in real life.

With the thought of seeing my first real fight piquing my curiosity, I picked up my pace, reaching for my phone to snap a few photos for my best friend, Jessica. She'd eat this up, that was for sure, and I could already hear her harassing me if I didn't get footage of this. She was always yammering on about going viral and whatnot, but the only viral things I cared about were advanced reader copies from my favorite fantasy authors.

Hitting record and lifting my phone, I turned the corner at the end of the aisle and entered chaos. One woman lifted her tote bag and smacked another across the face with it, while a third grabbed two of the water bottles out of the other's tote, and turning, she raised them in the air in victory. Without looking, she barreled away from the crowd.

In other words, directly at me.

I only had a moment to squeak out a warning cry before a mustard-yellow water bottle with *Boujee Bitch* written on it caught me in the eye.

And then everything went black.

Chapter Two

ROSIE

Epiphany by way of water bottle and subsequent black eye is not the way I recommend going.

Nevertheless, I suppose one doesn't get to choose such defining moments in their lives, do they? At least I didn't. But suffice it to say, when I came to, surrounded by store employees and a few shoppers who'd cared enough to stop to check on me—or in one notable case to *film* me—I finally understood that I really did need to change my life.

And just in case I wasn't fully getting the message from the universe? Well, the video of me taking a water bottle to the eye had gone viral. Much to John's and Jessica's delight.

For differing reasons.

"Babe, the store is getting so much attention for this," John said, gleefully scrolling the comments on the video while I nursed an ice pack on my eye. No concussion, thankfully, but I'd still gone and gotten checked out at the hospital. Davidson's Discount didn't have stellar health insurance, but they also weren't the least bit interested in a worker's compensation lawsuit, so John's dad had popped me in the car and taken me himself. Only when the day was over did I hear from John, when he'd shown up at my apartment an hour after Jessica had arrived.

Empty-handed, unlike my best friend. Zero text messages, unlike my best friend.

Jessica, being who she was, had arrived with ice cream, popcorn, and the promise of a *Lord of the Rings* marathon as needed. John had barely looked up from his phone since he'd walked in the door, dropping an absent-minded kiss on my forehead as he passed me and pulled a beer from the fridge.

I caught Jessica's glare from my one good eye.

"*Break up with him.*" She mouthed this to me, while his back was turned.

It was a familiar refrain, one I'd largely ignored because breaking up with him would also mean breaking up with my job, and despite hating working at the store, I enjoyed having money to pay my bills. Just a small catch-22 there.

I pressed my lips together. Every other time Jessica had insisted I break up with John, I had pushed her off, not ready to make that call. But today? Well, let's just say, as phones pinged with more incoming notifications about the viral video of me going down, I didn't want to play nice anymore.

I *hated* working at that store.

And John was a distraction at best.

I'd been treading water in my life for too long.

"John?"

John looked up from his phone. He was an average-looking man, nearing his thirtieth birthday, with the beginnings of a slight paunch. A beige boyfriend for bland Rose Withers. Suddenly I wished desperately for the courage that my romance heroines had in their fantasy books.

"Yup, what's up?"

"Don't you want to know if I'm okay?"

"I already know. Dad said you were fine."

"She's got a black eye the size of my hand forming," Jessica said, lifting her chin at him. "That is not okay."

"I mean, I know it's not great. But it's just a bruise, isn't it?" His eyes drifted back down to his phone, and he grinned.

Jessica turned back to me, widening her eyes.

"You didn't bring me anything." I enunciated clearly and raised my volume, just to make sure he heard me.

John looked back up, squinting for a second as he thought about my words.

"Um, you didn't ask me to, did you? Maybe I missed a text. My phone's been blowing up."

"No, just like, something thoughtful. Because I was hurt today. It was traumatic, John. I was knocked unconscious, *John.*" I emphasized his name to keep him focused on me and not returning to his phone.

"Yeah, but you're fine. Stop making this a bigger deal than it is." John rolled his eyes as though I was as hysterical as the mob that had fought in his store earlier that day. I pressed my lips together and took a deep breath through my nose for courage. This was now unavoidable.

"Please leave."

"Okay." John shrugged one shoulder, still scrolling his phone. "If that's what you want."

"And don't ever come back," I clarified, finally catching his attention.

"You're breaking up with me?" This time when he looked up, confusion crossed his face. It was the same look he'd given me when we'd run into each other at Trader Joe's reaching for tiny bags of dark chocolate peanut butter cups. I'd thought it was a fun meet-cute. Turns out that was the most fun we'd ever really had in our relationship. John was obsessed with watching and betting on sports—all sports—and I didn't know a rugby ball from a golf stick. Or club. Whatever they were called.

We'd fallen together more so out of casual interest and then the pattern of hanging out had just stuck. At least we hadn't progressed to moving in together. I'd kept my little apartment that I'd had since I'd graduated university six years ago, with a degree in literature and creative fiction and no clue how to use it. The timing had been crap, per usual in my life, as we'd hit a recession and there wasn't much work for a nerdy Lit grad whose people skills extended to asking new acquaintances if they dog-eared the pages of their books or used bookmarks. What? That said a lot about a person, in my opinion.

"I am."

"What? Why?"

"Because you're an insensitive prick who has never been the type of partner that a beautiful and smart woman like Rosie deserves. From day one you've ignored every one of her needs, putting yourself first over and over, and finally, she's seeing the light. Don't let the door hit you in the ass on your way out."

"Oh sure, you'll listen to her, over me?" John finally showed an ounce of annoyance, pointing at Jessica. The two had never gotten on well, with Jessica hating how little attention he paid me, and John bothered with how much of my time I gave to Jessica. But when it was a toss-up between blindly watching sports or hanging with my best friend, Jessica usually won out. I suppose that should have told me what I needed to know, but I'd just reassured myself it was okay to have different hobbies than my boyfriend. It was fine until it wasn't, which had happened long ago. Again, I'd just sort of molded myself into this pattern to the point I didn't really recognize who I was anymore.

Getting smacked in the face with a forty-ounce aluminum water bottle had a way of waking one up to the faults in their life, I guess.

"Please leave."

"You know you'll be out of a job, right? My parents will never keep you on if we're broken up."

"Even better." Jessica, my knight in shining armor. "She's too smart for that job anyway. Now get out before I make you get out."

John stormed from the apartment, the door slamming on its hinges, and I blew out a breath, my eyes still closed. He hadn't even put up a fight. What did that even say about our relationship? Taking a deep breath, I took inventory of my emotions to see if this was really going to shake my world or not.

"Rosie? You okay?"

"Yeah, I am. I really am. I should have done that a long time ago."

"As I've been telling you." Jessica was positively cheerful at this point. Clapping her hands, she stood. "Out of all your bland boyfriends, he has to have been the worst. I think you're regressing."

"Bland is safe."

"Bland is boring." Jessica put her hands on her hips and glowered down at me. "When are you going to give love a chance? Real, honest, earth-shaking love? Because you just broke up with a boyfriend and barely batted an eye as he left the building. I don't even see a sheen of tears there."

I squinched up my face and tried to pretend I was sad.

"Don't even try." Jessica pointed a finger at me. "You need to get over your hang-ups about love. The right man is going to make you revise your opinion."

"Love is for my romance novels, Jess. Not for me."

"You can't keep letting your mother's choices determine your path."

"Hardly," I scoffed, grabbing a throw pillow to hug at my chest. My mother was flighty, irresponsible, and fell in love with someone new every week. I'd had a revolving door of stepfathers before I could even crawl. "Maybe I'm just waiting for my knight in shining armor."

"Well, you're sure as hell not finding him at Davidson's Discount Store. Now, do you think you can have a drink? This calls for a celebration, and I brought G&Ts."

"I don't have a concussion and I don't have to work tomorrow, so I don't see why not."

"Even better. I'll get glasses. I brought supplies with me just in case you needed it, unlike your dumbass ex-boyfriend. God, I love saying that. Ex-boyfriend. Finally! Oh, by the way, I brought your mail because there was an envelope too big to fit in your mailbox. What did you order from Scotland?"

"Scotland?" I sat up from where I'd reclined on the couch and gingerly took the ice pack off my eye. "Nothing that I know of."

"There's an important looking mailer from Scotland with your name on it."

"No kidding?" I pursed my lips, thinking. "My mother's side has some family in Scotland, if I remember correctly. But otherwise, not much that I can think of."

"One way to find out." Jessica plopped on the couch next to me, wincing as she looked at my face. "I'm going to suggest you don't go out in public for a while."

"That bad?" I sighed.

"I mean, it's not great. We can try some makeup on it tomorrow." She handed me an icy gin and tonic and then bent over to pick up the envelope off the coffee table. Depositing it on my lap, she clinked her glass against mine.

"What are we celebrating? Me losing my job or me getting a gigantic black eye?" I touched it gently, wincing at the pain that ran down my face.

"To new beginnings."

"I'll take it. To new beginnings." I took a sip of the cocktail before handing it back to her and lifting the envelope. "Hmm. Hefty. I wonder what this is."

"One way to find out."

I ripped the top off the envelope and slid a thick stack of papers out that looked a lot like a contract. Squinting, I tried to make sense of the words.

"Here, you read it. It's hard to focus with just one eye. I think this is from a solicitor."

"Ohhh, the plot thickens." Jessica grabbed the papers and began to read out loud.

"'Dear Ms. Withers—'"

"Oh jeez, that sounds so formal."

"'We are writing today to inform you of an inheritance.'"

Jessica and I both squealed.

"A what?" I gasped.

"Your great-aunt Moira MacDouglas has left you her bookshop in Kingsbarns, along with a yearly stipend to operate it. To claim your inheritance in full, and to have the property transferred to your name, you'll need to run the bookshop for one full year of operations. Please contact me after you have reviewed the enclosed contracts and advise on your decision regarding this inheritance. Should you choose to not accept it, we'll move on to next of kin."

"Holy shit," I breathed, dropping my head back on the couch, my heart pounding in my chest.

A year in Scotland.

A year running a bookshop in Scotland.

It was like, all of my dreams come true. At once.

"Say you'll do it." Jessica was bouncing on the couch, clutching the papers in her hands.

"But what about my apartment ... you ... all this?"

"You're month-to-month on the lease here. And let's be honest, it's not a great apartment."

I looked around at my shoebox apartment. No matter how many paintings I hung on the walls or rugs I threw on the floors, it was threadbare at best. I'd only stayed because the rent was cheap, and I wasn't the best at change.

"It's not, I know. But it's all mine." After sharing an off-campus house with chaotic co-eds at university, this apartment had become my sanctuary in the first year after I'd graduated. Never once did I come home to random men in the kitchen or the remnants of an all-night rager all over the house or in the bathroom. Maybe, at some point in the last few years, it had also become my hidey-hole from social activities.

"And I'll come visit. You know I'm killer at finding travel deals."

It was true, too. Jessica was one of those that lived *A Big Life* on social media, constantly jetting off to exotic locales. I'd joined her once, on a trip to Mexico, and I had to admit—we'd had a blast. But then my student loan payments had kicked in and the discount store didn't exactly pay top dollar to their employees, let alone a healthy vacation package. I'd been stuck here for the last two years with no fancy umbrellas in my cocktails.

Now, it seemed it was finally my turn.

"I want to do it." I rushed the words out before I could change my mind or make a list of a thousand reasons why this might be a bad idea.

"Yes!" Jessica pumped her fist in the air. "Finally. Go live your life, Rosie. Seriously. This is so absolutely perfect. It's like you made room in your life for a new opportunity by kicking John out and, boom, here it is. I love how the universe works sometimes."

I didn't roll my eyes, because I was used to Jessica's woo-woo stuff, but I was far too pragmatic to think that this had all happened on the same day for a reason. If life worked that way, I would have signed with a literary agent the moment I graduated university and published a bestselling book by now.

"Scotland." I picked up my glass and drank deeply, excitement fizzing inside me like the sparkles in gin and tonic.

"It's going to be amazing. Life-changing. I can see it now. You might even meet a man in a kilt."

I craned my head to look at Jessica.

"Why would I meet a man in a kilt?"

"Because statistically speaking you're more likely to meet a man in a kilt in Scotland than anywhere else."

"Yeah, but it's not like they run around in them every day. Do they?" I wrinkled my nose as I thought about it. I truly had no clue the kilt-to-man ratio in Scotland, let alone the day-to-day occurrence of wearing said traditional garments.

"We can only hope. You can pick yourself up a Scottish McHottie and run your own bookstore."

"I'm not picking up any hottie." I pointed my finger at her. "My judgment can't be trusted."

Jessica pursed her lips as she thought about it.

"Granted your past doesn't speak highly of your decision-making abilities when it comes to romantic partners."

"John wasn't as horrible as you made him out to be."

"John was tepid on a good day. He'd never even read Tolkien or watched *Game of Thrones*. I wonder what you two even had to talk about?"

"I did get him to watch *Schitt's Creek* with me."

"Hmm, I'll give him half a point for that."

"But then he said he didn't like how Moira spoke." Remembering that comment now, I realized I should have broken up with him on the spot. Jessica gasped, holding a hand to her chest, offended.

"How *dare* he. Moira Rose, nae, Catherine O'Hara is a national treasure."

"I know. I think that was the beginning of the end."

And that was week eight of a two-year relationship. Good God. I took another sip of my cocktail and held the cold glass against my throbbing eye.

"Also, your aunt's name was Moira too. I mean ... could this be even more perfect? Ugh, just think of all the hotties. I want you to be bathing in men."

"That sounds awkward at best. I can barely fit in a bathtub, let alone adding copious amounts of men to the equation." It was true too. Blessed with a body that fashion magazines liked to call "curvy" when they really meant fat, bathtubs and I were not usually on speaking terms. I preferred it when the hot water actually covered my knees and breasts.

"We'll just make you a list. Like a dos and don'ts list for picking men. Or a wish list of sorts."

"Damn it, Jess. You know I love a good list." They were so neat and orderly, and I always got a little dopamine hit when I crossed an item off.

"That I do." Jessica squealed and jumped up from the couch. "I'll get paper and pens."

I closed my one good eye and sighed, letting her have her fun. It was how she would handle me leaving the country, if she felt like she had some sense of control over my future. And knowing me, this would be the first of about seventy lists I'd likely make before my departure arrived. A soft thrill of anticipation worked through me.

My departure.

I was going to do this.

It was time for me to live *My* Big Life.

Chapter Three

"**B**loody hell."

I dropped my binoculars from where I was watching for the arrival of the snow buntings on a particularly drizzly gray day at the beach in Kingsbarns. Icy wind buffeted me, bringing the salty sting of the sea with it, and angry clouds hugged the horizon. I was waiting for the telltale sign—the flash of white wings against a moody winter sky—as the first sign of the holiday season arriving. I'd always likened the snow bunting's winter call to Christmas bells, a bit of nostalgia from my mother, I supposed, who'd dragged me to this beach year after year to look for these cute birds.

She'd loved Christmas, and even when the birds arrived some years as early as the end of September, she'd taken it as her cue to start decorating for the season. While I didn't decorate, or carry on much with any traditions, really, I still went to look for the snow buntings. The males always arrived first to set up their territories before the females, and my mother would note how nice it was they'd care for their partners. Hearing their call reminded me of her laughter, both a gentle note on the wind, and it was my way of honoring her memory. But now, I had a bigger problem on my hands than my grief.

Across the wide expanse of damp sand, a puffin was struggling ashore, which was all sorts of wrong. He should be out to sea, not clambering onto the beach with one wing askew. This could only mean one thing: he was hurt and needed help to survive. Without an ability to dive for food, he stood little chance of survival. Racing to my car, I grabbed a soft towel and strode quickly back to where I'd seen the wee puffin fighting.

It squawked at me as I approached, hopping away with one wing bent, but I just tossed the towel lightly over it and scooped it up before it could struggle much more. I didn't want the poor thing to be in more pain than necessary, and I made soothing noises as I held its body secure and made my way to the car.

Two hours and one vet visit later, my new puffin friend and I were eyeing each other in my back garden.

My friend Niall, a vet, had not been optimistic about the bird's ability to return to the wild, but one could hope. Something had clipped the puffin's wing, and time would tell if a good molting would change his future. Whether the puffin ever flew again was another matter entirely, but for now, the wee bird should be out of pain and was healthy enough.

He was young.

With just two grooves on his bill, he was likely just over four years old and nearing when he'd first start looking for a mate. Now, it looked like he'd be spending the winter in my backyard, unless I could find a bird rehabilitation center that could take him in. In the meantime, my heart quite simply couldn't handle the alternative—to euthanize him—so he'd come home with me in a carrier and now we had to figure out what to do with each other.

The first of which was trying to build an enclosure that would keep the wee lad safe from any predators, as well as keep him from wandering away while I was out. The second? I'd need to make a stop at the fishmonger to make sure he was well fed.

I should name him.

The puffin eyed me, turning his head back and forth, and scraped one of his webbed feet on the bottom of the carrier.

Of course. They liked to burrow. I should try to make him a makeshift burrow and then maybe a pool of sorts so he could still be in the salt water. Luckily, I had the perfect back garden for this sort of thing. My house was set just behind the sand dunes that overlooked Kingsbarns Beach, and one of the selling points, at least for me, was that a low rocky cliff edge narrowed to a point where salt water trickled through craggy rock piles to form a wee wading pool of sorts. It was tiny, no more than three to four meters across both ways, but if I could figure out how to fully enclose it, the puffin could have a wee paddle about, maybe even catch a few minnows that snuck through when the tide was high.

The puffin rattled its bill at me, clearly wanting to be let out of the carrier.

"Not yet, lad. I have some work to do."

Luckily, I had a shed full of miscellaneous building materials, as part of the cheap price on this seaside cottage had been its desperate need for repair. I'd spent the last three years shining it up, and it was almost finished. I hadn't planned to basically become a builder in my downtime, but I had to admit, it suited me. I'd learned that I quite liked working with my hands, and every project had been a reason to expand my knowledge. Between YouTube videos and trips to the bookshop, I'd been well equipped with tools to teach myself how to build.

Except the bookshop had been closed for almost a year now, requiring me to stop at the shop in St. Andrews to source my materials, and I had to admit I missed my wander down to Two Sisters for a cup of coffee before my stop at Highland Hearts, our local bookshop in Kingsbarns. A frivolous name to be sure, but the owner, Moira, had been anything but staid.

"I've got a plan for you," Moira had always singsonged to me when I'd seen her at the shop, swirling by in a swath of frilly skirts and bright jumpers, several reading glasses caught in her bird's nest hair. She'd never gotten around to telling me what her plan was, and I supposed I should have expressed more interest at the time. Frankly, she'd intimidated me. She'd decorated the shop for every holiday, and it had been practically a social hour whenever I'd gone in there. At the very least, it had forced me to interact with people outside of my colleagues and my students, and slowly I'd grown to be on a first-name basis with many people in the small village. I tried to avoid the bookshop on Thursdays, when an equally terrifying group of women, the Book Bitches, descended upon the store wearing punny T-shirts and doling out life advice left and right.

I'd narrowly escaped their ruthless attempts at matchmaking, and it had taken me the year since the store had closed to recover from being questioned about if I would wall slam a woman or if I was more of a "take it slow" kind of lad. Even now, I flushed at the thought. I'd had to go home and look up wall slam to see if it had meant exactly what I'd thought it had meant and then had lost an hour of my time to some dirty videos on the internet that left me taking a cold shower and clearing my browser history.

And to answer the question, it appeared I was both.

Not that I'd ever tell the Book Bitches that.

They needed to stick to their book club, and not to matchmaking. The last thing I needed was a woman in my life. One divorce had been enough and at the ripe old age of thirty-four, I was happy for my space.

By the time I'd finished gathering materials to build a pen for the wee bird, made up of chicken wire, two-by-fours, and piles of rocks and fresh grass for a burrow next to the wading pool, I had just enough time to go get him some food from the fishmonger before they closed. Torn between leaving him in the carrier, or bringing him with me, I did what any logical bird-loving man would do. I took him with me. What if he wanted to pick out his own fish?

Right, I probably wasn't allowed to take a bird into a fishmonger, what with health and safety rules, and maybe being a hermit was getting to me if I thought that was acceptable behavior. Either way, the bird sat in his kennel on the front seat and eyed me through the door.

"I promise, you'll be happy with our next stop."

The bird rattled at me, gnashing its beak together to likely tell me what a jerk I was, but that was probably due to hunger. There was no way he'd been diving for food with that clipped wing of his. Once at the fishmonger, a tiny shop outside Kingsbarns, I rolled the window down to let in the cool air.

"I'll be just a minute. I promise."

The puffin made that chattering sound again and I rushed inside, not wanting him to hurt himself more by going crazy in the wee kennel in my car.

"Hiya, Alexander, how's it going then?"

"All right. So, I've rescued a puffin, and it looks like they eat herring. Do you have any I can feed him?"

The fishmonger nodded. "Sprat too. Their favorite are the sand eels, but we can't get those. I'll get you sorted."

I liked this fishmonger. No long chats or intrusive questions about my life, he was all business. I was in and out in just a few minutes and happy for it as the puffin was making increasingly annoyed sounds from my car.

"I'm here. I'm here." I held the bag up like the bird had any idea what I had. But at least it stopped its complaining. "All right, you're probably starving. How about a wee snack to tide you over on the drive?" Digging in the bag, I unwrapped one of the packets marked herring, immediately berated myself for opening fish in the car as the smell filled the air, and the puffin danced closer to the door of the carrier.

"Here. Try this." I slipped a fish through the door, and he snapped it up so fast I drew my finger back. "So you are hungry."

I fed him a few more through the gaps in the cage door and then started the car, humming all the way home.

Next time the Book Bitches cornered me about my love life, I could tell them I *had* taken a bird home. Snorting, knowing that very few would find me funny, I glanced at the puffin who seemed to regard me with a much friendlier look in its eyes.

"Well, mate. Shall we find you a name?"

Chapter Four

ROSIE

Scotland? You've never even left your hometown.

Running a bookstore? You need real business acumen for that.

Meeting new friends? That means you'll have to actually talk to people.

Dating? Nobody will be as good as sweet John.

No, those weren't my insecurities in my head beating me up on the long flight to Scotland. Those were actual comments John and his family made when I'd picked up my last paycheck. Why they still hadn't figured out direct deposit, I do not know, but I was forced to do the walk of shame to the back office to pick up my check while the other employees eyed me either with envy or scorn. It was hard to tell when I refused to make actual eye contact with anyone. There, John and his family had descended on me, picking apart my plans to move to Scotland all while I'd sidled closer to my employee mailbox and tried to retrieve my check. There wasn't a word of praise or thanks or support between all of them, not that I was surprised. But it would have been nice for the ego to think I'd be missed. *I was good at my job. Their loss.* However, I didn't stoop to their baiting, though it had taken a level of control that even I wasn't aware that I had, and somehow, I'd managed to leave the store without burning it down behind me. I hear arson charges make it hard to board an international flight.

The flight and the subsequent taxi ride to Kingsbarns seemed anticlimactic at this point. They'd both gone smoothly, and even though I'd never flown internationally before, I'd researched the process thoroughly and had made enough lists to guide me through the experience. Now, pleased that I'd navigated things fairly well thus far, even with jet lag, I let out a little sigh of relief as the sign for Kingsbarns came into view. The taxi drove about another block after the sign and pulled to the side of the road.

"This is Kingsbarns. The shop is down that wee lane."

I blinked at the village that seemed to stretch a few blocks at most. Whirling, I looked out the back window where the rain misted down in fine sheets. This ... this was the town? Surely there had to be more to it than this.

"Is this ... it?" I asked, leaning forward in my seat until the seatbelt stopped me. I'd been so consumed with packing my apartment, travel research, and making sure my passport arrived in time that I hadn't looked up much about Kingsbarns. A mistake on my part, it seemed, as this place was tiny. How would a bookshop even prosper in such a small town? Biting my lower lip, I tried to quell the rising panic that put me in a chokehold.

"Aye, this is the main bit. There are plenty of cottages on farmland and whatnot spread out around here as well." The driver turned and indicated the card machine for payment before popping out of the front door and rounding to the trunk for my luggage. I slipped my card in the reader, trying to do a quick calculation on the dollars to pounds conversion, and then froze when there was no option to tip on the reader. Easing the door open, I winced at the icy wind that sliced across my face.

"Sir, there's no spot for a tip?"

"Aye, nae bother, hen."

I blinked up at him, my mind taking a moment to digest his words through his thick accent. Had he called me hen because I was round? Or was it because my hair fell somewhere between brown and copper? Maybe it was both. Maybe I looked like a fluffed out broody hen in my rumpled sweatsuit and likely untidy hair.

"I feel bad," I explained, and the man gave me a quick smile.

"Americans do love to tip. It's appreciated, but not necessary."

"Okay." Right, I'd read about this, it just went against my very nature not to tip. Sighing, I resigned myself to accept the situation since I hadn't had time to break the hundred-pound note I had tucked in my wallet for emergencies. I hadn't wanted to travel with too much cash on hand, and I'd been told ATMs were readily available in Scotland. Though, looking around this small village, I wasn't certain I would find one easily. I made a mental note to investigate buying a car or a bicycle, some sort of transportation, and grabbed my suitcases. Following the taxi driver's directions, I stepped into the road with my luggage.

A horn sounded.

I screamed, tripping and falling in a puddle on the sidewalk. The car continued past, and I stayed on all fours for a moment, catching my breath. My shattered reflection, broken by drops of rain, peered back at me in the puddle. Not an ideal start. And I realized that not only was I dangerously close to tears, but I was also making a fool of myself. Sniffing, I stood and wiped the dirt from my pants the best that I could, and immediately saw my mistake as another car whizzed past.

Like a fool, I'd looked the wrong way crossing the street and had almost gotten myself killed two seconds into my adventure. Must be rush hour here. *My Big Life* had very much almost become My Short Life due to stupidity. Well, that and jet lag. Taking a deep breath to steady myself, and wiping the rain from my face, I crossed the road with care toward the narrow lane that the driver had indicated. Too small for a car to pass through, and lined with cobblestones, the street seemed to be from another world entirely. Pushing my emotions down, I tried to focus on the good—as though I was my very own main character in a fantasy novel. Maybe around the corner I'd find a castle and—

I screamed again as I rounded the corner and slammed face first into a brick wall.

Well, not exactly.

More like a very muscular chest that might as well have been a brick wall. Tripping as I scrambled back, mumbling apologies, strong hands gripped my arms and caught me before I fell to the ground once more.

"Careful there, lass."

Oh. My. God.

I swear my insides melted into one puddle of gooey liquid lust as I blinked up at this gorgeous man with dark hair and piercing blue eyes. Helllllo, *Outlander*. Hell yes, I'd binged that series with Jessica before I left, preparing myself for any and all magical encounters that I might have in Scotland. And this man ... this man who might as well have walked off a movie set had just called me "lass" and was looking at me with ... well, it wasn't desire, that was for sure. More like concern that he'd run into a serial killer on his way to ... wherever hot men like him went in this small town. Which, of course, I'd need to figure out where that spot was once I'd recovered my ability for speech. Just for observational purposes, of course.

"Lass? Are you bleeding?" Oh my God, he was leaning closer, was he going to kiss me? My heart rate picked up and my lips parted. I let out a breathy little laugh like I was some damsel in distress needing rescuing, which, by the way, I was not. I was meant to be the warrior, not the damsel, according to my novels. I blinked when he brushed at my cheek.

"Bleeding?" I squeaked out and then looked down at my hands. I'd scraped the palm of one of them when I'd fallen in the puddle mere seconds ago in my other already forgotten embarrassment. Had he seen that? "Oh, I scraped my palm. Oh no, I'm sorry. Did I get blood on you?" I leaned closer to peer at his jacket, and he took a step back.

Because of course he did.

The man had no idea who I was, and here I was putting my nose to his chest while dripping blood.

"Nae bother. It's waterproof." The man shrugged off my concern and I wanted to linger here, in this icy rain, which was beginning to penetrate my very core, and find out more about this handsome stranger on the street. Because, I mean, that's how it was supposed to work, right? I'd run into him, we'd make a fun joke, and then before you know it, we'd be skipping across the fields and reading books together with a pot of tea between us. Caught up in the fantasy, I beamed up at him, fluttering my eyelashes a bit, the blood and dirt on my face already forgotten.

The man moved and I did too, thinking, again, that maybe he was coming in for a kiss. When my lips met his shoulder as he tried to angle around me to get past me on the sidewalk, I realized my grave error.

Seriously, how jet lagged was I? This had to be the most awkward thing I'd ever done. I was blaming Jessica for this one. She was the one who'd gotten me all wound up about finding my perfect man in Scotland, and no matter how many times I told her that I couldn't be trusted to pick a good match for myself, let alone believed in true love, she'd somehow managed to get in my head.

To the point where I was imagining romantic kisses in the rain with random Scottish strangers.

Instead, I'd basically assaulted the poor man as he tried to get past me. He looked down at where my lips had met his shoulder, his eyes rounded in shock, and then we both did that awkward little dance when you were trying to get around someone on the path, but you both moved in the same direction at the same time.

Finally, the man gripped my shoulders.

"Stay." It was an order. *I'd sit up and beg if this man ordered me to.* I swallowed, my throat thick with nerves.

He walked around me, freeing the path. When I looked over my shoulder, he was glancing back at me.

"Are you lost then?" He was still walking away from me, and I couldn't blame him, not after that embarrassing stunt I'd just pulled.

"Nope. All good. Thanks." I jabbed a thumb over my shoulder. "Just off to the bookstore."

At that, he stopped walking.

"It's closed."

"Oh, yeah, I know. It's just that it's, um, mine now, I guess. Well, kind of. If I stay the year. See I inherited ..." I trailed off as the man tilted his head at me. Of course he wasn't asking me for my life story. "I'm fine. Everything's fine. Have a great night. Sorry about the, you know ..." I waved my hand in the air and then, because I apparently couldn't be trusted to speak, let alone cross a street safely, I grabbed my suitcases and all but ran down the lane. Barely noticing the charm of the narrow cobblestone path, or how it spilled out onto a large swatch of green with a single stone cottage, I almost kicked the empty flowerpot over to get to where the solicitor had told me the key would be.

My hands trembled, from cold or nerves I couldn't be sure, and the key slipped a few times before I got the door open and dragged my two large suitcases in behind me. Slamming the door, I stood with my back to it and took a few shaky breaths.

I was scared to open my eyes.

I'd been so fixated on this one goal, this one new huge thing, this *Big Life* that I was going to live, that I wasn't ready to see if I'd royally screwed up by accepting this inheritance. My great-aunt Moira, apparently from my mother's side, had wanted me to have this. It appeared she'd been trying to get in touch with me over the past few years, but my mother, fickle and hare-brained that she was, had never bothered to open her mail.

Who didn't open their mail?

The same woman who had met my father at the wedding she'd crashed with her best friend, had a one-night stand, and had never bothered to get his name. The same woman who picked up and followed a band, or a new hobby, for an entire summer at a time, largely forgetting her teenage daughter left to fend for herself. The same woman who was currently somewhere in South

America on an ayahuasca retreat to rid herself of all her traumas.

I hadn't even known she'd left until I'd received a postcard two weeks later. It was always like that with her, and she'd flit in and out of my life like a hummingbird, and I'd come to regard her as more of an absentminded sister than a mother who offered any real guidance in life. So, no, it wasn't a far reach that Moira hadn't been able to find me. But it was sad that I'd never been given a chance to meet any of my kin. It wasn't like my mother had been much for family, and I'd never met my grandparents either. Nevertheless, it had all checked out, once I'd had a lengthy call with a very kind solicitor who I'd wanted to ask if he'd be willing to adopt me as his granddaughter, and now here I was.

In Highland Hearts, dripping rain, dirt, and blood likely everywhere, my eyes screwed so tightly shut that my cheeks hurt from the tension.

This is not what the main character would do in your fantasy novel.

At that, I steeled myself and opened my eyes.

Oh, ohhhhh. Tears did spring to my eyes this time.

It was, quite simply, perfectly imperfect.

I wasn't sure I would have been able to handle it if the shop had been all glossy and sophisticated. But no. No, *this* was a shop that a heart could warm to. Give me curious corners cluttered with odds and ends and nooks piled high with pillows and stacks of books over sleek and pristine any day. A bookshop should be a discovery, an adventure of sorts, and Moira, it seemed, had understood that. A single lamp had been placed on a mahogany table with a red leather high-back chair tucked behind a vintage cash register. The lamp, with a fringed shade and holes cut in the fabric to resemble stars, beamed warmth into the shop. A beacon of welcome. I crossed slowly over to the table Moira must have used as her check-out counter. A note, along with a small bottle of whisky and a tin of shortbread cookies, sat beneath the lamp.

Welcome to Kingsbarns, Rosie. I've turned the heat on, and you'll find your wee flat at the back of the shop. The village is looking forward to having the shop open once more. We hope you'll make a happy home here. Regards, William Stuart.

The solicitor had been kind enough to leave a welcome gift for me. I smiled gently, trailing a finger over the table, noting that I'd still need to give the place a solid clean. Next to the note was a stack of leather-bound notebooks, which I assumed would be Moira's ledgers, and I would make sure to dive into those first thing tomorrow. But first, I needed to get my bearings. Things needed to be done in order, of course, and I couldn't just jump into running the business when I hadn't even unpacked, could I? Reminding myself that I'd made a list of tasks to accomplish on my arrival, I pulled out my phone and scanned my next task.

Unpack, shower, make sure all the doors were locked.

I hadn't exactly budgeted time in my list of to-dos to wander around the shop in awe, dreaming over all the curiosities I was sure to uncover.

But I was the boss now. Surely, I could just give myself a moment to explore. The shop was just too charming to breeze right past it and put my clothes away.

"Just a few moments. Then I'll get back on schedule." Jessica would be kicking me right now, likely dragging me back out in the rain to try and find more hot Scotsmen, and as if on cue my phone rang. Answering, I beamed as Jessica gaped at me.

"What happened? You're all dirty."

I'd already forgotten my fall in the puddle with the distraction of my new shop.

"It's nothing. I fell in a puddle. And then ran face first into the finest man I've ever seen in my life. Covered in blood and dirt. But never mind that. Look, Jess, just look!" I turned the camera around on my already blabbering best friend, stopping her questions with a view of the shop as I walked around. The bookshop was essentially one big room, but bookshelves created a maze of sorts so every time you turned a corner there was a new little nook to be discovered. Vintage chairs upholstered in turquoise and mustard flower fabric were tucked into one corner beneath a window piled high with books, a lamp, and vases of dried flowers. In another corner, a disco unicorn head was mounted on the wall, and velvet floor poufs to curl up and read on were scattered on a faded jade oriental rug.

"Oh my God," Jess breathed. "You're never coming back, are you?"

"It's incredible, Jess. Just like … look." I held the phone up to show the stone walls and thick beams that crossed the ceiling. "The building itself has to be from the 1800s."

"I wonder if it is haunted."

"I could only be so lucky." I loved ghost stories, which in turn fueled my love for fantasy and paranormal romance, and I'd always secretly wanted to experience a ghostly encounter in real life.

"Only *you* would wish that. Seriously though, I need you to back up and tell me about that man. And why you aren't currently having a drink with him somewhere. Did he meet any of the criteria on our list?"

"You mean the man I bled on and then accidentally kissed on the shoulder? The one who practically ran away from me? That one?" I was going to ignore her comment about the list we'd made for the type of man I was looking for in my life. As noted before, I couldn't be trusted to pick a man for myself.

"I mean, yes, I suppose that doesn't make for a great start. But hey, at least you know there are hot men in town."

"One. There is one hot man in town. And based on the size of this place, likely the only one." I sighed and pointed out the window. "There are like, twelve buildings total here."

"Ohhh, even better. Small towns give you a great opportunity to meet new friends. Like sexy men to *acci-*

dentally shoulder kiss." Jessica's laugh sounded through the shop.

A book fell at my feet.

I jumped back, looking up at the shelf above my head. All the books were neatly shelved, even though they didn't look to be in any discernible order. But the books on the shelves? Neatly tucked away. None hanging haphazardly or wildly askew. I looked from the shelf to the book on the floor and back, Jessica's ramblings just a murmur in the background.

Hmm. That was odd.

"Hey, Jess. I'm absolutely dead on my feet and want to get out of these wet clothes. Can I call you once I'm all unpacked and tucked in?"

"Absolutely. Gah! I'm just so excited for you. Keep me posted on everything, including sexy strangers on the street."

"On it." With a quick goodbye, I pocketed my phone and bent to pick up the book.

It was a green, weathered leather book with an intricate Celtic heart etched on the cover, and there was no title to be seen. I turned the book over, searching for any words on the binding, but there was nothing. Flipping it over, I gasped.

For one second, a glow—almost a shimmer or a sparkle of sorts—danced in the air. Like when sunlight speared through a dusty window, catching flecks of dust in the beam, so too did these sparkles drift around the book. But there was no sun, and frankly, there was barely any light in this corner of the shop. Confused, I lifted the book and tucked it on the windowsill underneath the disco unicorn. I could shelve it tomorrow when I gave the shop a proper clean.

Turning, I headed for my luggage only to have the slam of a book hitting the floor stop me in my tracks.

My heart rate picked up and I turned, eyeing the Celtic heart book that was once more on the floor.

"Right, I must have just put it down wrong. It's dark in here and I'm very tired." I explained it to myself like there was any logical reason that a book was throwing itself off the shelf at me. Scooping it off the floor, I waited for any shimmers in the air. When none came, I nodded to myself.

"See, Rosie? You're just imagining things. Come on now, you're off schedule. Get back to it."

With that, I took the book with me and put it next to the bed in the bedroom I found through an arched doorway at the back of the shop. Making sure I'd locked the front door, I bent my head to unpack before I finally allowed myself the luxury of a long shower. By the time I was done, I was ready for bed, and I was asleep before my head hit the pillow.

Chapter Five

ALEXANDER

"The American is here? The one who will run the bookshop?"

I hadn't meant to stop at The Royal Unicorn for a pint. Truly. My focus had been on stopping at Two Sisters before they closed to grab a toasty, and then I'd be on my way home. Instead, running into the random woman on the street, the one with luminous green eyes and a mouth made for kissing, had rattled me so much that I'd ended up veering off into the pub instead of trekking back home in the damp night. It was dark already, though it was now just past five in the afternoon, but we'd entered winter hours in Scotland, and we were lucky to have daylight up to mid-afternoon these days. When I'd wanted to sip a pint by the warmth of the fire at the pub and ruminate on why this woman had kissed my shoulder, instead I'd been confronted with some of the Book Bitches. Maybe all of them. I had a hard time keeping track of who was in the club and who was out, but I was told that Sheila was back on the outs for poking fun at one of the trashy books they read.

Esther told me this, an elderly woman with sharp eyes, a short bob of gray hair, and a jumper that read *Smart Bitches Read Smut*. What does one even say to that? I wasn't much for romance novels either, but I also knew when to keep my mouth shut. The last thing I needed was to be eviscerated by this woman who still terrified me from our encounter a year prior. I'd mostly been successful in avoiding conversation with her since, but it seemed like today was not my lucky day. In more ways than one.

"Aye, that's what the lass said."

"What did she look like?" This from another one of the club, Shannon, I believed, with a jumper that proclaimed she was a Book Dragon.

"Um ..." Mouthwatering. Heart-stopping. A goddess in a tracksuit. Curvy and flustered and dirty, and I'd wanted to dive my hands into her messy hair and pull those lips against mine. *I'd never reacted so viscerally to a woman before. Even my ex-wife.*

"A woman." The perfect height for kissing.

"American." With the sweetest accent.

"Darkish hair." That I'd love to have my fist wrapped around while she was on her knees before me.

The hell, mate?

Esther snorted.

Had she read my mind?

"Men are the worst at observation."

A point I'd dearly love to argue, what with my position as a software engineer at the university largely relying on my powers of observation, but that would mean more conversation with these women whom I sincerely hoped would leave me alone before they brought up my prowess, or lack thereof, in the bedroom again.

"What's her name?" Meredith asked.

"Didn't ask." I sipped my Guinness, waiting for the inevitable next question.

"Young? Old?" Esther asked.

"Um, medium, maybe? Younger than me probably."

"How old are you?"

"Thirty-four."

"Hmm, that is young. I hope she doesn't ruin the shop. Make it like ... trendy or something." Another woman, Cherise, plopped down at the table with a fresh glass of wine. Cherise's jumper said she was a Bookaholic. It seemed the Book Bitches preferred pun-based clothing.

"What's wrong with being trendy? We're on TikTok. And wee Wallace has an Instagram account." Esther nodded toward a cat that was currently sleeping on a stool at the end of the bar. Above him a picture frame sat with a wee dram of whisky poured at the ready. A way to honor the former owner, I was told, and I admired the sentiment. It would be nice to be remembered when you were gone.

"Was she pretty?"

I blinked at Esther, realizing she'd asked me the question twice now, and lifted my pint again.

"Isn't that subjective?"

"Fine. Did *you* find her to be attractive, Dr. MacTavish?" Esther's eyes sharpened and I groaned inwardly.

If I said no, somehow it might get back to the lass from Highland Hearts that I thought she was ugly or something. This town was full of gossips and news traveled fast. If I said yes, then I suspected these women would try to set me up. They were developing a bit of a reputation for enjoying matchmaking, likely due to all the romance novels they read.

"Of course," I said, and Esther's eyes lit. "But I find all women to be beautiful. Don't you agree?"

Esther narrowed her eyes at me and muttered something that sounded dangerously close to "cheeky bastard." I grinned into my pint.

"You're quite sweet, aren't you?" Shannon leaned closer. "Why aren't you married yet?"

"Tried it out. Didn't take."

"Och, you just picked the wrong woman then."

Didn't I know that?

Instead, I just shrugged a shoulder, refusing to be drawn into a conversation about my past that I wasn't interested in revisiting. Tara *had* been a poor choice as a partner, but for a moment, she'd made me feel fun and exciting when she'd drag me on adventures until I grew too boring for her when I'd needed to finish my PhD studies. Soon her adventures had included other men, and while I could tolerate a lot in a relationship, infidelity had been a dealbreaker. Which she'd well known. I just wished she'd broken it off instead of lying to me, but Tara had loved a dopamine hit, and seeing me get mad had lit her up inside.

I enjoyed my quiet life now, and I didn't intend for that hard fought peace to be disrupted.

"So I rescued a puffin today." It was time to steer the conversation elsewhere, otherwise the women would continue prying at me, and I really didn't want to have to skull my beer just to get away from their nosiness. Gasps went up, and I took a sigh of relief. Crisis averted, even though it meant the whole pub had turned at my words—there was no way to avoid conversation tonight now.

The Royal Unicorn was a small pub, recently and lovingly restored by the owner Reed, and his girlfriend Harper. With thick stone walls, some pretty black and white photography of Kingsbarns through the ages, and a cheerful fireplace in the corner, it was the perfect place to cozy in on a cold winter's night. It was also another hub for village gossip, aside from the Two Sisters coffee shop, and a stop at both during the day would catch most people up to speed on any major goings-on in the surrounding areas. If you were interested in who had taken ill recently, who was shagging whom, or whose son was off to university, well, then this was your place.

That being said, living as close to nature as we all did,

and with very little else going on in Kingsbarns, there was more than one person who enjoyed birding like I did. A puffin rescue would be the talk of the town, that was for sure.

"What happened? Did he survive?"

"Wrong time of year for them to be this close to shore."

"Where did you take him?"

"Will he be okay?"

"How did you catch him?"

The questions lit up the pub and I tried to answer them the best I could, smug in the knowledge that I'd outwitted the Book Bitches.

"He's had his wing clipped, and I am working on building an enclosure for him. But I'm keeping him in a smaller pen while his wing heals, and then will gradually introduce him to the outdoors more to see if he can fly again. If not, well, I guess I'll keep him if I can't find a sanctuary that takes them in for life."

"How old is he?" This from a man named Gregory who worked in the local government office.

"Young. Maybe four or five? I need to name him."

"I always thought they looked like potatoes."

We all stopped talking and looked at Cherise who seemed to be a wee bit tipsy. Esther reached out and pulled the wine glass away from Cherise.

"You think the bird—a *puffin*—looks like a potato?" Esther demanded, derision in her voice.

"Not the grown one." Cherise hiccupped and waved

a hand in the air. "You know. The young ones. The pufflings. They look like a fluffy potato."

The pub was silent as everyone looked at each other.

"She's not wrong." Meredith held up a picture of a fluffy puffling on her phone. "Also, I forgot the babies are named pufflings and now I'm in love all over again."

"You should name it Tattie," Esther declared, and the pub cheered.

"I ... wait, what? I can't name it Tattie." I was not going to name this distinguished bird, Tattie, after potatoes. Surely I would offend the poor thing.

"And why not? Tattie is a damn cute name." Cherise hiccupped again, and Harper poured a glass of water at the bar.

"I mean, it is a cute name. But I was thinking something more prestigious."

"Like what?" Gregory asked.

"Mm, maybe like the pirate? Since he came in off the seas? Captain Kidd?"

"Not bad, not bad." The pub collectively thought it over and I took another sip of my pint, pleased with myself. Captain Kidd was a *great* name for an esteemed puffin.

"No. Tattie." Cherise sniffed, her voice a touch wobbly, and I realized she was close to tears. Shite, I was horrible with women's tears. They just completely undid me, and I had no idea how to handle that level of emotion. Which usually meant I froze and agreed to whatever the woman wanted, so long as they put the water streaming from their eyes back inside their bodies.

"But he isn't a puffling anymore," I said, my tone gentle, a last-ditch effort. "He no longer looks like a potato. You'll have to come meet him."

"It's Tattie." Esther's voice was dangerously low, and she tapped the back of my hand, so I met her eyes. Seeing she was dead serious, I sighed.

"Right. Tattie it is then."

Cherise grinned, a radiant beam of sunshine, and the pub cheered once again.

Bloody hell.

Why had I decided to stop in here again? Making my escape, with the promise that I would update everyone on my puffin, who I couldn't quite bring myself to call Tattie, I ducked into the rain. Maybe I'd just tell others that was his name but call him Captain Kidd in private.

Resolved, I bent my head to the rain and walked toward home. The light in the window of Highland Hearts gave me pause. It was nice to see it there, even if I was entirely unsure of the new owner. She'd seemed a touch odd, skittish even, and out of sorts. Not that I was one to talk about other people and their awkwardness. I spent my days coding and building software. My people weren't renowned for our social skills.

I wanted to see if she was okay. Was she lonely? Scared? Nervous?

Shocked at my thoughts, I forced myself to keep walking. That was entirely unlike me. I made a point of not diving into other people's business, and wondering if the newcomer to Kingsbarns was scared in her bookshop was not a normal thought for me to be having. Of course she wouldn't be scared. Kingsbarns was a safe town, we looked out for each other here, and Highland Hearts was a lovely, albeit eclectic, place to call home. She'd be just fine. Whatever her name was.

Speaking of names, I needed to test out this Tattie business on the puffin. By the time I got home, my wool cap was soaked, and I'd lost any warmth I'd taken from the fire at the pub. I'd put the puffin in the back mudroom attached to my house, as they were well used to the cold, yet it didn't feel right to leave him outside on his own. When I spied him sleeping in his pen, I made to tiptoe back out, but his eyes sprung open. The wee lad hopped to his feet and moved closer to the door, clacking his beak at me.

"Tattie?" I asked.

The puffin regarded me and then bobbed his head backward and gave out a low call that sounded like a deep belly laugh. It was the first I'd heard it from him, and it sounded like an old man laughing at a funny joke.

"Captain Kidd?" I tried, hopeful. The puffin just tilted its head, then gnashed its beak at me.

"Tattie?" I asked. Again, the chuckle call.

Sighing, I went to get him some herring.

A puffin named Tattie. Could this day get any weirder?

Chapter Six

ROSIE

I went from sleeping to awake so smoothly that I barely noticed the transition, instead blinking at the ceiling as my brain scrambled to figure out where I was. It was still dark, or darkish, so I presumed I'd awoken in the night, and I rolled over to stare at the cheerful pillow with two puffins dancing around a heart.

Right. Scotland.

I was in the bookstore in Scotland, and I'd basically gone face first into bed last night after I'd unpacked and showered. At least I'd unpacked. Proud of myself for sticking to my list, I stretched lazily, pleased that I'd woken so early. At least I could get a start on the day and hopefully get a jump on my cleaning. Picking up my phone, my eyes widened.

It was eight in the morning. *How?* How was it still dark? Usually, I'd be up with my coffee by now, having gone through my morning routine of lemon water, light stretching, hand weights, face serum application, and finally a cup of coffee as my moment of silence before I had to talk to people all day at the store. Honestly, I didn't much mind the talking to people all day, it was just that I didn't like the subject matter. I never really knew how to answer questions about if a ceramic pig pitcher would make a good centerpiece or not. Taste was subjective, wasn't it? Who was I to tell someone if it would look good on their table or not? I'd often deferred to just telling people what I thought they wanted to hear, but largely, the conversations at Davidson's were mind-numbingly boring.

I had high hopes that wouldn't be the same at a bookstore.

Annoyed that I was already behind schedule, I rushed through my stretching and serum application. I'd need to source a set of hand weights, and I hadn't had time to go food shopping, so lemon water and coffee were out. I'd been told there was a coffee shop in town, so at the very least, I could pop down there and get breakfast while I got my bearings on where the supermarket was and what I needed.

"Chill, Rosie." I took a deep breath and reminded myself that I didn't need to be on a schedule. Yet. It would take time to find a routine here and a few basic things needed to be set up before I did so. Like getting groceries, figuring out transportation, getting internet hooked up—all those kinds of things. I just needed to ease up on my rigidity and it would be fine.

I could be flexible.

It was a mantra Jessica had made me repeat, over and over, while we'd made a list of what I was looking for in a man. Largely because I think she was scared I was going to just settle into another relationship with someone and then refuse to change it because the person had become a part of my routine. Because that was really what had happened with John. Once he'd become a part of my day-to-day, it just was what it was. Even the occasional sex had been bland ... *mediocre.* Did that mean I was medi-ocre at sex as well? After all, he'd walked out my apart-ment door without as much as a backward glance. He was part of my life, but it took Jessica to remind me that it wasn't normal to fit people into your schedule simply because it was what you'd grown used to.

She was right, she was always right, and now here I was in Scotland with a new job and a master list of "requirements for a man" hidden in my purse.

Which was where it was going to stay.

I groaned as I pulled on a fresh pair of jeans, a button-down white shirt, and a Fair Isle sweater vest over it. Braiding my hair back in two French braids on each side of my head, I put on dangly sapphire earrings and strapped my Apple Watch at my wrist. Even getting dressed couldn't quite pull my mind away from how I'd awkwardly kissed a stranger's shoulder yesterday. It didn't matter what requirements he'd met on my list. Because the list was staying in my purse.

I was not to be trusted with picking a match.

That was abundantly clear.

Before John there had been Jeff. A John look-alike, Jessica swore. Before Jeff had been Zach. And before him Tristan. All of whom had seamlessly worked themselves into my life and basically become a background fixture until something, or someone, ahem, *Jessica*, had pointed out what I was sacrificing for the sake of routine.

I jumped as a book fell off the bedside table and hit the floor with a loud bang.

"Damn it, that has got to stop happening." Picking up the Celtic heart book, I brought it with me to the shop. I'd add it to the pile to reshelve, but for now I placed it on the table that Moira had used as her check-out counter. Pausing, I took in the shop. In the soft light that filtered through the windows, the space felt welcoming and cozy, and I couldn't wait to open it to the world. It was such a different feeling than working at the discount store, where I'd hated opening hours. Here? In this beautiful shop full of beautiful stories? Yes, I wanted to share the space with actual humans. This was a place to be proud of, even if it needed some elbow grease before it was set to rights.

Walking around the back of the mahogany table, I pulled out the red leather chair and sat, testing how it felt. I needed to learn how to work the vintage cash register and see if there was a credit card machine to be found anywhere. Surely, there were bank accounts to be opened and ledgers to be read, but since I was giving myself permission to go off schedule, I decided to just take a deep breath and gloat a bit.

Well, maybe gloating wasn't the right word. More like, enjoy? Just enjoy this cool space that I'd been lucky enough to inherit.

A bang sounded and I jumped, slamming my hand against my chest.

"Yoo-hoo!"

Holy hell, was that someone knocking at the door? Jeez, I was jumpy. Taking a deep breath, I pasted a polite smile on my face as I unlocked and cracked open the door.

"Sorry, we're not open yet. I just arrived last night."

"Oh, we know it, honey." A trio of women pushed past me, and I automatically stepped back, still traumatized from the water bottle incident, and gaped at them as they hauled full tote bags to the table.

"Ladies," I began, needing them to leave so I could get back to my already revised schedule.

"We know you're not open. But we've got Book Club starting here on Thursday, so you'll need to get the shop back in order. We've brought groceries, cleaning supplies, and our charming personalities." The three elderly women beamed at me as I blinked at them in confusion.

"I'm sorry ... did the solicitor hire a cleaning service of sorts?"

The women hung up their coats one by one on a coat rack I hadn't even noticed and only then did I see their shirts.

I have puffin to declare except my genius. My lips

quirked up at the words on one woman's shirt with a puffin wearing glasses and reading a book.

The next woman's shirt read *Much Ado about Puffin*.

The third said *Puffin Compares to You* and had two puffins, beak to beak, with a heart.

Was this a deranged birding club? Why were they all wearing puffin shirts? Didn't they say book club? Were they hoping we had books about puffins?

"I'm the only one that has professionally cleaned in my life, but these two can hack it. I'm Esther." Genius Puffin shirt grinned at me. "This is Shannon and Meredith."

"Cherise was too hungover to come by this morning, though she claims it's cramps."

Esther snorted. "It's been a good twenty years since she's had cramps."

"Umm." What did one say to that? I gestured at their shirts. "Puffin fans, are you?"

"One of the locals rescued one yesterday so we're showing our support for wee Tattie as he gets back on his feet. Or on his wing, I suppose?" Esther scrunched up her nose as she thought about it.

"Tattie?" My eyebrows winged up.

"A perfect name for a puffin," Meredith assured me.

"What's a tattie?"

The three women gasped like I'd just threatened to slit their throats if they didn't leave the store. Granted, I might have been thinking something along the lines, though a touch less gruesome to be sure, but I'd never outright say such thoughts.

"Neeps and tatties?" Shannon gaped at me.

"I don't know what you're saying to me."

"Such a shame." Esther clucked her tongue at me as she began to unpack the grocery sack. "Neep means turnip, and tattie is what we call potatoes here. You really don't know much about Scotland, do you?"

"Unfortunately, no. I wasn't given much notice about my inheritance, so, yeah, my research on Scotland has been a bit rushed." Did bingeing *Outlander* count as research? "Though I do hope to see some men in kilts."

The women turned on me as one, excitement in their eyes.

"You're single then?" Shannon rubbed her hands together, reminding me a bit of the Grinch plotting to take down Christmas. Speaking of ... I'd need to start getting holiday decorations sorted since it was almost December.

"Ladies." I raised my hands in the air to try and stop any more personal questions. "You haven't even asked me my name yet. Let's start there before we jump into my personal life. Also, I'm already behind on schedule soooo ..." I made a big show of checking my watch.

"Well, what's your name then?" Esther demanded.

"Rose ... er, I mean, Rosie. My name is Rosie." Excitement filled me. Finally, I could introduce myself how I wanted to be called. "Rosie Withers. Moira was my great-aunt once removed I believe on my mother's side."

"Welcome to Kingsbarns, Rosie. We're the Book Bitches and we're going to help you get Highland Hearts up and running again."

56

"You are?" My mouth dropped open at Esther's proclamation. Since when did these women have any say in my business? *And did they really just call themselves bitches?* "Do you work here?"

"Goodness, no." Meredith laughed, waving a hand in the air as she took out a pile of neatly folded rags. "It's just what we do. We got The Royal Unicorn up and running again too."

"The Royal Unicorn?" Was this another thing like the neeps and tatties I was supposed to know?

"The local pub. In fact, you might want to meet Harper, the woman who brought it back to life. She's American. Came over here to have a Scottish pub experience and fell in love with the owner." Esther's eyes gleamed as she looked me up and down. "You didn't mention if you were single or not?"

Right, this was getting to be a bit much. I needed a moment to get my thoughts sorted about their intrusion. Yet, at the same time, I couldn't quite bring myself to kick the women out into the cold. They knew this town and they'd known Moira. Maybe they could be of some help.

"Listen, I'll be totally honest with you. This is my first morning, I'm a little overwhelmed, and I'm still trying to figure out where to start on opening the shop, let alone talking about my love life. I have a list of things I need to do and I'd feel much more comfortable if I could just get on with it."

"List?" Shannon rocked on her heels in excitement. "I love a good list."

I paused. Ah, maybe I'd found my people.

"If you really do want to help, I won't say no. But I can't promise to pay you as I don't even know the finances yet of the shop."

"No payment needed." Esther waved that away. "We're retired and we miss having the bookshop open. Give us this list and let's see how we can help."

"Well, first thing was food, to be honest." My stomach grumbled and Meredith beamed, taking the sack of groceries.

"I'll get brekkie sorted. Tea or coffee, Rosie?"

"Um, coffee, please." My eyebrows rose once again as Meredith breezed away into my personal flat, and I heard cupboards opening in the small kitchen in the back. This was weird, wasn't it? Random women in my shop and new home? Making me breakfast?

"After we've had a cuppa, you can tell us about your love life. Highland Hearts was known to be quite the romantic spot." Shannon picked up a dust rag and disappeared behind a bookshelf.

"Was it? What was with the name?" If they were going to cook and clean for me, I might as well get some information from them. Rounding the table, I sat in the leather chair and pulled the ledgers closer to me. I couldn't open until I knew what the finances were, as well as where the bank accounts were held.

"I think it was because she loved romance novels. There's more shelves of romance books here than any other genre, and Moira didn't care. She hosted all sorts of parties here, even speed dating sometimes, and she just loved love. I think it's a lovely name. Will you change it?"

"Oh, I hadn't thought about changing the name." I paused and looked up at Esther and noted the concern on her face. "I think I have enough on my plate without a rebrand, don't you? Plus, I read romance. I mean, more fantasy romance with magic and whatnot, but I can't argue with her love for the genre. I think Highland Hearts is super cute for a bookstore name."

"She reads smut!" Meredith crowed as she came in with a tray of cups and pastries.

"You'll do just fine here," Esther promised me.

"I hope so." For some reason, their approval warmed me, and I realized just how much I wanted this to work out. I couldn't go home, not to the discount store, and not to the life I'd been living. Well, treading water at best. No, Highland Hearts was my new home, and I was determined to make a success of it.

"Now ... about your love life."

I grinned and shook my head, pointing at the cup of coffee Meredith put in front of me.

"Coffee first, ladies. I need to figure out these accounts long before I figure out my love life. Or lack thereof."

"Hear that, ladies? She's single!" Crows of delight met Esther's words and I sighed, pinching my nose. Between these ladies and Jessica, I'd be married before the end of the week.

"No dating. No men. No love life. Just work."

"Boring," Shannon called from where she dusted the disco unicorn.

"For now," I amended. "Let me get my bearings, okay?"

"That's fair. Och, let's talk Christmas. What are the plans?" Esther asked.

"I have a list." I pointed to the list, refusing to be distracted by Christmas. "Follow the list and we can get to Christmas decorations. I promise. I can't open if I don't have any money. That has to come first."

"But the Winter Windows competition starts soon."

At that I looked up, squinting at where Shannon teetered on a step stool. "The what now?"

"The Winter Windows competition. All the bookshops in this part of Scotland decorate their windows for Christmas and the winner gets money for a charity of their choice."

"And St. Andrews has won the last two years." Esther clucked her tongue.

"Posh bastards." Meredith flounced back to the kitchen, and I raised an eyebrow. *St. Andrews was for the posh, got it.*

"List first. Party second. Then we'll make a decorating plan."

"Party? Wait ... what party?"

"You have to throw an open house, don't you?"

"But why? Everyone's been in here, I'm sure."

"To meet you. Plus, we like a party, don't we, ladies?" Esther nodded at me as the women chimed in.

"Right. Okay. Party. I'll make a note of it." I pinched my nose as the women grabbed the list and disappeared to the other side of the shop, muttering to themselves while I gripped the side of the table and took a few steadying breaths. I was the one in charge here. And I just needed to sort a few things out, and apparently, delegate better to my unasked-for volunteers.

My eyes caught on the Celtic heart book and, despite my need to dig into the ledgers, I reached out and traced my finger over the etching on the cover.

A shiver of ... something ... zipped up my arm. It was stronger than static electricity, but not as strong as being electrocuted. Chalking it up to nerves and excitement, I bent my head to the ledgers, letting the women's chatter fall into the background behind me.

Highland Hearts. My new home. It felt ... right. Like maybe I'd finally found the path that I was looking for. I might even have time to keep writing that fantasy novel I'd given up on two years ago. I was in charge of my time now, and nobody else, and that alone was worth celebrating. Looks like I'd be planning a party for sure now.

Chapter Seven

ROSIE

By the time I'd ushered the Book Bitches out of the shop, declining their invitation to the pub because, honestly, I just needed some silence, my energy was waning. However, I couldn't complain. Not in the slightest. The Book Bitches had blown through my list at a terrifying speed, and I had to admit, their help had been invaluable.

Half the time I hadn't even needed to speak. They'd chattered in the background, and despite struggling to understand what they were saying given their brogue, I managed to absorb *some* information both about the village and my great-aunt Moira. Clearly, *Outlander* slowed down the Scottish speaking so the non-Scots could actually understand them. *I must tell Jessica that.*

Turns out that my great-aunt had been eccentric—a label I'd secretly coveted. *How can I lean into that more?*

Certainly the bookshop reflected an eccentric personality. Even though the shop had been dusted and polished until she shone, there still wasn't much logic to ... well, anything really. At best I could say, the books seemed to be separated by genre, but they weren't in alphabetical order by author or title name that I could discern. At one point, I'd hoped they were shelved by color when I found six pink books in a row, but nope, that had been an anomaly. Esther had suggested that Moira had thought bookshops should be a discovery for people. An adventure. But the lack of organization made my skin itch a bit and I vowed to at least categorize the books by author name and keep them separated by genre.

Still, I had boxes and boxes of odds and ends to go through on top of stock that needed pricing, piles of secondhand books, and at least ten bins of holiday decorations. I was told Moira had gained notoriety for her decorating prowess, and many people made a stop on holidays—any holiday, it seemed—just to see what she'd come up with. That part gave me pause, since I'd never quite had a hand for decorating, but I hoped I'd find inspiration in the copious amounts of bins in the stockroom.

I hoped people would like me.

The thought struck me as I bent beneath the table and pulled out another box, and I leaned back on my heels in surprise.

I hadn't much thought about being liked back home.

Madison was a fairly big city full of students and businesspeople, and it was easy to fade into the background without needing or wanting to make an impression on anyone. But here? Where it was clear the community was tight-knit? Yeah, I wanted to be liked. Even if I wasn't ready to go to the pub or start dating, I wanted Highland Hearts to be a welcoming spot for everyone where I was in control of the atmosphere.

And I couldn't wait for discussions with customers about literally anything other than plastic tableware. For that to happen, my patrons needed to like me. *No pressure or anything, Rosie.*

Humming, pleased I didn't have to unbox a new shipment of Live Laugh Love faux wooden signs, I bent to the box again.

"Ow!"

The Celtic heart book, which had been perched on the front table, smacked me on the back of the head before it fell to the floor. I'd been meaning to look at it all day today, but I'd gotten caught up in ledgers and business paperwork. Thank God for good solicitors, because William Stuart was a blessing in disguise. In the top ledger, he had noted the up-to-date bank balance, as well as the information for the bank accounts, utilities, and internet services. The benefit of living in a small town? One phone call and I'd arranged a quick meeting at the local bank to verify I was the new owner of Highland Hearts and I'd been cleared for business. The credit card machine still worked, internet was back up and running, and my Spotify playlist now played Lumineers through the small speakers tucked on a shelf behind the table.

The bells over the door jangled and I winced, annoyed that I hadn't locked up after the Book Bitches had left. Rubbing the back of my head, I pasted my customer service smile on.

"Hello?" A woman in her mid-fifties or so with a tense expression and a whisper of faded laugh lines at her eyes glanced around the shop. She wore a serviceable black canvas coat, jeans, and Wellies. She took a step forward, and then back, and then forward again before firmly shutting the door behind her against the rain that pummeled the side of the shop. *Interesting.* She seemed nervous.

"Hi, sorry, I was just cleaning out from under the table." I stood up.

"Oh, there you are. When I heard you were open again, I just had to make a stop here before I lost my nerve. I'd been working myself up to this for months now, you ken?"

I tilted my head at her, unsure how to respond. She'd been nervous to visit a bookshop? Pursing my lips, I thought it over. Perhaps she experienced some form of extreme social anxiety? I'd seen it with several people in my literature program in college. Most had been happier buried in a book than speaking to actual humans, and honestly, I couldn't say that I blamed them at times. I supposed it would be natural for some customers here to be more on the timid side. Determined to be a welcoming environment for anyone who stepped over my threshold, even if I wasn't yet open, I waved her closer.

"Well, I'm not technically open yet. I just arrived last night and I'm getting the lay of the land myself. Is there something in particular that I can help you with?"

"Aye. There is." The woman stepped forward until she stood at the table and then dug a hand in her coat pocket. Pulling out a twenty-pound note, she slid it across the table to me. "I'd like to order the Highland Hearts Special."

"I'm sorry, the what?" It felt like I was in a state of constant confusion today, and people just kept throwing me curveballs.

The woman looked around the shop and lowered her voice, even though nobody else was there.

"The Highland Hearts Special."

"Is that a ... book?" Had the shop published its own book that I didn't know about?

"It's ... it's ..." The woman's hands fluttered in front of her as she tried to come up with an explanation. When a sheen of tears hit her eyes, I stepped forward and put a hand on her arm.

"Hey, hey, it's just fine. Everything's just fine. I'm sorry that I don't know what that is, but truly, I will figure it out. I'll find what you need. If you can just give me your contact information? I'm sorry that I don't know off the top of my head what this is, but I have a lot to learn. And look"—I gestured to the stack of leather-bound note-books on the table—"I have loads of information and instructions to read through. I'm sure once I get through it, I'll be able to help."

"You're certain?" The woman swallowed.

"Of course. Absolutely." I had no idea what I was promising, but I wasn't going to let this poor woman go out into the rain in tears. Should I offer her tea? That seemed like a polite thing to do.

"Can I put a tea on for you? Maybe I can find what you're looking for while you have a cup?"

"Och, I couldn't possibly stay. It's already taken so much to come here. Lovely shop, though. I'm glad you're opening it back up. I, well, honestly, it's just been right difficult to get myself here and, well. Right. I should just go." The woman turned.

"Wait, please. Let me get your information first." I grabbed the first notebook I could find and a pen and opened it.

"Right, it's um, Edina. And I'm meant to tell you my favorite book is *The Housemaid*. By Frieda McFadden. I'm told you'll need that information."

"I do? Is that the book you're looking for?" I peered around the shop. While it was much cleaner than it had been this morning, the books were still not grouped by genre.

"No. I want the Highland Hearts Special." Edina gave me a long look, as though she was telling me something else entirely, and then gave a brisk nod before scurrying from the shop. Her twenty-pound note was still on the table. Picking it up, I ran it through my fingers.

I couldn't quite count this as my first sale when I wasn't even sure what I'd sold. Or what that exchange had been all about. Tapping the bill against my finger, I paced back and forth in front of the table. What was I missing here? What did *The Housemaid* have to do with Highland Hearts aside from we were a bookshop? Pressing my lips together, I dug in a small chest of drawers behind the table and found a paperclip. Clipping the money to the page of the notebook with Edina's information on it, I sat down and tapped the pen against my lips.

That had been odd.

My phone rang and I answered, grinning at Jessica's face.

"You're looking better today. See the hottie again?"

"Nope, I haven't even left the shop yet." I mimicked shuddering. "It's scary out there."

"If you don't get out and track that hottie down, I'm going to fly over and drag his ass to your shop and force him to read you Armentrout by candlelight."

I fanned my face. "You're getting me all hot and bothered."

"I'll give you a pass since it's your first day, but I expect you to be dating by Christmas."

"This is the worst time of year to start dating someone." I stood up and walked around the shop, admiring a small glass-blown statue of a fairy that was perched on the corner of one shelf. That was one thing I liked about this shop. Every time I looked somewhere I discovered something new. And I hadn't even gotten to cataloging the book selection yet.

"What? Are you insane? This is the most romantic time of the year," Jessica gushed as she walked down the street, cars honking behind her. "Hot cocoa while the snow falls outside, kisses under mistletoe, cozying up in the cold. I mean, how could it not be romantic?"

"Meeting new people around family holiday time puts a ridiculous amount of pressure on a new relationship, not to mention having to buy a gift for someone you've just met. No, it's way too intense," I argued.

If I was honest, I wanted to stand on my own two feet and ... reinvent myself. I didn't want bland anymore. This was such a huge opportunity to let go of past unhelpful habits, seeking out the "safe" man to avoid deep connections. And I didn't need a man to fulfill any fantasies. *Books did that already.* So, dating was out. Because new Rosie was in.

"Please, dating is not for the weak, Rosie. You need to gird your loins and whatnot. Jump right into the fray. Kiss men left and right. Break hearts. Sample the local flavor. Have at it. Nobody knows you there, so it's the perfect chance to play as much as you want."

"That sounds terrifying." I gulped. "You are out of your damn mind if you think I'm going to ride a train of men through this tiny town. I don't even know anyone yet. The last thing I want to do is step on any toes."

"You wouldn't be stepping on toes, you'd be sitting on poles."

A throat cleared and I jolted. Whirling, my mouth dropped open to see the sexy sidewalk man standing in front of me, his eyebrows raised to his hairline.

"Um—"

"Just think about how hot they'd be in bed ... with that Scottish accent?" Jessica continued, clearly not looking at my expression on the screen. Wordlessly, I flipped the camera and she stuttered to a stop as the man's image filled the screen. A squeal filled the air. "Is that the hottie you shoulder-kissed?"

"Have you forgotten how phones work? He can hear you!" I hissed before unceremoniously ending the call before she embarrassed me further.

"Right. Can we pretend you heard none of that?" I blinked at the man hopefully. Damn it. He was just as sexy today as he'd been yesterday, even though I'd kind of hoped I'd hallucinated the entire meeting due to lack of sleep and stress.

"Not likely, no." But he flashed a grin to lighten his words, and I took a soft inhale. The smile lit up his entire face, transforming it from somewhat surly to warm and welcoming. Smile lines crinkled at the corner of his brilliant blue eyes, and I reached up to pat my hair, wondering if I was a mess after cleaning all day. "But I promise to keep your shoulder kink quiet."

"It's not a—" I barely resisted stomping my foot. "Apologies, *sir*, for my extreme awkwardness yesterday. I blame stress and jet lag."

"It's Alexander, but you can call me *sir* if you'd like."

Of course he'd have a sexy name too.

"Rosie," I said, weakly, and gestured to the shop. "We're closed." I could hear Jessica screaming in my head to shut up and invite him in for a look. Or a quick tumble.

"I wasn't sure you'd be up and running yet, but I saw someone leave the shop, so I took a chance." Alexander rocked back on his heels, hands in his pockets, and I took a moment to ogle while he glanced around the room.

Broad shoulders? *Check.*

Sharp jawline with just enough scruff to be sexy? *Check.*

Moody blue eyes? *Check.*

Thick dark hair that I wanted to run my hands through? *Check.*

"Is …" My voice cracked and I cleared my throat. "Is there anything that I can help you with?"

"Puffins."

"Um, hmmm." I pressed my lips together. It wasn't in my customer service nature to dismiss something a customer was looking for. "I can't say that I've yet spied a puffin section, but there doesn't really seem to be actual sections so I can't properly respond to that. Yet. *Yet.* I will be able to soon. I promise."

A hint of amusement flashed in Alexander's eyes.

"No, Moira wasn't much for organization, that's the truth of it."

"Are you the one that rescued Tattie then?" Curiosity won out, even though I really just wanted the shop to myself for a while so I could catch my breath and recalibrate to this new life that I'd started. And I was so tired. I'm not even sure what time it was here, let alone what time my body clock thought it was.

Alexander winced.

"Bloody hell. I can't believe they named him that. You heard already?"

"The Book Bitches visited the shop today."

A visible shudder ran across Alexander's shoulders. "Terrifying women."

Delighted that I hadn't been the only one who'd thought that, I fist-bumped his shoulder.

"Yes, thank you. And yet I also kind of love them."

Alexander stared down at where I'd bumped his, admittedly very muscular, shoulder and my stomach dropped.

First I'd kissed his shoulder.

Now I'd fist-bumped it like we were long-time friends.

Ever heard of personal space, Rosie?

My cheeks pinkened and I stepped back, clearing my throat.

"Anywho. Puffins. I'll see what I can find."

"I'm looking specifically for enrichment exercises for an injured puffin."

"Maybe Tattie would like a game of Wingspan." I grinned at him, my inner board game geek delighted with my joke, since Wingspan was a bird-centered board game and had puffins in it, but he just blinked at me. "Um, the board game?"

"You think my injured puffin would like to play a board game?"

"No, I ..." I lifted my hands in the air. "It was a joke."

"Oh." This time it was Alexander's turn to look embarrassed. "Sometimes I miss those."

"It's okay. I mean ... it was a niche joke. Easy to miss," I said, rushing to reassure him.

An awkward silence fell between us, and my brain whirled at ways to fill it. For some reason, I didn't want him to go, and at the same time, I wanted to be alone in *my* shop to try and process all these emotions swirling inside me from making such a huge change.

"Um, so I can also look if I can order something in for you?" I rounded the table and opened the ancient laptop that had come with the store and grimaced as it beeped angrily at me. Yes, I know computers are not sentient, but I heard anger every time I'd tried to get this damn thing up and running. "Never mind. Stupid computer."

"You're having computer problems?" Alexander's tone lit up like I'd just told him he'd won the lottery. I nodded, raising an eyebrow at the change in his demeanor, and turned the laptop to face him.

"Ah, cheeky bastard. I see what you're on about." I stared at him as he bent to the laptop, mumbling to himself, his fingers flying rapidly over the keys. Beeps sounded and Alexander grimaced. "Och, it's giving me a wee battle."

More beeps rang out, and I watched, entranced, at Alexander's steadfast focus on the computer.

What would it be like to have him look at me with that level of focus?

Heat flushed through my body, and I turned away, silently rebuking myself. I could *not* fall for the first tall, dark, and handsome man that walked through my door. No matter what Jessica said, I was on a sabbatical from men. My choices simply couldn't be trusted. Rosie 2.0 was here.

"Listen, it's tied itself up."

"Tied up?" I repeated, my thoughts short-circuiting as they went down a decidedly different route than what he was speaking about.

"The computer?" Alexander gestured to the laptop, and I smiled brightly at him.

"Oh, right. Yeah, I have no idea how to fix it."

"It's a wee beastie, that's for sure. I know the programming on this one, but I need to check a few things. I'll be back to work on this sometime this week." Alexander stood and strode to the door.

"Wait ... you're going to work on my computer?"

"Aye. It's what I do." Alexander opened the door and paused in the doorway. A brisk wind entered the shop, carrying the scent of rain. "Right. I'm off. Good luck finding poles to sit on."

"Damn it." I banged my head against the table as he promptly closed the door, the gentle tinkle of bells seeming to laugh at my dismay.

I was never going to be able to show my face in this town.

Chapter Eight

ALEXANDER

Good luck finding poles to sit on.

I can't believe I actually said those words out loud. I just couldn't help myself, the image of this lush woman wrapped around my waist making my thoughts scramble, and now I felt like an absolute arse for bringing it up.

As I mentioned before, I'm not the best in social situations. Give me computers and they made sense to me. Logical, orderly, and usually presenting problems that weren't hard to solve.

Navigating social cues and subtle nuances? Not my top strength.

It was one of the reasons I tended toward the quiet side. Less likely for me to blurt out awkward things like suggesting the pretty new lass in town have fun finding men to sit on.

I blamed whomever she had been speaking to on the phone. Once I'd heard the words "sit on" I'd done nothing but picture Rosie in my lap, and what a deeply annoying time for my libido to come roaring back after a three-year hiatus.

Icy rain slapped my face, and I welcomed the sting of it, a mild form of punishment for thinking heated thoughts about the newcomer when I'd sworn off women after my divorce. Dramatic? Maybe. But unlike a few friends of mine who liked to bury themselves in endless rounds of dating after a breakup, I much preferred to nurse my wounds in private.

Buying the derelict cottage had been a great choice for me, giving me a project to work on where I could see measurable growth, all while pulling me away from sitting too long in front of my computer.

"Maybe Tattie would like a game of Wingspan."

My pulse kicked up in excitement. When I wasn't busy working on programs, I had two main passions—birding and games. Neither of which are the most glamorous hobbies, I guess. Again, see reasons why winning the dating game wasn't likely for me.

Which I was fine with. I'd been fine with it for three years now. Divorce, well, it sucked. And even though it had been the right decision in the end, I now furiously protected the peace I'd created in my life. I'd taken a gamble on love, it had kicked me in the arse, and I was content to live life on my own. A decision that not many people understood, which was also why I tended to hang out more in nature than with people.

That was obviously reflected in my asinine comment to Rosie. Sighing, I turned toward Two Sisters, my go-to coffee shop and wee takeaway at the end of the main road in Kingsbarns. The town itself was nothing but a speck of dust on the map, blink and you'd drive through it, but I loved its remoteness all the same.

It gave me the peace and space I required. I couldn't blame that necessity completely on Tara. After all, as they say, it took two to tango, but my pride had been battered, and it was the quiet of a tiny town that had provided some sense of solace.

"You're so boring. Who wants to go look at birds anyway?" Tara's jibes came back to me. She'd been more for fancy nights out on a surprise trip to Paris than she had been for quiet walks in nature.

Perhaps I just wasn't meant to be someone's partner.

Kingsbarns was an introvert's dream and the history of this place helped me heal after my divorce, yet at the same time I could be down to Edinburgh in a couple of hours when I was craving city life. Which obviously, wasn't all that often.

Streetlights shone in murky puddles that dotted the pavement, the darkness of winter afternoons making the icy rain seem that much colder, and the wind carried the hint of the sea with it. Lights glowed from windows in cottages that lined the street, and the faint strain of a Christmas song carried to me across the small cobble-stone square.

I used to love Christmas. Before my ex-wife had turned it into a high-pressure competition of who could buy each other the best present. Spoiler alert—I never won.

For the last three years, I'd spent Christmas alone, even though I knew it would have upset my mum. She'd loved Christmas and would have hated how dismal the time had become for me. I'd never considered myself a highly emotional person, but losing my mum, and then being betrayed by my *then* wife, well, it had brought to the surface a lot of messy feelings. I'd needed time to recover from both. Interestingly, I didn't miss my ex-wife, but I sure missed my mum.

We'd been a small family, just the two of us, for as long as I could remember. And now the familiar guilt of not honoring her favorite holiday tugged at my heart as I pushed through the door of the coffee shop.

Warmth blasted my face, along with mouthwatering scents of cinnamon, and something spicy—perhaps a curry—assaulted me and my stomach grumbled. I'd been busy all day researching how to care for a puffin, along with spending some time making sure Tattie was as comfortable as he could be with his wee wing injury. It hadn't been until I'd been passing the bookshop that I'd thought about enrichment exercises, which is why I'd poked my head inside.

Only to find the stunning Rosie gossiping on her phone about sleeping with men. She was refreshing, like stumbling upon a fragrant garden—an oasis—in the middle of a barren landscape. A veritable landscape of dips and curves, rolling hills to be explored, and my hands had ached, actually ached, to reach out and touch her. I'd had to shove my hands in my pockets to stop the impulse, and I swear my shoulder still burned where she'd fist-bumped me.

"Alexander! Just the man we need."

I stiffened at my name being shouted, and then took a deep breath before pasting a polite smile on my face. Turning, I found the Book Bitches, along with a few others, jammed around a table in the corner.

"Oh, hello there." I waved at the group. Cherise nodded at me, looking a little pale, as she gripped her cup of tea with both hands. I suspected she was feeling a bit worse for wear today after her indulgence the night before. Maybe now would be a good time to bring up changing the puffin's name that had been assigned to him against my will.

"We were just talking about you," Esther said, nodding at an empty chair at another table. Did they think I was going to join them? I wanted to pick up my takeaway and go home.

"Have we revisited the name Tattie? Sure, it was fun last night, but you can't possibly think I should call the puffin ..." I paused as I was met by stern looks from the group.

"*Of course* his name is Tattie," Shannon reassured a tense looking Cherise. I noticed they were all wearing puffin shirts and sighed. There was no way around it. Either I broke a few grandmothers' hearts and called the puffin Captain Kidd, or I just accepted his fate as being Tattie the puffin.

"We even put our puffin shirts on to support him today. How's the wee lad doing?" Esther asked, again pointing toward a chair. Resigning myself to a prolonged visit, I dragged a chair over to the table.

"Can I get you a cuppa?" One of the Two Sisters materialized by my shoulder.

"Chai, please."

"Coming up."

"The wee lad is doing fine. He's eating and getting acquainted with his spot. Hoping his wing heals up. I'm trying to befriend him but also not get him so used to people that he won't go out into the wild if he heals well."

"Sure that's a tough balance, isn't it then? We'll have to come see him." Shannon beamed at me, and I blinked at her as terror gripped my heart. Somehow I knew once I let these women invade my sanctuary, they'd never stop coming around.

"Um, best not to excite him too much for now. His wing is in a really delicate place."

"Mm-hmm." Esther peered at me like she could read every one of my thoughts. "Well, keep us updated on the wee lad. In the meantime, we were just talking about you."

"So you mentioned." I accepted the cup of chai with a brief smile of thanks and put it on the table to cool. Trepidation filled me. If I was on the Book Bitches' radar, that could mean anything really.

"The Winter Windows competition is starting. Next

week. And we are not prepared." Esther gave me a look like not only should I know what she was talking about, but I also was meant to do something about this.

"Well, good luck with it all." I picked up my tea and blew on the top, hoping to cool it down faster so I could be on my way.

"That's where you come in. We need someone to program the lights. If we're going to go big this year and beat St. Andrews, well, it has to be something fantastic. And you're a programmer, so you'll be just the lad to help us out."

"Um." I choked on my sip of tea and put it back on the table, coughing. Esther slammed me on the back, and my eyes widened. The woman had some power to her. "What's the Winter Windows competition?"

"Seriously?" Shannon leaned forward, surprise on her face. "How could you not know what this is?"

Because I moved here three years ago and am basically a hermit?

"All the bookstores in the region compete for the best windows in the month of December. There's judging each weekend leading up to Christmas. Four weekends of judging. St. Andrews always ends up winning and we want to break that streak."

"What do you win?"

"Money for a charity of your choice." Esther waved that away, the light of battle in her eyes. "It's not about the money. It's about the bragging rights. Highland Hearts has come in second or third place for years now, and we know that we can win with some added flavor."

"And I'm the added flavor?" Despite myself, I was amused.

"Yes. Your technical capabilities, plus Rosie's fresh outlook, will bring us over the finish line."

"Have you asked Rosie about this?"

"We're getting there." Cherise glared at me. Right. Don't upset Cherise seemed to be the name of the game this week.

"Ladies, what you need is an electrician. Not a programmer." Slapping my hands on my legs in the universal sign that I was done with the conversation, I made to stand.

"Nope, we need a programmer. Look at this." Esther pulled out her phone and clicked on the TikTok app, and then pressed play on a video. Leaning in, I watched as a house, positively drenched in lighting, flashed in tune to a rock version of *Jingle Bells*. "See? This is what we need. Next level."

"That's an entire house decorated in lights. I thought this was windows only."

Esther glared at me.

"It's just the concept, Alexander. Get with it."

"Apologies." I barely restrained a grin.

"So, you'll need to come up with a program that can do something like this once we decide on a theme."

"Um." I scratched my jaw as I thought about it. I likely *could* figure this out easily enough, but it would be putting me right in the path of temptation. In other words, one very sexy bookseller that I had no right thinking dirty thoughts about. "December is days away. Why didn't you talk to Rosie about it?"

"We are. Tomorrow. We felt she needed a wee break after we were there all day today," Shannon said, taking a bite of her biscuit. At the sight of food, my stomach grumbled, and I stood up before I got sucked into further conversation.

"I really need to run. Let me know if Rosie decides to join this competition. If she needs the help, I can see what I can come up with." I couldn't even believe the words leaving my mouth. Not only was I volunteering to join the competition, but I was also pulling myself out of my peaceful hermit-ville to work on a project with the Book Bitches.

The women clapped in excitement.

"You're our hero," Esther declared. And damn it, that felt good to hear. Even if it meant having to actively avoid conversations about my non-existent dating life with this group of women, I was still happy to help.

"Have a good night, ladies." My takeaway bag was waiting on the counter and my puffin was waiting for his dinner.

"Tell Tattie we send our love."

I grimaced and then sighed. At some point I just had to accept this. I nodded over my shoulder.

"Aye, will do."

Chapter Nine

Rosie

Wine was needed.

It was the only thing one could do after uprooting one's life and moving to another country only to awkwardly kiss a man's shoulder in the rain and later have him wish you luck in your journey to sit on many men.

My assumption was he was declining the role of that position if he was wishing me luck on *that* particular journey, but that was neither here nor there.

I'd say fingers crossed I'd never see Alexander again, but since he was apparently coming back to fix my computer, and I needed to find a book about puffin enrichment of all things, I would just have to work past my embarrassment. In fact, maybe I just needed to embrace it. So what if I wanted to sit on all the men? I mean, I didn't. But hypothetically speaking, I should be allowed to do so in this day and age and not be judged for it.

Realizing that I was standing in the middle of the bookshop having a mental argument with myself about a woman's right to sleep with as many people as she wanted, I snapped my head up when the door opened again.

Seriously. This town had, like, ten houses from what I'd seen in the pouring rain last night. How could so many people be stopping by already?

A tall man, with perfectly round glasses, a shock of white hair tucked under a knit cap, and kind eyes smiled shyly at me.

"I heard the shop was open again. It's taken me some time, but I'm ready now."

"Excuse me?" I tilted my head at him in question.

"Och, well, you know. I needed some time. But Myrna wouldn't have wanted me to stay a widower forever, and I'll admit, I'm quite lonely." The man shrugged and reached inside his pocket. "I decided to make the wee journey down here. I'd like the Highland Hearts Special."

I blinked as the man handed me a twenty-pound note.

"Sir. I'm not sure ..."

"Och, and I'm meant to, what was it ..." He looked up at the ceiling for a moment, lost in thought. "Right, right. You'll need a favorite book of mine."

"I will?" Curiosity filled me. What was going on in this town? And why were people coming in and handing me money without buying books?

"Aye. So I'm told. Forgive me. I'm new to all this." The man waved his hand in a circle in the air.

"As am I." I waited, hoping he'd expound more on what a Highland Hearts Special was.

"Right." The man snapped his fingers. "Is anyone else here?"

"Um, no." Why? Was he going to threaten me or something? Even though he looked to be in his mid-seventies, he still seemed sprightly enough. Maybe if I took out his knee, I'd have a fighting chance.

The man leaned closer and dropped his voice.

"*Pride and Prejudice.*"

Was he speaking code?

"The book?"

"Och, of course. Though there's been a few fine adaptations as movies, hasn't there?"

"I mean, it depends on which one you're discussing. But I'm partial to the one with Keira ..." I trailed off and slapped my forehead. "Sir, I'm sorry. Let's back up. I'm not even open yet. What, exactly, is this for?"

"It's for the Highland Hearts Special." The man blinked at me behind his glasses, and we fell into an awkward silence. How many times today was I going to sit and stare in uncomfortable silence at someone in this shop? Resolving myself to locking the door and flipping the lights off until I could figure out just what the hell this Highland Hearts Special was, I grabbed the notebook on the table with Edina's information.

"Right. Your name?"

"Daniel."

"Nice to meet you, Daniel. I'm Rosie. How best can I contact you?" After taking down the man's information, I looked up at him.

"Do you think this will work?" Daniel asked, his expression hopeful.

"I don't know," I said, honestly, because I had no idea what the Highland Hearts Special was. But if it was bringing customers to the shop in a relatively small town that likely saw little to no foot traffic, well, I was going to damn well figure out what it was.

"That's fair." Daniel's mouth turned down, sadness slipping across his features. "Worth a shot, I guess."

"I'll be in contact soon." I wished I could reassure him that I would help him, whatever I could do to take that sad look off his face, but I also didn't want to lie. It was clear there was something else going on here that I needed to discover.

"Thanks, Rosie. Welcome to Scotland, by the way. I hope you enjoy your new home." With that, Daniel took his leave and I locked up after him, flipping the main lights of the bookshop off. Now, just the lamp with the fringe shade glowed behind the front table, and I paused to look around the shop in the semi-darkness.

This *was* my new home.

For some reason, that hadn't fully registered until Daniel

had said it, but even though my lists had been torn apart and I was wildly off the schedule I'd written for myself, which was basically chaos in my world, I felt good. Trailing a hand over a bookshelf, I smiled at a small figurine of a witch with a batch of red hair, grinning at me from a corner of the shelf.

The sound of a book hitting the floor made me jump.

Already I knew what book it was.

"This is *not* normal." I said this out loud to the shop, craning my neck to peer at every dimly lit corner that I could see. I'd meant what I'd said about being excited if the shop was haunted, but it would be nice to have some evidence of it, so I didn't think that this was all just hallucinations born of jet lag. "But I hear you. Loud and clear, all right? I'll read the book."

Picking up the Celtic heart book, I noted an envelope sticking out of the corner. Maybe that was the reason whatever ghost that lingered here was basically throwing a book at my head every chance it had. Excitement coursed through me. This was a proper adventure, not like back home at the discount store where going viral over a water bottle was the most exciting thing to happen to the store in years.

I had myself a real ghost. *Jessica will not believe this.* And now I'd been led to look at an envelope specifically sent to me to review. *How is this my life?*

Humming softly to the music in the background, I put the book on the table and went to open a bottle of wine that the Book Bitches had brought me. Pouring a glass, I snagged another one of the pastries from breakfast, a buttery from what I was told. Delicious was what *I* called it. Munching on flaky yumminess, I returned to the front room with my glass of wine and, snagging the book, I wandered to the disco unicorn corner. There, I dropped onto one of the comfy floor poufs, more like a bean bag chair really, and put my wine on the windowsill and took a deep breath.

"Right, commence new adventure."

I slid out the envelope.

It was addressed to me. My heart picked up speed and I danced my fingers across the flowery script on the envelope, a silly little thing I was sure, but for a moment I felt like the ink warmed beneath my fingers. Taking a sip of wine for some liquid courage, I slid the flap of the envelope open and pulled out writing paper with an ink design of roses in the corner.

My dearest Rosie,

Do you mind if I call you "my dearest?" I suppose it's a bit of a presumption, seeing as how we've never met. And yet, I feel as though I know you anyway. You and I, well, my child, we're alike more than you'll ever realize. Two peas in a pod, some may say. How do I know this? Well, I stalked you. Now, don't be alarmed. It was in the nicest sense of the word, of course. Darling William gathered the information for me, and I'd just been meaning to reach out when I'd been warned that my time here wasn't for much longer. That's the way of it, I suppose, but I'll tell you what a fun life I've had. I hope you will too, particularly since I've left you more than this bookshop.

I paused and took another sip of my wine, sinking deeper into the cushion. There was more to this inheritance? The solicitor had been very thorough in his contracts and whatnot, so I was certain he wouldn't have missed anything.

If you're the kind of woman that I think you are, I'm hoping this news will bring you excitement, not fear.

"I mean, with a line like that ... how can I not be nervous?" I mumbled, taking another sip and smoothing the paper out in my lap.

This cottage that the bookshop is in has been standing here for almost two hundred years. Prior to that, a wee stone circle was situated just at the base of the back door. The

*couple who built the cottage, the woman was a
well-renowned midwife. One day, she saved the
life of the baby of a mysterious traveler, who'd
gone into labour early and was quite unwell. As a
thanks, this traveler, who saw the kind heart of
the midwife, bestowed upon her a very special
gift. One which has been passed down to every
owner of this cottage since.*

I tilted my head at that, nerves kicking low in my
stomach. This letter had taken a turn, and I wasn't sure
how I felt about it.

*It was a gift of magick, you see. But a very
special kind. Those holding this gift can bring
two lonely hearts together to find love. The traveler, knowing how much the gentle midwife loved
love, bestowed upon her the gift to help others
find their happiness. This, my child, has now
been passed down to you. But, because I am who
I am, and you are who you are, I was able to
learn a little iteration of this magick that
became quite popular around Scotland for those
in the know.*

. . .

"Oh my God. It's the Highland Hearts Special," I breathed.

Not only are you now a matchmaker, but your ability will come from matching people by their favorite books. Now, it's not an easy task. Just because two people like the same book doesn't mean they'll complement each other elsewhere. Sometimes it's the polar opposite book choices that strike up the most interesting of love matches. The magick will help you, if you work with it, and you'll be able to see just the right pairings as you learn. While the bookshop was a great joy in my life, helping people find love was my greatest gift. One I hope that you, too, can enjoy. Best of luck on this new journey, and remember, above all else, have fun. Life is meant to be an enjoyable adventure, not bland and boring. And what could be more exciting than magick? Sparkle on, sweet Rosie. You'll do just fine.

Holy hell. I took a deep breath, and then another, before reading the letter all the way through again. My hands trembled slightly as I slowly opened the cover of the Celtic heart book. I gaped at the list of names that greeted me.

Each page held two names, and what books had brought them together. "Oh, these are all matches. And their books. Oh, okay, I see, I see. These are like, case notes." Moira had noted her reasoning behind the pairings on each page, as well as the magick she'd used to help with the match. "And like little love spells. Spells. Oh my God. Actual spells."

There were things like salting a room to rid it of negative energy, a love knot charm, a love letter written in rose petal ink, a full moon tea and so on.

"Surely this can't all be real?"

A book fell on the floor by my feet, and I started. Happy I'd returned my wine to the windowsill, I glared at the empty air around me.

"Enough with the book throwing. You're going to knock me unconscious one day." It wasn't lost on me that I was speaking to air ... *possibly a ghost.* Interesting that I thought my life was bland only a week ago.

Bending forward I peered at the title of the book with a cute rom-com couple on the front. "*Believe in Love.* Right, catchy title. And I get it. Okay, loud and clear. Just no more book throwing. Please."

I had no idea if it was Moira who occupied the bookshop or if it was the magick doing this, but the last thing I needed was a concussion by way of overzealous magick tossing books at my head.

Even as I thought it, I bit back a small squeal of delight.

Magick.

Seriously. How freaking cool was that? I mean, I didn't actually know the first thing about magick, but I'd certainly read a lot of books with magick in them, so I mean, did that make me qualified? Somewhat qualified? At the very least, I wasn't horrified by this development.

In fact, I was pretty damn excited.

My eyes caught on the cute rom-com book on the floor again, and then back to the list of couples that Moira had helped in the book. My heart fell.

It wasn't just about magick.

This was about people's lives. Their hearts. Their hopes and dreams.

And I, well, I was an unreliable matchmaker. I couldn't even pick good men for myself. How would it be possible that I could help others with their love lives when I didn't even believe in a happy ending for myself?

And that was the crux of it, wasn't it? I picked up my wine glass and drained it, sadness washing through me. Jessica had been telling me for years that my mother had soured my view on love, and I'd always laughed it off. But now, after another failed relationship with a boyfriend who had barely excited me, I had to admit there might be a kernel of truth to what she'd said. At the end of the day, I had a hard time believing that true love existed.

Sighing, I dropped my head back and threw an arm over my face. *Your research might prove to be wrong, Aunt Moira.*

I was going to be the worst matchmaker ever.

Chapter Ten

Rosie

It wasn't jet lag that had me waking up at three in the morning and staring at the ceiling where Moira had hung faux green vines.

It was Daniel's sad eyes.

And Edina's hopeful expression.

I'd accepted their money, hadn't I? It was officially a transaction, even though I hadn't known what I was getting involved in, and now I felt a responsibility to see this through.

Or I could just refund their money. It wouldn't be hard to explain that I wasn't cut out for this job and they'd likely have better luck on a dating app.

I pictured Daniel trying to upload photos to Tinder and shook my head in the dark room. It would be like leading a lamb to slaughter. That poor man would be torn apart on the dating apps, if my brief experience on them had taught me anything.

People were not their kindest selves when hidden behind a screen.

Which didn't mean that I thought all people were bad. Contrary to that thought, I actually landed more in the default thinking that most people were good, albeit being around people at times annoyed me. But that was a *me* thing, not a people-hating thing.

I scrubbed a hand over my face, swiping at the screen of my phone to see that it was now four o'clock. Obviously I wasn't getting back to sleep, so I might as well take this time to be productive. Surely this time of night would not bring me any visitors knocking at my door. Energized by the thought of actually working through some of my lists without interruption, I hopped in the shower, did my morning routine using two heavy books as hand weights, and got dressed. Today's outfit was a cute pair of purple, wide-leg corduroy overalls and I paired it over a red, frilly almost sheer blouse. Piling my hair in a messy bun on my head, I wrapped a silk scarf around my tresses, and out of habit, patted some lip stain on my lips. Again, it wasn't like anyone was going to see me at this hour but, knowing my tendency to lose track of time once I was hyper focused on a task, it was best to dress as though someone would come knocking. That way I wouldn't be caught in my faded sleep shorts and ratty Minnie Mouse T-shirt.

After I brewed a cup of coffee and snagged another buttery, I walked out into the shop and pulled the chain to light the fringe lamp. Dropping into the chair, I put my coffee down, buttery in one hand, and reached for my list with the other.

I stopped, mid-reach, as my eyes landed on the Celtic heart book. I'd put it on the table the night before, promising out loud to the shop that I'd look more deeply into it the next morning, and it had stayed put through the night. Except for one small difference. Now, a magnifying glass attached to a long gold chain was on top of the book.

Finishing the pastry, I wiped my hands on the paper towel I'd brought with me, and then reached for the magnifying glass. It was small, maybe three or so inches in length from the handle to the top of the glass, and hung from a thick gold chain. The handle was ornate, gold vines twisting around a pink quartz heart, and lightly etched flowers lined the circle of gold around the glass.

"Isn't this pretty?" I was a sucker for fun and unique pieces, and this looked to be vintage. Immediately, I pulled it over my head and beamed as I held it up to my eye.

Blurriness greeted me through the lens.

"Oh, right. Duh." I laughed at myself. I was trying to hold it like a pair of glasses when it was meant to be held against the papers. A thought occurred to me. "So if this was left with the book, am I meant to use this with magick? With the love spells?"

The speaker behind me flicked on and began to play Mariah Carey's hit single, *All I Want for Christmas is You.*

I winced.

"Admittedly this song is a banger, but I'm also about to hear it four thousand times in the next month, so can we not?" The song switched to instrumental Christmas music, and I nodded in relief. "Thank you. Whomever you are."

I still wasn't certain if the shop was sentient, if there was a ghost, or if the actual magick that lived here was what was making the calls. I'd read enough fantasy books that anything and everything could be charmed or hold magick, so I was holding out on landing on any theories until I collected more evidence. Speaking of which ...

Pulling out a fresh notebook, I opened it and started a new list of magickal observations. It wouldn't hurt to take notes to reference. Once I noted the few oddities I'd seen so far, I put my pen down and reached for the Celtic heart book.

"Okay. I'm going to use this magnifying glass"—I held up the glass around my neck—"with this book."

The music kept playing so I took that as a positive sign and opened the book to a random page.

"'Susan and Sean.'" I read the names out loud at the top. "'Susan is a single mum who doesn't believe in love after divorce but hopes to find a father to be a good role model for her son. Her favorite book is *The Hunger Games*.'" I tapped the magnifying glass as I thought about the book that was a global phenomenon.

"'Sean has never been married but comes from a big family, and he's looking to settle down. He loves working with his hands and specializes in building custom cabinetry. His favorite book is *Four Blind Mice* by James Patterson.'"

And their books brought about a match? How? One was about a woman sacrificing herself in a game of death to protect her sister and another was about a hero cop who solved murders.

Remembering the magnifying glass, I held it over the page, though I could read the words clearly enough without it.

Protect.

The word hovered briefly in the air beneath the magnifying glass, above the page, glimmering softly in the dark shop.

"Holy shit," I breathed, putting the glass down and catching my breath.

If this was some magickal ink trick, well, it was a damn good one. Taking a healthy gulp of my coffee, I leaned forward and studied the words written on the page. Nowhere was the word "protect" written that could be seen. Even if it was invisible ink or something like that, there was no reason it would hover off the page in such a manner. Holding up the magnifying glass again, I sucked in my breath when the word "protect" lifted off the page and danced in the air beneath the lens.

That was the common link.

Both of these people liked to protect others. To nurture. Which would make them good partners, of course, because neither would feel like what they were giving wasn't being reciprocated.

"Ohhhhh, okay, okay, okay. So, I'm looking for ways

that their ideologies complement each other. I think I get it. This is so cool." Excitement zipped through me as I flipped the page and read another pairing.

"*Eat, Pray, Love* and *Climbing Mount Everest*?" Before I used the glass I wanted to see if I could guess the commonality. "Hmmm. Travel?"

Holding the glass up, the word *adventure* popped off the page.

"Not bad, not bad. Okay, so it's like finding a common thread. Even if the books are different. I think I get it now." Pleased at this new discovery, because it made matchmaking seem a touch less daunting, I hummed my way through reading several other matches. "This is fascinating."

Updating my list of magickal observations, because already my mind was spinning with potential book ideas for my half-finished novel, I paused, tapping the pen against the paper.

"Wait, how long does this all take?"

Would I just have to wait for someone to walk in the door and ask for the perfect book? Or was there a data-base of previous people who had ordered the "special" and were waiting to be matched? I glared at the computer, certain that the info I needed was in there, and sighed. In theory, this could work. But in practice, match-making, particularly with the use of magick, sounded like a full-time job.

A notebook in the pile of ledgers on the table shook.

"Listen, I feel like I'll get used to this assistance at some point, but honestly, this freaks me out a little. Or startles me, I should say." It was true, too. I wasn't scared by what was happening in the shop. Excited. Interested. A bit on edge. But scared? No. Because the magick or ghost or whatever was here didn't feel evil. There were no scrapes down my skin or bloody words showing up on my mirror.

If I had to be exposed to magick, well, this was the perfect kind.

Unless a falling book took me out one day.

That would not be good. I'd already had one blunt force-induced epiphany this year, and I wasn't really looking for another. Pulling the notebook closer, I flipped it open.

"And we've struck gold."

It was a list of Moira's customers along with their orders, preferences, and contact information. Certain pages had little red hearts at the top. Taking that to mean she'd matched them, I cross-referenced the names in the matchmaking book.

"Yup, okay, I see. And the rest? Surely they all can't be single?" That's when I noticed an individual letter at the top of each page. S. M. W. D.

"Single. Married. Widowed. Divorced."

This was starting to fall into place. I had to admit, I was absolutely transfixed with the possibility of being able to bring people together over their shared love of books. My fingers paused as I came across Alexander's name.

Alexander MacTavish.

Sighing, I reached for my coffee. His full name

sounded even sexier than just his first. Telling myself that this was simply professional curiosity, in case a perfect match came in for him, I checked the letter at the top of his page.

"Divorced. Hmm, I wonder what happened."

None of my business. I then scanned his purchase history. His listed favorite book had a question mark after it, but it made my heart dance.

The Hobbit.

I mean, it wasn't unlikely that *The Hobbit* was *many* people's favorite book. It had been my gateway into reading fantasy and magick books after all, and I am sure many others. But still, it was a foundational block for my love of reading and seeing that next to his name made me warm to him.

"Let's see, what else, Dr. MacTavish? My, you have a varied reading list, don't you?"

It was as eclectic a list as mine. It seemed the man bounced from science fiction to murder mysteries to self-help books. I paused at one title.

"*Get Divorced, Be Happy.* Aww, poor guy. At least he sought some advice for it." I had to admire a man that reached out for help, even in the form of a self-help book, after a breakup. Not all men, frankly all people, were sufficiently in touch with their emotions to do so.

"*Losing a Parent.* Navigating grief. Oh, buddy. That's a tough one too. Jeez, you've had some wounds, haven't you?" It made me think back to our stilted conversation yesterday. I made a note to try and be as gentle with him as I could. Who knew what level of grief he was currently dealing with? Discreetly, I checked the dates next to the sales. *Over three years ago.* I hoped he was in a better place now.

Even so, I made a mental note not to add him to my dating pool. He hadn't come in and asked for the "special," and it was clear he was taking some well-deserved healing time.

"It's astonishing what information you can glean from someone's book choices."

Curious, I flipped through until I found Esther's page. Or pages, I should say.

"Oh, you're a hopeless romantic." I laughed at the endless list of romances she'd purchased through the years, everything from deeply erotic books that I'd read and had even made me blush to sweet, clean closed-door romances. It seemed that Esther didn't discriminate in her romance choice, she just wanted everyone to find love.

I wondered if they'd like to be involved with the matchmaking.

Turning the thought over, I paused as I saw Esther's favorite book.

Pride and Prejudice.

"Is that right? *Interesting.*" I drew the word out as I thought about Daniel. They were similar in age, from what I could guess, but I wondered how his sweet nature would do with Esther's battering-ram approach to life. Would she just steamroll the poor man?

"I'll think on that one." In the meantime, I needed to get these accounts sorted so I could have my first proper day of business. Which also meant I needed to take stock of what books were in this shop.

The disorganization was surely going to keep me up at night. While the Book Bitches had done a great job getting everything cleaned, dusted, and sorted yesterday, I still had entire shelves of books that had no rhyme or reason to how they were put away. I suppose that was the easiest way to do it, just shove a book onto a shelf when you were done with it, but no way was my brain ever going to allow me to function in a shop without some sort of order.

The music flipped off.

"Oh, don't be in a huff about it. If you want me to stay here, I need to do some things my way. And I can't run a shop and make a profit if I can't track the stock. It's as simple as that."

The music flipped back on.

Mariah Carey again.

"Cute. But I'm taking that to mean you agree with me, even if you're annoyed about it."

The volume increased and, despite myself, I laughed.

"Well, I'd promised myself a new adventure, didn't I? I guess this is what I get. A sarcastic ghost and a match-making business."

Chapter Eleven

Alexander

Was it too early to knock on the bookshop door? It was just shy of eight, and even though I knew the shop didn't usually open until mid-morning, I had a solution for Rosie's computer problem. If running the business was hedging on using that ancient laptop of hers, it wasn't going to go very smoothly.

Rosie opened the door looking like a bouquet of flowers in purple overalls and a frilly red blouse that upon closer inspection revealed the lacy outline of her bra. Pulling my eyes away from that enticing sight, I tilted my head at the bird feeder she held in her hands.

Was this woman purposely trying to make me fall in love with her?

Between her delicious curves, her colorful clothes, and now, apparently an interest in birds, I was going to have a tough time falling asleep tonight.

"Oh, Alexander. Hi. I wasn't expecting anyone. Actually, never mind, I was expecting everyone." Her nose crinkled as she rolled her eyes at me.

"You were?"

"I don't think it seems to matter if I have my sign flipped to open or closed. People seem to just wander in whenever they want."

"Oh." Shite, I'd screwed up by coming this early. "I can come back."

"No, no. That wasn't a dig at you. More at me and being rigid."

The word rigid at her lips did weird things to my gut and I had to take a deep breath.

"Whenever there's something new in a small town, it's quite a big event." I still stood on the doorstep, the morning air crisp and cool at my shoulders.

"I'm gathering that. It appears I'm going to have to adjust to ... many new things." She glanced over her shoulder at that and then back at me.

Was someone with her in the shop?

And why did that instantly annoy me? I knew next to nothing about this woman and it was more than likely she *did* have a partner.

"Someone there?" Damn it. I couldn't help but ask.

"What? Oh, no. Nothing like that. Come in, come in." Rosie stepped back, the bird feeder still in hand, and I made my way past her, making sure my backpack didn't catch any of the random bits and bobs tucked in front of the books on the shelves.

"What birds are you trying to attract?"

"Excuse me?" Rosie looked at me blankly and licked her plum-colored lips. She probably hadn't even realized she'd done it, but it sent a jolt of lust through me.

"The bird feeder?" I gestured to her hands.

"Oh, right. Right. I have no idea. I just dug this out of a box as I was trying to organize. I don't know where to hang it or what to feed the birds. I've never had an outdoor space before."

"Really?" I tried to imagine not having nature to immerse myself in and couldn't. I'd grown up basically feral, running the hills and shoreline, and aside from university, had never lived in a city.

"Really. My apartment was a tiny one-bedroom that I've had since college. I was lucky it came with windows, frankly, since it was so cheap."

"No garden growing up?"

Rosie threw her head back and laughed, the sound sending a prickle of awareness over me, like someone blowing a soft breath across heated skin.

"No staying anywhere long enough. My mother was, *is*, impetuous, sporadic, and largely absentminded. She'd either grow tired of a place, forget to pay rent, or move on a whim. And I was just a second thought, a back-seat passenger along for the ride."

I tried to imagine my steady and graceful mother packing me up and moving yearly. I just couldn't do it. She'd enjoyed being settled as much as I had, and she'd provided an exceedingly stable foundation for me to grow on.

"That had to have been—"

"Exciting?" Rosie said, quickly, too quickly. "Of course, it was. Loads of new experiences and meeting new friends and all that."

"I was going to say tough." I kept my eyes on hers and saw the brief flash of pain before she turned away. From what I remembered of my boyhood years, it hadn't always been easy to make new friends.

"Oh, it was fine. I'm fine." Rosie waved a hand in the air.

It didn't seem like she was fine. It sounded like she'd had a careless mother who'd had a child who needed love and attention. But this was not a problem I could solve, nor really weigh in on, and I did my best not to offer advice when it wasn't asked for. So instead, I redirected the conversation.

"Do you know what kind of birds you'd like to see outside your window?"

"Um." Rosie pursed those pretty lips. "Happy birds. I'd like to see happy birds."

At that, I huffed out a small laugh.

"Any bird getting food in the winter is going to be a happy bird."

"Perfect. That's what I want then."

"I'll bring some feed by for you."

"Oh, no. I'm sure I can get some on my own. You don't have to do that."

"I have entire bins of it." I held my hands out to show

the size. "It will get you started, and then once you get an idea if you'll remember to fill it or not, you can start buying your own."

Rosie tossed me an affronted look.

"You'd think I'd forget to feed my birds?"

I grinned. "I'm only saying that it's easy to forget if it is not a habit for you. That's all."

"I would never let my birds down. They need me."

"You haven't even met them yet," I pointed out, taking off my backpack and hanging up my coat on the rack at the door. "What if they're a bunch of wankers?"

"How *dare* you call my birds wankers. Wait, what's a wanker?"

"I'm not!" I held a hand to my heart, holding back laughter. "I'm just saying ... what if they are?"

"I will have happy birds. The best birds in all the land. No wankers allowed." Rosie narrowed her eyes at me, and I held my hands up.

"That's fine then. Do you want me to make a sticker for your feeder that says that?"

"You've got a sticker machine?"

"Well, a label maker."

"Keep talking." Rosie fanned her face, and I laughed outright this time.

"I'm sensing you like organization?"

"I'm an absolute slut for it. I love lists, labels, neat little boxes that hold tiny little things. It makes my heart sing."

"A woman after my own heart. I'm a programmer," I explained, crouching to unzip my backpack. "Well, a software engineer. We love when things are logical and line up. It's built into our very DNA."

"That makes sense. One wrong line of code and the whole thing can crash, right?"

"Pretty much." Pulling out the laptop I'd spent a good portion of the evening refurbishing and installing programs on, I placed it on the table. Rosie eyed it suspiciously before looking up at me.

"What's that?"

"That, lass, is what we call a laptop. They are a new invention from the last forty years or so, but one that has gained popular traction around the world."

"I know what a laptop is." Rosie stomped her foot in the most adorable manner, and I grinned. Wow, that was like three smiles and two laughs before ten in the morning. It was more than I'd laughed in weeks. "What is *this* laptop?"

"This laptop is now yours."

"What? No. *No.* Alexander, I couldn't. I can't." Rosie put the bird feeder on the table and promptly picked up the computer to hand it back to me.

"Sure you can. It's easy. You just say, thank you Alexander, and we skip this whole song and dance where you pretend you don't need it to run the shop."

"You can't just *gift* me a laptop." Rosie squinted at me like she wasn't sure if I was all there. "You don't even know me."

"What would make you more comfortable about accepting this? Do you want to get to know me better? Och, go on then. Fire away."

"Fine. How did you come up with a laptop so fast?"

"I have a good twenty of them sitting around."

Rosie's mouth dropped open. "You do?"

"Yes, Rosie. It's what I do. This is an older model, but not too old, gently used, and honestly not worth all that much in today's market. But it's serviceable and will suit your needs just fine."

"Hmm." Rosie looked up at the air and then back at me. "How old are you?"

"Thirty-four."

"What's your astrological sign?"

My lips quirked. "Capricorn."

"Mustard or mayo?"

"Depends on the situation."

"Sandwich." Rosie narrowed her eyes at me.

"Mayo."

"How many pillows for sleep?"

"One is sufficient."

Rosie scoffed and shook her head. "If you live in a prison."

"How many pillows do you use?"

"At least three. I like one for my head and one on either side of me so when I turn, I can wrap around it."

Instantly my mind went to images of a sleep-flushed Rosie, all soft and round and warm, and I had to pull my mind away because the very thought made me a little dizzy.

"Rock music or hip-hop?"

"Both. Depends on the mood."

"Concerts or raves?"

"Concerts."

"Board games or video games?"

"Both."

"Correct choice." Rosie beamed at me. "Favorite book?"

"Recently or ever? That's tough. I read all over the spectrum."

"Now and all-time."

"Hmm, I really enjoyed Richard Osman's newest, but *The Hobbit* is a classic for a reason. It made me believe in fantasy lands and that I, a humble boy, could defeat the big baddies. I used to race across the fields and build forts that were like hobbit holes and then defend them with a branch."

"A warrior at heart, eh?" Rosie sized me up. Did I puff out my chest a little? Yeah, I did. So what?

"I think we all hope to be the hero of our own story." I was getting a little too close to my own personal wounds for comfort, but there was no way for Rosie to know that.

"True enough. Favorite date night meal?"

"I don't date."

"If you *did* date," Rosie amended with an annoyed little shake of her head that sent the mass of hair on top of her head tumbling about. I wanted to reach out and run my hands through the strands to see if it was as silky as it looked.

"It depends what the lady liked. I wouldn't cook her steak if she was a vegetarian, you ken?"

"So you'd cook on a first date?"

"Aye. Unless she'd want a fancy night out. Then I'd find a good restaurant."

"You'd let her choose then?"

"I'd like to surprise her a bit, but I think she should get some say in what we do."

"Brothers or sisters?"

"None, only child."

"Same!" Rosie reached out a hand and I realized she was trying to high five me. I tapped my hand lightly against hers and warmth raced down my arm at her touch.

"Is that enough for you to accept this gift?" I asked, wondering how long we'd be doing this round of questioning.

"Why birds?"

"Why birds what?" My eyebrows rose.

"Like, why are you into them? I thought it might just be the puffin you rescued, but you said you have buckets of birdseed so you must like them."

"Oh." I took a moment to think about it. Uncomfortable, I rubbed at a spot on my chest. "Many reasons, I guess. My mum loved them. She used to take me out every winter looking for the snow buntings, her favorites. Which is how I found the rescue puffin. I still go out, even though she's passed on."

Rosie's eyes softened with sympathy, but I rushed on before she could interject.

"And I guess, I don't know, I kind of like the gamification aspect of it? There's this website, you see, that you can track all your finds. By your home, when you travel, that kind of thing. And you get ranked the more birds you find. It ends up being like a big scavenger hunt. It also gives me an excuse to get out in nature, particularly when the weather isn't great. Which is quite often here. It'd be a lot easier to just hunker in every day through the winter. But birding forces me to get out and explore."

"Wow, I wasn't expecting all that. So it's more than just liking birds."

"Aye. Also, I do think they're pretty cool. But not enough to drag me out of bed and into the icy winter. I think it's the gaming aspect that drives me to do that. I want to up my rank."

"Makes perfect sense to me." Rosie nodded. "Fine. I will begrudgingly accept your kind gesture so long as you accept mine."

"Which is what?"

"I won't be charging you for your books for the next six months."

"Och, come on, Rosie. You need to make money too."

"Nope, you'll not convince me otherwise. Take it or leave it."

Looked like I was going to be reading on my Kindle more often to save her from giving away too many free books. Giving up, I nodded.

"That's fine then. Now, show me this bad boy."

"It's pretty self-explanatory. I didn't password protect it because I figured you'd want to set one, so we can do that now." Crouching by the table, I fired up the computer and ran my hands over the keyboard until the settings screen popped up. "Here, enter your password."

I turned away, closing my eyes so she'd know I wouldn't look, and then silently berated myself for doing so. She pressed close to me, all warmth and heat and lush curves, and I wanted to lean into her softness. I wanted to peel those silly purple overalls off her body and see if the shirt was as sheer as I thought it was when the corduroy material wasn't covering her breasts. It made me ache, her being fully covered, yet teasing with glimpses of something more.

"All done." I realized that Rosie had repeated herself and I turned, finding her face close to mine.

Our eyes caught.

The moment hung suspended, the music dimming in the background, and I ached to lean forward for just a small taste. Her lips begged to be kissed and I, to my absolute surprise, wanted to be the man to do it.

The bells at the door rang and we sprang apart.

"Well now, what do we have here?" Esther barked from the door and my face flushed as I bent to dig in my backpack for the charger.

"Just delivering a working computer," I said, taking far longer than I needed to pull out the charger that was neatly packed on the side of my bag.

"Isn't *that* nice?" Esther singsonged, and I rolled my eyes. *So it begins.*

"Ladies, to what do I owe this pleasure?" Rosie asked, deflecting the attention. Putting the charger next to the computer, I rose and turned.

Meredith, Cherise, Shannon, and Esther stood clustered by the doorway, each carrying a box or a bag, except for Esther. Esther had a whiteboard in her hand. The women were already chattering among themselves, ignoring us, as they hung up coats and carried the boxes and bags over to the table.

They all wore Christmas jumpers.

Pursing my lips, I checked my smart watch. We had two days until December, so not technically Christmas month yet, but that didn't seem to stop these ladies.

Meredith's shirt had two bottles of gin tied together with a big Christmas bow and it read *Gin-gle Bells*.

Shannon's had a cartoon drawing of a Christmas cookie with *Out here looking like a snack*.

My favorites were Cherise's and Esther's.

Cherise's had a puffin holding mistletoe with *Merry Puffin Christmas*.

Esther's had two puffins dancing with a Christmas tree in the middle and it read, *Puffin around the Christmas tree*.

"Love the jumpers," I said.

"We didn't want wee Tattie to feel like we didn't support him." Esther sniffed in Meredith's direction.

"What? You didn't tell me it was another puffin day. Plus, you were hogging the cricut machine."

"You make these?" Rosie asked, delighted. "Oh, these could be fun for the shop. We should sell them."

Esther carried her whiteboard across the room and set it on an empty shelf behind the table. Rosie looked at me and I shrugged.

"It's time for a meeting." Esther clapped her hands together.

"Would you hold on? Can I put the kettle on?" Without waiting for an answer, Meredith disappeared past Rosie and into another room and Rosie waved a hand weakly in the air.

"I can do it. That's my—" But it was too late, Meredith was already gone.

"Did she just go into your private flat and make herself tea?" I lowered my voice and leaned closer to Rosie.

"She did. I have no idea how to handle this."

"Want me to say something?"

"God, no. And break their hearts? I think they know how much power they hold simply because everyone is too scared to stand up to them."

"Agreed."

"Um, what is all this?" Rosie pitched her voice higher and leaned a bit closer. I caught a whiff of her scent, something soft and seductive, reminding me of steamy summer afternoons.

"We needed to give you some time to get your feet under you yesterday. But, now that you're all sorted, it's time to get down to brass tacks." Esther put her hands on her hips and glowered at us. Rosie recoiled.

"Are we going to war?" Rosie whispered.

"You can consider it such," Shannon warned.

"What is happening?" Rosie looked at me.

"I think it's the—"

"It's the Winter Windows competition. St. Andrews wins every year and, well, we're sick of it. While Moira did a great job decorating, she didn't change it up enough, which is why St. Andrews always edged us out. But not this time. Nooooo, not this year. We're going to take those posh twats down." Esther sliced an arm across her neck and Rosie's eyebrows winged up her forehead.

"We're really doing this?"

"It's just a decorating competition," I said out of the side of my mouth.

Esther slammed a hand on the table and Rosie and I jumped.

"It's not *just* a decorating competition, lad. It's the most elite bookshop holiday window decorating competition in the world."

"Are there many bookshop window decorating competitions? Is there a database somewhere that I can track previous wins?" I asked. Rosie snorted quietly and warmth filled me. I considered that comment a win, even if it earned me a glare from Esther.

"It's that kind of attitude that's going to lose us the prize. Don't make me demote you."

"You're a part of this?" Rosie looked up at me.

"Involuntary volunteer," I whispered.

"I heard that." Esther turned to her whiteboard and uncapped a marker. The marker squeaked as she wrote "Destroy St. Andrews" in large block letters.

"There's the Christmas spirit." I nodded.

"Is it even Christmas if you're not plotting someone else's demise?" Rosie wondered out loud.

"The true meaning of the holiday season," I agreed.

"Esther's going to put you on her naughty list if you two keep it up," Cherise warned us.

"Why do I feel like Santa's naughty list and Esther's are wildly different?" Rosie asked.

"Oh, they are. Neither of you go on my naughty list because both of you together couldn't handle me. Now, on my shite list, yes, I'll put both of you there if you don't straighten up and focus on the task at hand."

My mouth dropped open, as did Rosie's. We looked at each other and came to a silent agreement that neither of us wanted more information about Esther's naughty list.

"Um, how is the competition judged? Are there rules?"

"There's an independent panel of judges who aren't affiliated with the participating shops. There are no rules except it has to be a holiday theme of sorts. And there are four windows, one for each weekend, to draw crowds to the store."

"Crowds?" Rosie paled a bit.

"It's very popular. And good business for the bookshops."

"What was St. Andrews' winning window last year?" I asked.

"A literary Nutcracker."

"What does that mean exactly?" I accepted a cup of tea from Meredith and leaned back against the table. When my shoulder brushed Rosie's and she didn't move, I realized that I enjoyed her closeness. It felt … companionable. Like we were in this together, a team against the overwhelmingness of the Book Bitches.

"They made different famous literary characters and then staged them as parts in the Nutcracker."

"Ah, I see. Okay, okay." Rosie tapped a finger against her lips. "So if I do this, it's going to take considerable time and effort because it can't be basic."

"What do you mean *if* you do this?" Esther demanded. "You *will* do this."

"Will I?" Rosie arched a brow.

"You will. And you'll love it. And we're going to go bigger and better and more extravagant than anyone's seen before!"

"For a wee window competition? Isn't that excessive?" I asked, earning Esther's wrath.

"*Your* questions are excessive."

"Right. My apologies." Soon she'd tell me I was excess baggage and I'd likely be kicked off the team. Yesterday, I'd wanted nothing to do with the Book Bitches and their competition, but today, after seeing Rosie in her bright clothes and subtly indecent top, my interest had been piqued.

Which it shouldn't be. Because I'd sworn off dating and women. I was finally at peace with my life and there was nothing wrong with being single, or with being content with your life as you know it.

"Well, it certainly could be a way to drum up more business over the holiday season." Rosie worried her bottom lip, as she glanced outside to where rain pelted the windows. "And I had planned to decorate as Moira left loads of boxes. Why not? I'm in. St. Andrews is going down."

I internally groaned at her phrasing of choice and looked away. Clearly my libido was back in full force. We were talking about Christmas decorations of all things. There was nothing sexy about decorating. If anything, it just led to arguments and tangled strings of lights.

"Right, team. Let's workshop some ideas." Esther held a marker to the board. "Nothing is a bad idea."

"Willy Wonka," I said, even though I had no idea why.

"What? That makes zero sense." Esther shook her head.

"I thought there were no bad ideas." *Immediate betrayal by my teammates, I see.*

"No, it's not bad, Esther. You could do all sorts of fun things with the candy and have golden tickets tucked in the books. It's not a bad idea at all." Rosie bumped my shoulder and I smiled smugly at Esther.

"Noted." Esther wrote it down.

"A giant pop-up book," Meredith suggested.

"*Narnia*," Cherise tossed out.

"Gingerbread houses but made out of book covers."

"Enchanted forest."

"*Alice in Wonderland*."

"Jane Austen."

"*Sherlock Holmes*."

"Christmas under the sea."

"Christmas around the world."

"Christmas in space."

"Stop!" Esther cried, putting her hand in the air. She finished scribbling the last of the suggestions that the group had shouted out. "That's enough. For now. There are some good ones in there. Well, some. Christmas under the sea?" Esther rolled her eyes at Shannon.

"Och, it would be great fun. A mermaid Christmas? We live right at the ocean."

"I mean, I kind of like it," Rosie said. "Could there be puffins?"

"Ohhh, I'm in." I grinned as Esther's cheeks mottled. "All for Christmas under the sea?"

Four of us raised our hands. Cherise started to but dropped it at Esther's expression.

"Well, I see I've been outvoted. Fine, then. But when this window ranks poorly, don't come crying to me."

"Och, go on then, Esther. You know it'll be just lovely. Don't be in a huff."

"I'm not in a huff." Esther sniffed and turned her back. She was a woman in a huff if ever I'd seen one.

"But you do the best designs. We have four chances. Isn't it best we start with the smallest idea and work up to the best? That way we can really wow them by the end of the month," Meredith said.

"I suppose." Esther turned and stuck her nose in the air. "But I'm putting pirates in as well."

"Naturally. We wouldn't want them not to get a Christmas gift either." Rosie nodded as though a pirate, puffin, and mermaid-themed Christmas window made any sense at all.

"It's going to be great. Esther will draw up the design and we can pick up materials. Once we have a design, Alexander can figure out the lights and the music."

"The music?" Rosie asked, arching a brow up at me.

"Aye. They want lights that change in beat to the music."

"Won't that be a tad annoying to listen to on repeat all day?" Rosie trailed off as Esther gave a deep sigh.

"Right, music it is." Turning to me, Rosie bumped my shoulder again. "Hey, is it possible I could meet your puffin? I've never seen one before and, from their photos, I think they are just too cute."

"Oh," I said. Caught, I didn't dare glance around as silence filled the bookshop. "Aye, that'd be fine. Just one person shouldn't be much disruption to him."

"Oh cool. That will give me something to look forward to after work. Now, let me just go grab some of those boxes of decorations." Rosie disappeared into the back room and silence filled the shop. I turned and made a great show of zipping up my backpack, refusing to look at the Book Bitches.

"Say, Meredith, wasn't it just yesterday that Alexander mentioned that nobody could come visit Tattie? That visitors would be too much excitement for the wee bird?"

"I believe it was, Esther. Just yesterday indeed. At the coffee shop."

Bloody hell.

"I'm sure one person will be fine," I hissed, keeping my voice low.

"So we can come by one at a time then?" Esther pressed.

Caught, I stared at them like a deer in headlights.

Shannon threw her head back and laughed while Cherise shook her head, making a clucking noise with her lips.

"I think the lad's got a wee crush."

"You know, we can help you with this." Esther marched closer. "We're practically legendary when it comes to our matchmaking."

"Matchmaking?" Rosie said, and I froze, feeling the blood drain out of my face. Nope, this was not what I needed.

"Ladies, I have to run. I have a Zoom call soon." I didn't. I was absolutely lying, but I needed an out. I was already past my limit for conversation for the day and it wasn't even ten o'clock. Slipping my backpack on, I made to leave.

"Wait." Rosie grabbed my arm. "How will I find your house?"

My cheeks burning, I turned and wrote my number down for her while the Book Bitches watched gleefully on. Barely able to say goodbye, I grabbed my coat and tossed it over my shoulders and backpack, not caring that I hadn't properly put it on.

The ice-cold rain that slapped my face was a sharp reminder to not get too comfortable.

"Bloody hell," I murmured again. What was I getting myself into?

Chapter Twelve

Rosie

"What, exactly, were you talking about with matchmaking?" I demanded, whirling on the women. They all turned away at once, digging in boxes, dusting shelves, and Cherise picked up a fairy ornament and held it in front of her face.

"Hello? I know you can hear me." Walking over, I took the ornament out of Cherise's hands, and she blinked up at me.

"What is that, dear? You know, I'm quite old. I must be losing my hearing." Cherise turned and ducked around a bookshelf, hiding from me. I knew who the head of this group was. Turning, I stalked across the room until

I was almost nose to nose with Esther. To her credit, she didn't flinch, instead she lifted her chin to meet my eyes.

"Is this about the Highland Hearts Special?" I asked.

Surprise entered her eyes. "What?"

"The matchmaking? The magic?" I waved a hand in the air.

The music flipped off.

As one, everyone in the shop turned to look at the speaker.

"Lass, what are you talking about?" Esther whispered, reaching out to put her palm against my forehead to check for a temperature.

"What were *you* talking about?" I demanded, batting her hands away. "I'm not sick."

"Matchmaking. We're known to be quite good at it. In fact, I would say we have a one hundred percent success rate." A smug expression crossed Esther's face and she tucked a gray curl behind her ears.

"With the shop? The Highland Hearts Special? You're a part of this too?"

"I have no idea what you're talking about."

The music flipped on again. This time it was the song, *Magic*, by the band, Pilot.

"Shit," I breathed.

"Are you wanting to tell us something, dear?" Meredith asked, keeping her tone cheerful as she sidled closer, giving the speaker a wide berth.

"Um, no?" My voice rose in question.

"You don't sound convinced. And judging from your

speaker over here, I'd say there might be something you want to maybe have a wee chat about?" Shannon asked.

"Nope, can't think of a thing." I pursed my lips and looked at the ceiling.

The song switched to *Little Lies* by Fleetwood Mac, and I closed my eyes, shaking my head.

"Your ghost doesn't seem to agree," Esther said, a cheerful note in her voice.

"This amuses you?" I raised an eyebrow at her.

"If it's a bit of magic you're in a fuss about, I wouldn't worry. Scotland's chock full of hauntings and magic and spells. Just wait until you go to Loren Brae. They're positively crawling with magickal beings."

"Excuse me?" My eyebrows rose.

"Och, lass. Wait until you meet Clyde. Cheeky bastard. He'll scare the bejeezus out of you." Meredith laughed.

"Clyde?" I asked, weakly.

"A ghost highland coo. Haunts MacAlpine Castle. He's a cheeky one, that he is."

"A ghost coo."

"Correct."

"What the heck is a ghost coo?"

"A coo, dear. You know, they produce milk."

"A cow?"

"Yes, a coo. A highland coo, to be exact."

"Right." I looked around. Was it too early for wine?

Seeming to sense my distress, Shannon pulled a flask from her purse. "Just a wee tipple to set you straight."

"I won't say no." I held out a hand and took a sip from the flask, the whisky burning a path down to my core.

Day two and I was already drinking in the morning. This did not bode well for my new adventure. To be fair, I'd never encountered magick in real life before so I'm sure some allowances could be made.

"So this old shop is haunted? Is it Moira?" Cherise wondered. She looked around, a hopeful expression on her face. "Oh, I hope so. I do miss her so."

The music switched to the Beatles. When *With a Little Help from My Friends* started, the women all gasped. Cherise fanned her face, a sheen of tears coating her eyes.

"Moira, you're here. Oh, we've *missed* you, my dear. We really have. A wee bit of sparkle has gone missing from our lives." Meredith saluted her with a coffee mug that had a picture of a cat riding a unicorn on it.

"This is the best news I've had all year." Shannon beamed and galloped across the shop, doing a little shimmy with her bum.

"Moira, you're derailing us as usual," Esther said, annoyed. "Ladies. You've got your assignments. Shannon, you're on fabrics. Meredith, figurines. Cherise, you're on sequins, glitter, and all the sparkles. Go on, go on. I need to draw this up and we barely have time as it is before the first judging." Esther clapped her hands and herded the women out of the shop, slamming the door after them. Turning, she leaned her back against the door and took a deep breath. And then another.

Worry flitted through me. Her expression was

unreadable. Gone was the brash woman who'd just been bossing her friends around.

"Och, Moira. I'm *so* damn glad you're here." It was just a whisper, and my heart twisted as Esther's ravaged expression of sadness turned to one of relief. When *Lean on Me* started playing from the radio, I had to turn away as tears sprung to my own eyes.

I hadn't had a chance to know Moira, but she'd clearly left a huge absence in these women's lives. I hadn't given a lot of thought to the legacy Moira had left behind. She'd left me her shop to run—*and to continue its mission to unite souls*—but she'd also left a hole behind in this community. She'd had friends who missed her and, for some reason, I had completely overlooked that facet of this whole thing. *What an extraordinary woman my great-aunt was.*

I wanted to make an impression like that, I realized with a start, as I glanced up at a photo on a shelf that I hadn't seen before.

Giving Esther a moment, I walked over and picked the frame up. It was the bookshop, twinkle lights strung across the wood beams that lined the ceiling, and there had clearly been a party going on. But in the middle, a woman swirled in a sparkly skirt with a smile that lit up the room. This must be Moira.

Nobody would have remembered me at the discount store.

But here? I could make a difference. I could bring joy to people's lives, through stories and community and parties and whatever, really. A bookshop was a hub of so many things to so many people and all I had to do was open the door. In this case, not *even* open the door and people would come in anyway.

"All right, lass, now that they're gone, tell me, what's this matchmaking business about? The Highland Hearts Special?" Esther looked over my shoulder and her expression softened at the photograph I held. "She was like that, you know. Just lit up a room. Annoying old bat. Scored all the men."

"Is that right? I thought she was single."

"And ready to mingle." Esther sniffed. "Nagged me all the time too."

"Something I'm sure you never do." I stifled a grin as Esther narrowed her eyes at me.

"It's not nagging if I'm right," Esther pointed out.

"Is that the way of it?" I hummed under my breath as I looked around the shop. "Do you think she'd care if I decorated more in here? I mean, it's already full of lovely pieces. But I was thinking of maybe a statement wall over here." I pointed to the wall on the other side of the room that was bare except for two abstract paintings full of pops of color. "Put up some wallpaper, add some lighting, maybe some fun chairs and a table in front of it? Create another little nook for people to sit down?"

And maybe a spot for one of their fancy tea kettles that just needed an electrical socket, and tea, so some people would stop going into my kitchen all the time.

"Moira loved changing things around. She moved bookshelves quite a bit. These all unhook and can be shifted about. You can create a different configuration,"

Esther explained, pointing up to hinges and hooks on the edges of the bookshelves that I hadn't noticed before. "I'm sure she'd be delighted that you would want to do the same. She loved surprising people with new and fun things when they came through the door. I think that was part of the draw of the shop. It wasn't just the books. Moira made it an experience to visit."

"I don't doubt it. I feel like every time I turn around I discover something new. It's the way a bookshop should be, in my opinion. I want to be charmed and delighted when I go through a door to a bookshop, you know?"

"Aye, I know it." Esther took the picture from me and moved across the room to stick it next to the speaker. "There. That's better. Now that I've gotten rid of the others, why don't you tell me more about this Highland Hearts Special?"

"Um." I wasn't sure if I was allowed to share this information. I'd clearly bungled it by saying something and now I wasn't sure what to do.

The music flipped to *Go Ahead* by Alicia Keys.

"See? Moira knows I'm good for it. Go ahead, lass, tell me."

"Well, from my understanding, it's a magick inherited through the shop owner." It actually felt like a weight shifted off my shoulders a bit. Not only had the discovery of magick been both daunting and exciting, but the pressure of having to match people I'd never met before was slightly terrifying. Esther might actually be a really valuable resource as I tried to fulfill the matches that I'd inad-

132

vertently agreed to help with already. I went on to give her a quick rundown of what I'd learned so far.

"Let me see," Esther demanded, when I told her about the magnifying glass. I moved around the table and took a seat in the leather chair, and Esther pulled one of the velvet fabric chairs to the table and plopped down in it. Stretching out her legs, she breathed a sigh of happiness. "Moira and I used to sit here for hours at a time like this. But she never told me about her matchmaking business. Probably because she knew I'd be better at it than her."

The lights flipped off for a second and I bit back a grin.

"Och, fine, fine. You could read people well enough." Esther waved a hand in the air and the lights flicked back on.

The music flipped to *Bitch* by Meredith Brooks, and I laughed out loud.

"Okay, Moira has a sense of humor. I like her." I pushed the notebook over to Esther and showed her matches. Then I lifted the magnifying glass from where I'd secured it in a drawer in the credenza behind the table. "And if you use this ... you should be able to see a word that connects the matches."

"Oh." Esther patted a hand at her heart before taking the magnifying glass from me. "Moira used to wear this around her neck every day. Will you?"

"I ... I think so."

"Good, you should. It will be like looking through her

eyes a bit." Esther held it up to her face and I grinned at her magnified eyeball looking back at me.

"Hold it over the paper."

When Esther did so and gasped, I figured she was seeing the same thing I had.

"So I can match people through their favorite book. And apparently, there's some sort of underground market for this because I've had two people come in already and slip me money along with their contact information. I have no idea where to start."

"Who?" Esther demanded, leaning forward.

"Let me see." I opened my notebook and looked down. "Edina and Daniel are the first two."

"Oh, Edina. Such a shame that one. Nasty divorce. She's just a shell of herself these days. Like watching a fallen leaf get tossed about by the winter breeze."

"But here's the thing. *How* do I help her? I think I've narrowed down two potential past clients that might be a good match based on their book choices, but there may be more. I didn't get very far before visitors arrived. Unannounced." I raised an eyebrow at Esther.

"Get used to it. I'm going to annoy you even more now that I know we get to match people with magick. Show me who you think for Edina." Esther tapped the book, stern as a strict schoolteacher.

"Right, okay. I tabbed them." Flipping through the book of past clients, I found the two I'd marked. "The first one is Samuel. His favorite book is *The Martian* by Andy Weir."

"And what's hers?"

"*The Housemaid.*"

"Och, that's a good one. But hmmm." Esther tapped a finger against her lips. "Not sure how they're connected, lass."

"The other is Randall and his book is *It* by Stephen King."

"Hmm. Small town. Horror. Maybe the small town link? Mystery in a small town?" Esther wrinkled her nose. "I know Randall and I can't say that I'm overly impressed by him. Are you certain he'd be a right match for Edina?"

"I literally know as close to nothing about these people as is possible," I pointed out.

"On the surface, I'd say *It* and *The Housemaid* would link. But it doesn't feel right. What would connect the other book instead?"

I leaned back in the chair and closed my eyes for a moment, thinking back. I'd read both *The Martian* and *The Housemaid*. An idea formed.

"They were both outsiders."

"What's that now?" Esther leaned forward.

"The protagonists. They were outsiders coming into a new situation. What do you know about Samuel?"

"He's nice enough. Quiet. Moved here a few years ago and manages the local Tesco."

"And Edina?"

"She's really kept to herself since the divorce. Her husband embarrassed her about town, if you catch my drift. She hasn't been out much."

"So both might be feeling a bit like outsiders?"

"Well, lass, write it down and use the glass. Let's see if you're right."

I did as instructed and we held our breaths. When I held the glass over my writing, a shimmery word appeared in the air, dancing across the page.

"Outsider!" I crowed.

"We've got ourselves a match." Esther high-fived me. "Och, this is great fun. Now, to make it happen." She rubbed her hands together gleefully and I realized the flaw in my plans.

"Oh shit. How the hell am I supposed to get them together? I can't just give her his number and tell her to call him."

"What about your opening party?" Esther suggested.

"You want me to throw a party on top of doing this window competition?" I asked. Seriously, did these women not understand that not only had I left my entire life behind two days ago, but I'd also just discovered magick? And I was supposed to be entering a cutthroat window decorating competition and hosting parties?

"Aye, lass. It's a good way to meet everyone in town. You can invite Samuel and Edina. Don't worry. I'll take it from there." Esther rubbed her hands together, and a gleeful light shone in her eyes.

"You're looking a little scary there, Esther."

"Thank you." Esther beamed at me.

"Not sure that was a compliment."

Esther's watch beeped and she glanced down, fiddling with it before standing and reaching for her purse. "I'm off to the dentist. I'll sort out the designs today and we can discuss everything later. Oh, and enjoy your time at Alexander's."

"Oh, thanks. I can't wait to meet his puffin."

"Mm-hmm. Is that what the kids are calling it these days?" Esther arched an eyebrow at me and then swirled out of the shop, letting in an icy blast of wind as she went.

"It's not like that," I called. But she'd already slammed the door behind her. I blinked at the empty shop, the speaker now silent as I took my bearings. I hadn't wanted a boring life. I just also hadn't expected so much activity before ten on a Tuesday. Taking a deep breath, I turned the magnifying glass over in my hands and then for fun, held it over the notebook again. When the word "outsider" shimmered in the air again, a rush of understanding ran over me.

"I get it. I feel the same way. But it won't always be that way. I can do this."

The speaker switched on.

This Must Be the Place by The Talking Heads filled the room. Maybe it was the whisky, or maybe it was the fact that I had a very cheeky ghost in my shop, but I jumped up and twirled across the room.

"Home ..." I sang.

Chapter Thirteen

Rosie

I had a blessedly quiet afternoon.

And I loved it.

Loved it.

I'd never had a chance to make my own decisions when it came to doing anything in a retail space before, and having the complete freedom to rearrange as I saw fit was honestly exhilarating.

Moira kept me company by serving up a wide variety of musical hits, and I'd started to call her DJ M by the end of the afternoon. That seemed to tickle her fancy and she'd started playing quite a mix of dance hits after that, and it kept me moving as I took stock of the shelves, made decorating notes, and mocked up different configurations for the shelves and furniture in the room. It was a clever system she'd devised, because—get this—the bookshelves were on wheels. I wasn't confident on unhooking them and moving them on my own, but at least I had the option.

The bookshop itself was one of those buildings with excellent bones. Which made sense, as it had been around for almost two hundred years. I wanted to change the flow of the pedestrian traffic in the shop, as I noticed people were getting clustered by the door when they first came in, and if I moved one bookshelf and created more of an S shape, people could greet me at the table and then wind their way through the stacks. I also was pretty set on creating another seating area under the statement wall I was going to build out. I wanted to frame quotes from a multitude of books and put them in mismatching frames and create a gallery wall of sorts. Add some fun sconces and a really funky wallpaper, and I was certain it would turn out cozy as could be.

But it was the back garden that kept drawing my eye.

There were two ways to enter the garden, either through my personal quarters, or if you walked in the front door of the shop and turned right, there was a side door on the opposite wall. It was there I now stood, tucked in the open doorway, studying the garden space as a blast of wind brought me the scent of the sea and damp earth.

From what I could tell, Scotland didn't have a lot of sunshiny days. However, back home, I was well used to long and nasty cold winters. Many of the restaurants and cafes had taken to creating outdoor seating in these small, clear domes with indoor heaters. I wondered if I could create a little weather-proof space out here, maybe offer coffee, and people could linger a while longer over their books. It was already a beautiful space, with a low stone wall coated in moss and vines, and a view across a rolling field at the back. Surely people would enjoy reading their books and staying a while here. I knew I would.

Going back inside, I made a note in my projects list to source quotes for a garden build-out. At the moment, I just didn't have the funds for it, but it gave me something to work toward. I was very goal focused, so I slotted it in for a potential end-of-summer project, pending funds. Glancing at my watch, I realized it was already late in the afternoon.

"Shoot, I'd better message Alexander." Honestly I could have kept working in the shop, I was so loving having the space to myself, but I also wasn't a fan when someone changed plans last minute on me, so I didn't want to do that to Alexander, particularly if he had planned any of his day around me stopping by. Picking up my phone, I texted him.

Permission to launch, sir?

Aye, lass.

Okay, my stomach shouldn't flutter at that, but I couldn't help it. Since nobody was around to notice, I squealed. There was just something about a hot Scottish man saying "Aye, lass" that excited me. Truly, I had no idea this was a thing for me prior to coming to Scotland, but it seemed I was uncovering new layers to myself every day.

Alexander pinned his location and I pulled it up to see how far it was from the shop since I didn't have a car. Belatedly, I also realized I hadn't been out to properly explore Kingsbarns yet. The Book Bitches had delivered so much food that I'd had more than enough to eat the past few days, and I'd been busy with the store. So, two new adventures for me today—exploring Kingsbarns and meeting my first puffin. Excited, I popped into my bathroom and checked my face in the mirror. Adding just a smidge more of eyeshadow and a dash of blush across my cheeks, I considered my outfit. I loved these overalls. Serviceable and cute, and they'd be perfect for a walk in the cold winter afternoon. The shirt might be a bit cold though. Considering, I grabbed my Fair Isle sweater vest and pulled it over my head, adding another layer of warmth. Switching my flats out for chunky leather boots, I grabbed a coat and an umbrella and swung a crossbody purse in brilliant red over my shoulder. Eyeing the map once more, I stepped out of Highland Hearts and locked the door behind me.

Tucked at the end of a short cobblestone lane, Highland Hearts looked incredibly charming with stone walls leading off on either side of it, and the soft glow of lights in the windows. Taking a step back, I held my hands up and framed it out like it was a picture.

It was going to look fabulous when it was decorated

for Christmas. Suddenly, I wasn't so against this Winter Windows competition. Why not have fun with it? It would bring people to the shop, and even though the shop was gorgeous and stunning on its own, adding some dressing would just sweeten it up that much more. Giddy at the thought, I hummed to myself as I jammed my hands in my coat and walked toward the main road, ducking my head against the wicked blast of wind that slapped at me. I didn't mind it though. It wasn't as cold as my winters back home, and there was something about being out in the elements that always excited me, particularly if there was inclement weather on.

At the end of the lane, I stopped and looked both directions on the main street. To my left, I could just see Two Sisters coffee house, the warm light from the windows a welcoming glow in the darkness of late afternoon. They'd already begun to decorate for the holidays, and twinkle lights winked around the door. Turning the other direction, toward the ocean my map told me, I stopped at a stone two-story building with a cheerful wooden sign hanging above the door.

The Royal Unicorn.

Ah yes, the pub that I had been told about. I needed to go in there and introduce myself to Harper, the American woman who had moved here last year. Maybe I'd stop in on my way back since it was literally around the corner from the shop. Humming, I continued on down the path that wound past cute one-story cottages, some already decorated with Christmas lights, before the road took me out of town. It really wasn't a large town, but it was bigger than I'd first given it credit for as now I could see where more houses were tucked farther back behind the main road. It was still small enough that someday I'd likely know everyone here.

What a thought.

I'd never lived in such a small town before, and already I could see it was going to be a wild adjustment from what I was used to. Back home, I was fairly certain I'd only known two of my neighbors in my ten-unit apartment building, and that had only been because we'd kept getting our packages delivered to the wrong addresses.

Maybe this would be good for me. Friendships hadn't come easily to me growing up, what with my mom moving me around so much, and I tended to be a loner who preferred a cozy night of reading my book over going out clubbing. Much to Jessica's distress. The best thing about Jessica though was that she accepted me for who I was, and I'd been lucky to keep her friendship. Now I wondered what it would be like to make friends in this small town. Would people like me? Would they know all my business? Would I end up being invested in other people's gossip? It was likely I'd hear it, between working at the shop and trying to make matches, so it might be a good thing for me to know and understand the people better that lived here. So far, I had felt so ... accepted. *Wanted.* And that was such a welcome feeling. Jessica could be right about me staying here.

Turning up the lane on my map, I followed a gravel road that wound along a field of tall grass that was battened down by the recent rains. It was darker now, and I could hear the ocean, but not see it. Annoyed with myself for not thinking this through, timing wise, I used my phone as a flashlight to follow the winding road until a turn revealed a stunning cottage tucked between two cliffs with rolling hills on either side of it. I stopped, my jaw dropping open at the sight. The outdoor lights lit up the surrounding area, allowing me to see around, and my heart clutched at the beauty of this charming cottage, brimming with light, on this wild and windy landscape.

The door opened before I could even knock, and Alexander winced when he looked down at the phone in my hand.

"Bloody hell. I didn't even think. I'm sorry." Shaking his head, he stepped back and ushered me in. "You're my first guest and I didn't think you might be walking."

"It's my fault, I keep forgetting how early it gets dark here." I handed him my coat and purse and took a deep breath. The house smelled like cedar and oranges, a refreshing scent, and warmth enveloped me. "Wait ... did you just move in? I'm your first guest?"

Alexander glanced at me from where he hung my coat on a rack by the door. I noticed a bench with boots beneath and automatically sat to take mine off.

"Oh, you don't have to if you don't want to," Alexander said. I looked up at him and caught him looking at my calf where I'd unzipped my boot, an unreadable look in his eyes.

"Nope. All good. I'm sure I picked up some mud along the way. Thanks for having me over after I rudely invited myself to see your puffin."

"Nae bother, hen." Alexander just stood in the small alcove, looking at me, and I glanced up at him as I stood.

"What's the whole hen thing about? Is that because I'm round?"

Alexander visibly blanched and then his cheeks pinkened. Rushing to explain, he waved his hands in front of him. "No, no, no. Not, no. It's not that you're round. I mean you are, but you don't look like a chicken. It has nothing to do with body ..."

He trailed off as I raised both eyebrows, giving him a bemused look.

Sighing, Alexander rubbed a hand over his face.

"Hen is just a term we use affectionately for women in Scotland. For example, we call a bachelorette party a Hen Do."

"Is that right? So are men cocks then?"

Alexander visibly swallowed.

"No, um, we're stags. It's called a Stag Do."

"So I can say 'nae bother, stag' and that's a normal phrase?" Delighted, I turned the phrase around in my head. I was going to call so many men stags now that I knew this.

"Och, no. Not really. I guess it's just the hen thing. We call each other lads or mates, but not stags."

"Hmmm. Double standard much?"

"I suppose. I apologize on behalf of my country."

"Accepted." Grinning, I stood up. "How come I'm your first guest?"

Alexander did that visible swallowing thing again

and I realized that I was asking a pretty nosey question for just having met someone.

"Sorry, you don't have to answer—"

"I don't socialize much ... anymore," Alexander said at the same time.

"Oh."

We stood, blinking at each other in the hallway for a moment, neither of us speaking. As the moment drew out, I wondered if this man maybe needed some help with socializing or if he just simply preferred life on his own. Or if there was another reason altogether why he was staring at my mouth the way he was.

"Do you maybe want to show me around? The place looks charming as can be from the outside," I suggested and that snapped Alexander out of his intense focus on my lips. Visibly jolting, he turned away, gesturing for me to follow, and a shiver danced across the back of my neck. I hadn't realized just how much his gaze had heated my skin until he'd turned away from me. It was like stepping away from a fire. It was a stark contrast to the indifference I'd felt from John ... *toward* John. How was it possible to feel such intense attraction to a man I barely knew?

"Honestly, I got this place at a steal. It was falling down, but the foundation and walls were solid. I hired a roofer to rebuild the top half of the place so it was nice and watertight, and then I've basically spent the last three years doing the rest."

"What do you mean doing the rest? You built this place?" I reached out and grabbed his arm, surprised. I'd thought he was a computer programmer. Yet the rippling

146

muscles under my hand told me he clearly worked out whether that meant in the gym or swinging a hammer.

"Pretty much." A shy grin crossed Alexander's face, and I had to pause and remind myself that I wasn't looking for a man. But I couldn't help noticing how handsome he looked tonight in a fitted green Henley that showcased his broad shoulders. His hair was still damp from the shower. "YouTube is great if you want to learn things."

"Wow." Turning a circle, I studied the main room. The front door opened to a small hallway that could be closed off by a door, and then you stepped directly into the main room of the cottage. The wall directly across from us speared up almost two stories with huge windows that ended in a point at the apex of the room, and a large stone fireplace lined the wall cornering it. Low-slung leather couches were placed in an L-shape so you could either sit and watch the fire or stare out the windows to the sea as your mood decided. I immediately wanted to sling myself onto the couch in front of the fire, pile one of the several tartan blankets tucked on the back over my legs, and fall into my never-ending to-be-read pile. "What a great room. I'd never leave."

"I rarely do." Alexander laughed. "Aside from work of course."

"Tell me more about your work? You program computers?"

"Among other things. I also teach, up at St. Andrews."

"Get out." I smacked his arm lightly, mainly because

I wanted to touch his muscles again. "You're a hot professor?"

"I have no idea how to answer that and not sound incredibly egotistical." Alexander winced and led me toward a door on the other side of the room. "Kitchen."

"Oh, I bet all the women in your class have a crush on you."

"God, I hope not," Alexander groaned, pushing the door open. "It's awkward enough having to speak in front of a room full of people."

"So why'd you do it?" I stepped through to a bright kitchen done in simple white cupboards, with a sky-blue mosaic backdrop. It was airy and clean, and had another tall window that likely showed the ocean as well. In front of it was a round table with four chairs and three computers on it.

"Teaching?" Alexander leaned against the counter and considered the question. "At the time I hadn't been happy in my job at the company I'd been at. Getting my PhD offered me more work options, but I also found that I liked helping people. I guess that is what outweighs the social anxiety of teaching. And I also took up freelance consulting, so I can supplement my income there as well."

I gaped at him and gestured to the kitchen.

"All while also building a home essentially from scratch."

Alexander laughed, his lips twisting wryly as he did a small shrug with one shoulder.

"Kept me busy." Turning, he went to the fridge. "Can I get you anything to drink?"

Right, conversation closed. I remembered the books about divorce and grief. The man clearly had just buried himself in work to get through the last few years. I couldn't say I blamed him. There were worse ways to deal with difficult times in your life, even if sequestering yourself on a cliff wasn't the most socially acceptable. That being said, he hadn't been entirely cut off from society, what with teaching and all, so I wouldn't put him in recluse territory yet.

"Sure."

"I have juice, wine, beer, and water."

"Wine would be great."

Alexander poured us both a glass of wine and then brought it over. Clinking the glass against mine, we both drank. It was a very smooth Malbec, and I appreciated the choice.

Alexander gave me that unreadable look again over the top of his glass. My skin heated. What was he thinking when he looked at me that way?

"And you?" Alexander startled me with the question, interrupting the silence that was drawing out between us again. It was as though he'd forgotten how to carry on normal conversations. Which, based on what he'd just explained about how busy he'd been with work and severe lack of socializing, tracked. "Your work? Before this?"

"Ah, yeah. The most bland job in the world. I worked

retail at a discount store. I quit when I got knocked out with a water bottle."

Alexander visibly blanched. "One of those big ones with the handles and the straws?"

"The very ones."

"I had no idea discount stores were so violent."

"Neither did I. Well, there had been hints of it." I laughed as I took another sip of the wine and studied a photo on the counter of a smiling woman hugging Alexander. This must have been his mom. "People got pretty pushy over the dollar bins of wrapping paper."

"Is that right?" Alexander gave me a disbelieving look.

"Seriously. It's because it's mostly a single-use product. Nobody wants to pay a lot of money for it. So they'd come to the discount store and load up, but would get pissy if someone else was there taking it."

"I had no idea. And why were you working there if you found it so bland?"

I sighed, twisting the stem of the wine glass in my hand.

"I'd lost my job as a technical writer because I was too fanciful in my wording. My ex-boyfriend's family owned the discount store, and it was an easy transition when I needed to pay the bills. In hindsight, a dumb one. I wasted two years of my life being bored out of my mind."

"You're a writer?"

"I am. Apparently not a very good one."

"Did you want to be writing technical descriptions?"

"No, I want to be finishing my fantasy novel."

"So how can you say you're not a good writer if you were using the wrong tools for the job?"

I blinked at him, surprised at how easy it was for him to state the obvious of what I should have seen a while ago. Losing my writing gig had been a blow to my ego and I'd let it poison my hopes of becoming an author some-day. But the two jobs were so different that I never should have conflated them.

Insecurity was messy like that.

"I have no idea. Nobody's ever phrased it quite like that before," I admitted.

"Will you write now? Now that you're in a better place that is? I'm sure the bookshop will be inspiring."

"Or intimidating. Seeing so many published authors on the shelves can be overwhelming."

"Or motivating."

"True. You're very motivational. Can I keep you around just to cheer me on every time I talk myself out of writing?"

"Of course." Alexander said it so seriously, even though I'd been joking, and warmth sent a funny tingle through my body. This conversation was dancing too close to some of my long-buried vulnerabilities, so it was time to change the subject.

"Ah, so where's this puffin of yours? Or were you just making that up to lure women back to your home?"

"You're the first person I've had here. Plus, you invited yourself," Alexander said, a serious note to his voice, as though he was trying to convince me that he would never invent a puffin to trick women into coming to his home. *Note to self: Alexander can be quite literal.*

"I know," I said, weakly, as I mentally laughed at our mutual awkwardness. While I'd always known I had some socially inept moments, it was refreshing to meet someone who seemed to have the same.

"He's this way. Come on, I'll show you."

Alexander turned to a door at the back of the kitchen and I followed him as he nudged it open and made a soft cooing noise.

"I don't like to startle him," Alexander said over his shoulder. "I'm hoping his wing will heal soon. In the meantime, I have him in the mudroom where it's cool enough for the weather he's used to, but safe from the elements."

A large dog crate had been placed in the middle of the room, with gray plastic sides and a slotted metal gate for a door.

"I don't like keeping him in this, but it's bigger than the box I started with."

"Oh my God, he's so cute." I gasped as the bird waddled to the door, making a clacking noise with his beak as he knocked it lightly against the wires of the cage, gnashing lightly against the metal.

"Tattie, meet Rosie."

Tattie paused and looked up at me, cocking his head, and I grinned down at him, fluttering my fingers.

"Here, you can feed him some herring."

"Just hand it to him through the bars?" I sat on the floor directly next to the carrier, and Alexander sat next to me, his shoulder lightly brushing mine as he handed me a container of fish.

"Aye. The wee lad loves it."

"Aww, I feel so bad for him in there." I plucked some fish from the container, ignoring the slimy feel on my fingers, and gently slid it through the door to an eager Tattie.

"He was worse off out there. Couldn't swim, couldn't fly. He wouldn't have made it."

"What does the vet say?"

"Something clipped his wing. Hard to say what, but in rare cases the feathers will grow back. He doesn't seem to think this will be the case."

"Aw, buddy." I frowned at the puffin currently devouring the fish I gave him. "What will happen to him?"

"If he can't fly on his own, I'll keep him."

"Here? In this?" I couldn't imagine that was a great life for a puffin.

"I'm building him an outdoor play park of sorts," Alexander admitted, and I glanced up at him, admiration growing for this man who would take time out of his busy schedule to build an entire enclosure for a puffin.

"Is that right?" Our eyes held, his face was not far from mine. "Isn't that a lot of work?"

"If he's going to stay here, he'll need a proper home. He can't live in this forever, and that's no way to live."

"So what will the play park be like?"

"I hope to have it combine as many natural elements as possible, like the salt water, grasses, rocky nooks where they like to burrow. But also lightly fenced to protect him from any predators."

"And that's it? You'll just have a puffin named Tattie? Living in your backyard? How long do they live?"

"I think like twenty years or so."

"That's a huge undertaking."

Alexander just shrugged a shoulder.

"The wee lad needed a chance."

"Will he be lonely?" I asked, plucking more fish from the dish and passing it to an eager Tattie.

"It's better to be alone than unhappy, don't you think?"

I realized we were talking about much more than a puffin. I chose my words carefully as I stayed focused on the little bird who clamored for more fish.

"But if he never leaves, and never gets a chance to get out there again, how will he know if he could be happy again?"

"He doesn't. But maybe he's young enough to not know what he's missing yet. Puffins mate for life, you know. He's just old enough to mate, so he likely doesn't have anyone missing him."

"They mate for life?" At that, I glanced between the bird and Alexander. Would these two end up growing old together? Being each other's stand-in mates so to speak because life had dealt them a tough blow?

"Aye. They'll go to sea for months at a time, but somehow always return to each other."

"The heart knows," I whispered, my eyes catching on Alexander's.

The moment hung, another silence where we stared into each other's eyes, until the puffin broke it by letting out a long low call that sounded like a man chuckling at a joke.

"Oh my God!" I exclaimed, looking down at Tattie. "Listen to you. Who is just the cutest, best puffin in the world? That was just the most adorable sound, wasn't it?"

Tattie seemed to agree with me, because he did it again, sidling back and forth in front of his door and preening.

"I think he's showing off for you."

"You're the most handsome 'lad' in all the land," I promised the *wee* puffin and gave him more fish. *Look at me using Scottish words.*

"I used to think it was easier to be alone. Easier to avoid maintaining friendships, that kind of thing," I said. "But now I'm not so sure."

"I am." Alexander stood slowly, and I followed suit, realizing my time with Tattie was done. "If you're alone, you can't get hurt. You can protect your peace. There's nothing wrong with a quiet life."

There was a world of pain behind those words that was none of my business.

I had my own problems to deal with, my own healing to do and revelations to unearth. It wasn't my job to fix this man when he seemed perfectly content with the path he'd chosen. And even *if* there was attraction there, I doubted that he'd act on it, and I should squash that too. I'd never been a one-night stand kind of girl, and this small village was not the ideal place to flex that unused muscle.

"Thanks for introducing me to Tattie. You'll have to let me know if I can help with the play park. It would be fun to see him in his element."

"I'll do that."

It felt like he was ready for me to leave now, and if he wasn't used to ever having visitors, that was likely the case. "Right, I should get a move on. Thanks again for having me by."

"Wait, I'll walk you home."

"You don't have to do that."

"It's dark and I have a big flashlight. Please. It will make me feel better if I know you get home safe."

Peering at the darkness behind his windows, I decided to accept.

"Actually, I'll take you up on the flashlight offer. My phone only did so much."

"Great, let me grab it."

I waved goodbye to Tattie, hoping I'd get to see him soon, and crossed through the kitchen and gorgeous living room where Alexander tamped the fire down. I wanted to tell him to leave the fire, to stay in his comfortable place where nobody could ever hurt him again.

Instead, I silently put my boots on and waited.

"Shall we?" Alexander appeared with a flashlight and his coat, and I smiled up at him. For as much as he said he preferred to stay in and not form connections, he'd already put himself out to help me several times now. Maybe he had a damsel in distress thing, but it was more likely this was just who he was. Sighing, I mentally rolled my eyes.

Why were the good ones always unattainable?

And then I shut that thought down, fiercely reprimanding myself. I wasn't here for love. I was here to start a new life full of books and a new career. Nowhere in my neatly written schedule had I slotted a space for falling in love.

Maybe Alexander had the right of it. Being alone was just easier.

Chapter Fourteen

ALEXANDER

I wanted her to read books on my couch while I worked on my computer.

Was that weird? That I wanted her to just be there? Next to me? Quietly existing in my space?

The way her laugh had hung in the air, causing lust to spear through me, had me harshly reminding myself how my last relationship had ended. I had worked so hard to find my peace, and now that I had it, was it worth giving that up for a woman I'd just met?

Assuming she'd even date me.

Which was unlikely.

Did she know just how stunning she was? Half the time when I found myself just staring at her, unable to speak, it was because all thoughts had left my brain because I was fixated on her beauty.

You told her she was round like a hen.

Silently groaning, I mentally berated myself. What the hell had I been thinking? I hadn't meant it like that, and I knew women could be sensitive about their bodies, and I didn't want her to think I was commenting on her body. Being a professor had taught me to be very cautious with my words, and I always tried to make sure I was being respectful. It seemed that Rosie flustered me, which was something I'd have to examine more deeply. Later. Not when the wind teased me with her scent and made my thoughts scramble in my brain so I struggled with my words.

"One moment," I said, stopping by my outdoor shed. I'd already grabbed a bag from the kitchen, and swinging the shed door open, I took the lid off the bird feed container and scooped some food for her birds.

"Is that for my happy sunshiny birds?"

"You've still yet to meet them," I pointed out as I closed the shed door. The night was clear, the clouds having blown out over the ocean, and a half-moon lit the fields around us.

"I can vouch for my birds." Rosie put a hand to her chest. "Definitely not of the wanker variety."

"Some are. Some steal eggs from other birds and eat them."

"No, they do not." Rosie's mouth dropped open.

"Aye, lass. They do." Rosie gave a soft little sigh that

didn't sound like distress at all. Instead it sounded like ... desire? Excitement?

Och, where was my head at tonight?

"Um, so. Tell me." I paused, trying to focus on something other than asking her to stay at my cottage with me. "Why Scotland? Why here?"

"Well, when Moira left me the bookstore, I just ..." Rosie shrugged. My flashlight had a wide beam, lighting up the road ahead of us, and gravel crunched under our shoes as we walked. "I was tired of playing it safe. Being predictable."

"Nothing wrong with being predictable." In fact, I craved it these days.

"I know it. If you love where you're at, I suppose that's just fine. But what if you don't?"

"Your work or your relationship?" A soft breeze rustled the grasses and I was grateful we weren't fighting the rain on the walk home. It was cold, but I loved walking on a crisp, cold winter's night.

"Both. I suppose it was a reaction to how I was brought up. My mom rarely stayed in one place for long, always wanting an adventure. She couldn't even tell me who my father was."

"Ouch, I'm sorry to hear that."

"It's fine." There was that shoulder shrug again. "I made peace with it a while ago. But once I went to college and found an apartment, I just settled in and stayed. I think I'm starting to realize now that I craved putting down roots so much that I settled for less than the best just because it was safe."

"Was it safe though? You got clocked on the side of the head with a water bottle."

Rosie's chuckle sent a shiver dancing down the back of my neck.

"No, I don't suppose it was. Safe because nothing challenged me and I could predict my days."

"And then suddenly Moira left you a bookshop in Scotland. Could you have turned the inheritance down?"

"I suppose I could have. But it was never a thought. Instead it felt like a lifeline. A way out from a bland relationship and a mind-numbing job."

"Why'd you keep dating him if he was so boring?"

"I didn't think he was going to be at first, but then we just stopped seeing each other. Sometimes I think people live with the idea of someone in their head because it's easier than looking at the reality of what is in front of their face."

Her words sliced through me. I absolutely had done just that with my ex-wife, thinking she'd be someone different and the things we wanted from life would someday align. It hadn't, and her easy rejection of the sanctity of our relationship somehow caused a snowball effect of hiding from them. *But if I were to consider dating again, I know it would be Rosie I'd want to try with.*

I hadn't been enough for Tara, though, and I hadn't fought to make it work.

"That, um, resonates with me." I cleared my throat. Rosie gave that low chuckle again, and then whirled, bumping her fist against my arm. She'd touched my arms

161

a few times tonight. Was she just a tactile person or had she wanted to touch me?

"Hey, do you think the Book Bitches are trying to hook us up? They keep giving us looks."

Relieved she'd brought it up, because there was only so long before those women went full matchmaker on us, I opened my mouth to speak.

"Because I am so not wanting to date anyone. I've sworn off men for a while."

I paused, recalibrating my thoughts. This was exactly what I wanted to hear. I'd already been more than happy with living my life solo, and had been blindsided by my attraction for Rosie. Knowing she wasn't looking for anything would make it easier to just keep her neatly in the friend zone.

"All good here. I'm horrible at dating."

"Are you really? That surprises me."

"Does it? Haven't we already had like ten awkward silences between us?" I pointed out and Rosie threw her head back and laughed.

"Yeah, but that happens between awkward people."

"You're not awkward. You're bubbly, and smart, and engaging." The words were out of my mouth before I could stop them, and I was glad that we were walking in the dark so she couldn't see my embarrassment.

"Seriously? You think that? You're too sweet." She fist-bumped my shoulder again.

"Except for the shoulder kink, I think you'd probably be great at dating."

"Alexander!" Rosie whirled, her mouth gaping open. "I am not obsessed with shoulders."

"It's not a bad body part. There are worse ones to have fetishes over."

"Oh my God. I take it back, you're probably bad at dating."

"Oh, I absolutely agree." I grinned into the night. "Don't even try and picture me trying to pick up a woman at a pub."

"A train wreck?"

"A flaming disaster," I agreed.

"Give me your best pick-up line."

We stopped at the end of the lane, looking both ways before we crossed the country highway, and continued on toward the wee village centre. Turning, I leaned down to her and gave her my best smoldering look.

"Is your name Google? Because you have everything that I'm searching for."

Rosie howled, bending over at the waist and slapping her knee, and I had to laugh along.

"Hey! It's not that bad."

"Oh, oh, it is though. It is. It's so bad." Rosie came up, wiping her eyes, and even though she was laughing at my expense, it still pleased me that I'd made her laugh. "Tell me that didn't work."

"It categorically did not work."

"What did work?"

"Long lunch meetings with a co-worker."

"Ah. Is this ..." Rosie let the question hang.

"My ex-wife? Yes, she'd been a co-worker while I was finishing my PhD."

"And—"

"What's your best pick-up line?" I asked, even though I knew I was cutting off her line of questioning. It was just that I was actually enjoying myself and I didn't want the presence of my ex to sully the conversation.

"Mine? Gosh, I don't think I've ever needed one." Rosie tapped a finger to her lips as we neared The Royal Unicorn. Voices and soft music spilled into the night air.

"I don't doubt it. A beautiful lady such as yourself likely gets hit on all the time."

"See? Now that's a much better pick-up line." Rosie patted my shoulder and I pretended to preen for her.

"What are we going to do about the Book Bitches?" I asked.

"We tell them we've agreed to just be friends. That there's no chemistry there."

Ouch. Feeling slightly wounded, even though this was exactly what I'd wanted, I nodded.

"Fair. Aside from your obsession with my shoulders." Rosie caught herself before she went to knock her hand against my arm, and I looked down at it pointedly.

"Damn it, you're right. I do touch your shoulders a lot." Rosie sighed.

"It's fine. I won't tell anyone." I winked at her.

"So, buddies then?" Rosie held up her fist and I met it, lightly bumping my own against hers.

"Buddies. The Book Bitches will have to set their sights on someone else."

"Say, buddy, want to grab a drink? I'd like to go in there and invite people to my party, but it might be less daunting with a friend." Rosie nodded to the pub.

"A party? Do I get an invite?" I asked, crossing my arms over my chest.

"Of course. I don't even know if I'm throwing it. But the Book Bitches seem convinced I am, so it appears I'm having an open house party this weekend."

I rarely went to the pub, largely due to that whole avoiding socializing thing, but suddenly it didn't seem so daunting if I was with Rosie.

"Aye, lass. Let's get a pint."

Holding the door for her, I noticed her blush at my words, or maybe it was the cold air, and she gave me a considering look before shuttering her eyes.

Unsure of the contradicting emotions swirling around inside me, I followed my new friend into the pub.

Chapter Fifteen

Rosie

"You here to pick up some birds?" a man sitting at a table just inside the door asked Alexander. He then laughed uproariously at his joke, slapping his knee.

"I could be available." Cherise blew Alexander a kiss and he cleared his throat.

"He's showing me the pub because I'm new in town," I interjected hastily. "And the birdseed is for my birds. I want to hang a feeder outside the shop."

"Och, you're the new girl then. For Moira's shop. I'm Gregory. An honorary Book Bitch." Gregory shook my hand and I smiled at him. He must be something if the book club let him join.

"Gregory helped save the pub last year," Shannon

explained from where she sat at the table next to him with the rest of the women. "We love him."

"Och, stop it." Gregory blushed and buried his face in his newspaper.

"What are you two doing coming in for a drink together?" Meredith asked, looking us both up and down, a gleam in her eye.

"Nope. None of that." I waved my finger at the table. "We're just friends. I asked him to come in here with me so I could feel comfortable inviting people to my party."

"Oh, so you are having a party? Smart." Esther nodded her approval, raising her glass of wine in the air. "When is it?"

"This weekend. Saturday. I'm going to have an open house party. I hope everyone can make it."

"I'll bake cookies," Cherise said.

"I'll make a signature drink," Meredith decided.

"I'll bring snacks," Shannon promised with a wave.

"Wait, you don't have to bring anything. I'm sure I can figure it out."

"It's not a bother." Esther waved a hand in the air. "We love doing this stuff."

"Rosie?" Alexander called from where he'd abandoned me to the Book Bitches and now stood at the bar.

"Be right back." I crossed the small pub, which was everything I wanted it to be. Charming tartan-backed chairs, a cozy fire, stone walls with black and white photos, and twinkle lights already strung along the wood beams in the ceiling. A gleaming wood bar, backed by a wall with a mirror and glass shelves lined with bottles, was tucked at one end, and there Alexander spoke to a pretty woman tending bar.

"So much for being my friend," I hissed to Alexander. "You abandoned me."

"Sorry, I panicked as soon as they brought up dating. I'll try and be stronger next time." Alexander grinned and then gestured to the woman behind the bar. "Harper, meet Rosie. Rosie took over the Highland Hearts bookshop."

"Oh yay! Another American here. And on a new adventure, just like me." Harper beamed at me, and I smiled back, enjoying her warmth and welcoming demeanor.

"You know what? I was ready for a big adventure. I'd been too settled into a boring life for too long. And what an adventure! A new country, a new store? I'm over the moon."

Harper beamed at me, but I caught Alexander wincing. He gave me an unreadable look before turning away and clearing his throat, again. That was odd.

"Well if there is anything I can do to help, please let me know. But I've heard the Book Bitches have already set up shop."

"They kind of just take over, don't they?" I laughed.

"Don't try and fight them." Harper shook her head, her long braid dancing behind her. "They're an impossible force of nature. But they did help me get this pub put to rights."

"How do you like running it?" I asked, settling on a stool.

A soft meow was the only warning I had before a cat butted its head against my arm.

"Oh, well hello, sir." A tabby cat blinked up at me with soulful eyes before insisting on more attention.

"That's our wee warrior kitten, Wallace. Though he's not quite a kitten anymore."

"What's a warrior kitten?" I asked, scratching behind his ears. "Does he catch all the mice?"

"He's absolutely horrible at catching mice. In fact, I think his favorite thing is to sleep all day and then terrorize us by running in laps around the flat at three in the morning."

"Maybe he's catching all the ghosts."

Harper glanced to a picture frame in front of an empty stool and then back to me.

Interesting.

"What can I get you?"

"A glass of red is fine if you have it. Cab or Malbec works."

"So you're big on adventure, huh?" Alexander asked as Harper went to fill my drink. His voice was steady, but I got the sense that I was missing something.

"Well, this is a big adventure for me. I needed to shake my life up and I did."

"There's nothing wrong with a small life." Alexander's voice was low, and the words were pitched into his pint glass.

"I never said there was. But it was time for a change. That's all." I was missing some sort of undercurrent here, I was sure of it.

"What happens when you move on? To the next adventure?"

"Based on my track record, I'd say I have a good ten years or so before I consider something of that nature. Assuming I can make this bookselling gig financially profitable for me that is."

"Here you go. First one's on the house." Harper beamed at me over the glass of wine.

"Aww, thank you. I'd like to invite you to my open house party I'm having this weekend. I'll stay open later than usual, if you want to invite other people in town. I figured telling people at the pub would be the quickest way to get the word out."

"I'll pop over before my shift and will spread the word. It doesn't take much to get news to people here." Harper grinned, leaning on the bar.

"Was that an adjustment for you or do you come from a small town?"

Wallace batted at my glass, trying to dip his paw in my wine, and I snatched it out of his reach.

"Sir. Rude." Harper tapped his forehead and he gave her a look as though to say he knew he was being cheeky and did not care in the slightest. "And it was an adjustment, living in a small town. But one that I found I welcomed quickly. I guess I'd been missing community is all."

"And why is he a warrior kitten?"

Harper's grin widened. "My boyfriend had me convinced that the Scots carried kittens into battle in their sporrans."

At that, Alexander huffed out a laugh.

"Is the sporran the purse thing around the waist?"

"It is not a purse, lass." Alexander groaned and pinched his nose.

"Hey, Rosie!" I turned as Esther called my name. The pub was almost full, and everyone looked at me expectantly. My eyebrows lifted.

"Yes?"

"If you had to put clothes on a seahorse, in this case, a Santa suit, which end would you put it on?"

My mouth dropped open and Alexander laughed outright this time.

"Oh, here we go," Harper murmured at my back.

"Seahorses don't have arms, do they?" I asked.

"Nope. Just little fins to propel them," Meredith said, squinting at her phone.

"So if you put them in a coat, they wouldn't be able to swim?" I couldn't believe I was having this conversation.

"That's what I said," Esther said.

"But their tail is kind of curly. You'd just put a one-legged trouser on them instead then?" Shannon looked up at the ceiling as she considered.

"Wouldn't that be a maxi skirt then?" Cherise asked.

"You can't put a seahorse in a Santa maxi skirt," Esther said, her hand at her throat, appalled.

"What if it is a she? Mrs. Claus?" Cherise argued.

"Did you know that the male seahorses carry the babies?" Gregory asked.

"See? The woman is the one leaving the house and

going to work while the man cares for the babies. That means she should get a Santa skirt," Cherise said.

"You want the seahorse in a skirt and no top?" Meredith asked. "What about, you know, her breasts?" Meredith held her hands in the air in front of her chest, as though we needed an explanation of what breasts were.

"I don't think seahorses have breasts," I said, wheezing with laughter.

"What about just a cap?" Alexander volunteered. "No outfit, just a cap. That way the seahorse can swim and yet is still in a festive spirit."

The Book Bitches looked at him, horrified.

"You want the seahorse to be naked? With just a Santa cap? What is this, *Magic Mike*?" Esther demanded.

"I have no idea how to answer that," Alexander hissed at my ear.

"Maybe you could hang some Christmas lights around its neck? Or tinsel?" I suggested.

"Hmm. Tinsel could work. Covering all the naughty bits." Shannon gave me an approving look.

"I seriously don't think they show any naughty bits," I said, my shoulders shaking with the laughter I was trying to keep inside.

"We can't get docked points for flashing seahorse privates to the judges." Esther glared at the room. Everyone nodded as though this made perfect sense.

"I'm never going to look at seahorses the same."

"And this, my new friend, is what makes small-town life never dull." Harper laughed behind me.

"What about a pufferfish?" I suggested. "They might look cute with a Santa hat."

"And how am I going to get a Santa jacket on him? His spikes will rip the material." Shannon spoke as though she was actually going to be wrangling a pufferfish into a Santa costume.

"Right, of course. My mistake."

"Maybe a crab or lobster should be Santa?" Alexander suggested. "Since they're already red?"

"Ohhhh." The entire pub took a collective sigh of relief, many sending Alexander nods of approval.

"I think you might have just saved Christmas," I whispered from the side of my mouth.

"But what about the seahorses?" Cherise's face fell.

"Could they be reindeer maybe? With antlers and little saddles?" I asked, and the room exploded with enthusiasm. I even got a few claps for my suggestion. "Why do I feel like I just won an award?"

"Let's just say that people tend to get very fixated on the small things here," Harper said.

"I can see that." A wave of sleepiness hit me, and I realized I'd been awake since before dawn that morning. "I think I need to go. As exciting as this discussion is, I'm still adjusting to this time zone."

"I'll walk you out," Alexander said.

"You don't have to." I nodded to his half-finished pint. "It's fine if you want to finish it."

Alexander drained the rest of the pint in one gulp and my eyes widened.

"Don't leave me here with them."

"Message received." I waited as Alexander settled up and we stopped by the Book Bitches on the way out.

"Oh, both of you are leaving at the same time?" Esther blinked coyly at me.

"Yes, that's what people do when they finish their drinks," I pointed out.

"Mm-hmm."

"Goodnight. Everyone, please stop by for my open house party this Saturday. The shop will be open all day, but I'll stay open after hours for drinks and snacks to get to know everyone better," I said to the pub and everyone waved us off, seemingly happy with their window design planning.

When Alexander turned toward the shop, I looked up at him. His eyes gleamed in the light spilling from the windows at the pub.

"You don't have to walk me from here. It's right around the corner."

"It's my job."

"You take this friend thing seriously." I fell into step next to him as we walked along the silent street. It was so quiet here. At home there would have been cars whizzing past, horns sounding, and likely a siren or two in the background. But here, I could just faintly hear the ocean in the distance, and the wind rustling the branches of a cluster of trees as we walked.

"I don't have many of them anymore."

"Lose some in the divorce?" I guessed and then clapped a hand over my mouth. "I'm sorry, that's none of my business."

"Och, it's fine, lass. And yes, I did lose some in the divorce. I guess they weren't much my friends anyway."

"Well, quality over quantity is what is important." I bumped his shoulder with mine as we stopped in front of the door to the shop. "Buddy."

"Mate."

I looked up at him, my heart tripping over his word.

"Mate?"

"We call them mates here. My mates. Not my buddy."

"Ah, oh, right. Okay, well, goodnight, mate." I stretched up on my toes to give his cheek a kiss just as a small bang sounded from inside the shop. Alexander turned toward it, and our lips met.

Holy ...

Desire raced through me. One moment, I was chilled from the icy wind, and the next I was burning hot. I'd never had someone light me up inside before, not from a single kiss, and I moaned softly at his lips.

When I realized what I was doing, I made to step back, embarrassment already creeping up, threatening to replace desire, when he wrapped a hand around the back of my neck and angled my head, deepening the kiss.

And with that simple act, Alexander forever eradicated the notion that awkward computer programmers with strained social skills wouldn't be sexy as hell. Because this man kissed like he knew every one of my hidden secrets, as though he'd dipped into my darkest desires and flipped a light on, causing every nerve ending on my body to stand up and shout in excitement. When his other arm came around my waist, pulling me against his body, I took the opportunity to thread my hands through his thick hair.

He didn't just kiss. He devoured. He tasted.

He played.

It wasn't just a kiss. It was a dance. Our tongues met, tasting, licking, teasing each other, and I moaned against his lips. I wanted more. So much more.

When we broke apart, panting, I waved my hands in front of my face.

"I'm sorry. I'm sorry. I just meant to kiss you on the cheek. I didn't mean ..."

"I know. I heard a noise. It was an accident."

I didn't know anyone who accidentally fell into a full make-out session like that, but I decided to let him off easily. We'd agreed to be friends, hadn't we?

"Yup, an accident. It happens. Right. I'd better see what that bang was from inside." Turning, I put my hand on the knob and ran straight into the door, hitting my forehead against the wood, because—duh—I hadn't unlocked the door yet.

"Oh shite. Are you all right then? Here, let me look."

"Fine. I'm totally fine. Really. Thanks for walking me home, mate." I wasn't sure what burned harder, the knot already forming on my head or the embarrassment in my cheeks, and I quickly unlocked the door, hoping to slip inside so I could die of shame in peace and quiet.

"Rosie. Wait."

Was he calling me back? Hope lifted inside me, but

when I turned, he was just holding up the bag of birdseed.

"Oh right. For my wanker-free birds."

"Are you sure you're okay?" Alexander squinted at my forehead. "Should I get some ice?"

"It's fine. Really. I'm just tired and clumsy and, right, just yeah. I'm done for the day."

"Goodnight. Sleep well, Rosie."

"Safe walk home and all that." I waved him away, closing the door and locking it quickly behind me. Leaning my back against it, I closed my eyes, embarrassment flooding me.

The speaker switched on and the song *Clumsy* by Fergie burst out.

"Oh, you too? Lovely. Just *lovely*." Grumbling, I went to find some ice to nurse my head.

I wasn't sure what to put on my injured pride though.

Chapter Sixteen

Rosie

The party was a hit.

To my surprise, after only being in Scotland for a week, I had a packed house at the bookshop.

Back home, I wouldn't have been able to even think of enough acquaintances to invite to a party to make it this busy, and here it just all felt seamless and ... easy. It wasn't effortless, as it had taken a ton of work to get the windows ready for the competition, to rearrange the bookshop to my new designs, and to prepare for the party. But the welcoming of strangers into my shop and new home? Well, oddly enough, it felt just right.

For the party, we'd decided to open the shop up, and instead of the S design I had originally considered for day-to-day shopping needs, we'd pulled the bookshelves to either end of the shop, creating a larger space for mingling. In one corner we'd piled the floor poufs next to a real Christmas tree that filled the shop with the scent of pine. The tree was nestled in a pot, its roots protected, and would return to the tree farm after Christmas. I'd pulled any extra chairs I had to the sides of the room, creating various conversation spots for people to have a seat and chat. The disco unicorn had tinsel wrapped around its neck and a Santa hat on its head.

But it was the windows that really drew the eyes.

True to their word, the Book Bitches had leaned into the Under the Sea theme and had worked tirelessly to bring it together. The main window next to the door was their crowning achievement, with the two smaller windows continuing the theme but on a smaller scale.

Alexander had shown up almost every day to help.

Neither of us had mentioned the kiss.

But I thought about it. Every night, when I finally was alone for the day and curled into bed, nestled under the thick duvet, the exhaustion of a hard day of work creeping over me, I'd imagine his lips on mine.

It had become my favorite thing to fall asleep to.

Something had shifted for me that day. I'd gone from thinking he was just a Scottish hottie that I could make jokes with Jessica about wanting, to craving his nearness. I'd moved out of a general awareness of his nearness to a full-blown crush.

Which, of course, meant that my clumsiness around him had increased. I'd lucked out by not having a bruise on my forehead from running straight into the door, but as I turned and almost knocked over a tray of shortbread cookies, I took a breath and steadied myself.

I hadn't been prepared for Alexander in a kilt.

It was like when I played a video game and accessed a new level I hadn't even known existed.

Alexander in his flannel and fitted jeans, climbing up ladders and hanging up lights, had been sexy. Alexander in a nubby gray sweater, with a kilt and thick-soled boots? Jessica would book a ticket on the spot if I sent her a photo of him. He'd gone from the friendly neighborhood bird nerd to the type of man that would turn heads on the street and stop conversations when he walked into a room.

"You're staring."

Jolting, I turned to glare down at Esther, who wore green velvet pants and a red sweatshirt that said *Merry Christmas Stud Puffin* over a puffin with an elf hat on.

"I have no idea what you're talking about."

I had been staring as Alexander had helped a young girl clamber onto a floor pouf so she could better see the window.

"How's that whole 'just friends' thing working out?"

"Fine. Why wouldn't it be?"

Esther trilled a note in the back of her throat, and I realized I'd need to divert her before she leaned into a cross-examination. I wasn't ready to talk about my feelings for Alexander. They were my little secret, something to be treasured in the dark, not brought out to the light of day. We'd both been clear that neither of us were ready or willing to have a relationship, and one accidental kiss didn't change that. At least from my understanding of things. He'd treated me with an easygoing air all week, friendly but not flirty, and I had to presume he'd also put the kiss behind him.

Compartmentalizing for the win. If only I had that ability.

Come to think about it, it seemed that everyone else in my life had that skill. My mom, my co-workers at the discount store who I hadn't heard from, John. Everyone else in my life had seemed to find it quite easy to walk away from me. *As if I'm inconsequential.* Well, that was one way to look at things. *But not tonight.*

"Look, Esther. There's Edina." I subtly pointed out the woman who we'd set our sights on matching this evening. She'd just inched her way into the party, clutching her purse and looking like she was ready to bolt at any moment.

"Och, poor lass looks like a deer in headlights. On it." Without a word, Esther barreled across the room and unceremoniously hooked an arm through Edina's, dragging her through the crowd of people so she'd be unable to leave easily.

"I suppose that's one way to do it," I breathed.

Alone for a moment, I pulled out my phone and snapped a few photos of the party before slipping out front. I wanted to photograph the windows from the outside, particularly because they were lit so beautifully, and add it to my new Highland Hearts social media pages.

For a moment, I was alone, and icy wind danced along my stockings, threatening to blow my skirt up. But I didn't care. The blast of cold against my skin invigorated me, and a soft thrill of happiness filled me. This place was mine. Happy voices and music spilled into the night air, with snatches of conversations pulled away on the wind. The exterior of the cottage had been transformed into a winter wonderland, and on cue, the music started from the speaker that Alexander had rigged outside the shop.

As *Under the Sea* began playing, I clapped my hands together, as giddy as a little girl on Christmas Day. Well, never the Christmas Days I'd had growing up, as my mother had more often than not forgotten about the holiday, but what I imagined the feeling would be like.

The main window showcased an enchanting underwater landscape. Faux kelp strands hung from the ceiling, intermixed with shimmering tinsel strands, to make it seem like a sparkly underwater world. Jellyfish, with sparkling tentacles, floated in the air. Between the kelp, underwater creatures danced, each one more sparkly than the next. I'd taken a stand on my pufferfish, and he'd been allowed in with a small Christmas bow tie. A lobster had been decided upon for Santa, and he was tucked inside a conch shell sleigh while being driven by seahorses with antlers on. One corner, a faux coral reef had been created, and on it sat a voluptuous mermaid, wearing a tinsel bra, with Christmas presents strewn around the pile of pearls she sat on. As the song played, the lighting changed, highlighting different corners of the window or flashing in tune to the beat of the song.

Propelled by whatever magic Alexander had programmed into it, the conch sleigh moved slowly across the ocean floor, and as the song wound down, sharks in Santa hats sprung from behind the kelp, silly grins painted on their faces. At the very top of the window, a pirate ship dangled, bobbing slowly across the surface of the water.

For an aging book club, a new store owner, and one determined computer programmer—we'd knocked it out of the park.

"Rosie! This is fantastic."

I turned to find Harper, along with two handsome men, standing behind me.

"Isn't it? I'm really in awe of how it all came together."

"No seahorse breasts to be seen," Harper observed.

"Nope. They managed to navigate that particular hiccup." We grinned at each other before she turned to the men at her side. "This cutie is Reed, my boyfriend and owner of The Royal Unicorn. And this is his friend Aiden who is visiting from Boston."

I registered Aiden's easy smile and interest in his eyes. He was handsome enough but didn't quite hold a candle to the kilt-wearing programmer inside.

"Are you enjoying your visit?" I asked.

"I am. It's a beautiful area, and I feel like there's so much to explore. How do you like living here?"

A funny little jolt hit me.

He was just on holiday, and I might as well have been, having been here for only a week. But it was a world of difference between living here and just visiting. And in such a short time I realized I'd already put down roots.

Esther poked her head out of the door.

"Judges will be here in twenty minutes."

"Oh, for the windows. Exciting!" Harper clapped her hands and we went to join the party. Two steps into the door, I was stopped by a nervous Edina.

"Can I speak to you?" Edina looked lovely tonight in wide-leg black pants and a soft emerald sweater with pretty pearl buttons. But her eyes were wary.

"Of course." I nudged her through the crowd and into my flat, closing the door behind us. "What's going on? How are you?"

"I think ... I think this was stupid. The whole thing was a stupid idea. Och, I'm not sure what I was thinking. Signing up for a matchmaking. Stupid, really." Edina paced, wringing her hands. "I don't even remember the first thing about dating. How am I supposed to just go on a blind date? I don't think I can do this. I'll just take a refund."

Damn it, I'd hoped to give her a chance with Samuel. He hadn't arrived yet, from what Esther had told me, and I had been excited to see if my first match would work.

"Sorry, no refunds," I said, cheerfully, and her head whipped to me.

"What do you mean, no refunds?"

"It's part of the policy. In the fine print." I was making this up as I went, but I didn't get the sense that I'd be able to placate Edina with words that everything would work out. She'd been told that before in her life and it hadn't.

"Where's this policy?" Edina demanded. "That's not fair. What if I don't want to be matched anymore?"

I shrugged. "Then you just say no when he asks you on a date."

"He? You have someone for me?" Despite her nerves, curiosity lit her eyes.

"Of course. It's my job, isn't it?"

A knock sounded at the door and Esther poked her head in.

"The local paper wants a photo with you before the judges arrive."

"Oh, wow. Okay. How do I look?" I automatically brushed my hands down my outfit.

"Bonnie," Edina said, and Esther agreed.

I'd been torn on what to wear that morning, not having much in the way of Christmas-themed clothes, and had settled on a satin slip skirt with a whisper-soft cashmere sweater in red that hugged my curves. I'd teased my hair into bouncy curls and hung sparkly drops at my ears. I'd slicked on red lipstick that matched my sweater exactly and felt pretty good about myself.

Breezing past the crowd, I caught a brief smile from Alexander before I ducked outside and posed for the photographer in front of the bookshop. *My bookshop.* The very thought thrilled me.

Even more so that I'd been inspired to pull out my own languishing manuscript and start editing what I'd written. The bones of the story were good, but I had so much more to add now. Ideas swirled in my brain, and I'd started waking up earlier than usual just to spend some time alone with my manuscript in the morning.

So many changes in such a short time. At some point, I knew I needed to process all of this on a cellular and emotional level, but for now, I was just riding the high of discovering a whole new life waiting for me that felt like me turning a key to unlock a door.

"Famous already," Alexander said at my back, as the photographer waved goodbye. Turning, I grinned up at him. We hadn't had much chance to speak once the party had kicked off even though I found my eyes straying to him more than once.

"You can say you knew me when." I flipped my hair over my shoulder.

"Aren't I the lucky one? Will you still talk to us plebs when you're known around the world?" His smile reached his eyes now, much less forced than it had been the first time I'd met him. It seemed he was becoming better at socializing, at least from what I could tell, as his somewhat tense demeanor had eased some under the Book Bitches' constant yammering this week. Once you got over how terrifying they were, it was surprisingly easy to be around the women. You could talk or not talk. It didn't matter much to them as they would just chatter right over you. I found myself tuning out of their conversations as much as I joined them.

"I'll consider it." Looking him up and down, I gave him an approving nod. "You, sir, look smashing tonight."

"Och, thanks." Alexander glanced down at his kilt and shrugged. "Figured it was festive enough."

"It works."

A look passed between us, and I couldn't help but think about the last time we'd stood in this spot, and how his lips had inspired many a naughty dream that week.

Car doors slammed and I turned to see a group of men and women, all with clipboards, approach.

"Oh, this must be the judges. Can you get the ladies?" I squeezed Alexander's arm before turning to greet the group of judges. The door swung open behind me and the women clambered out, silent for once, as I explained the concept.

"Hello, welcome to Highland Hearts. This week's window concept was Under the Sea." I raised a hand and Alexander started the song.

A sound of approval came from the judges as the lights danced and twinkled, the conch shell moved, and the sharks darted among the kelp. At the end of it, they made notes on their clipboards before stepping closer to look at the figurines.

"Also, we're having an open house party, and you're all welcome to stop in for a drink and some food."

The judges looked among each other and then bent to converse among themselves. One popped his head up.

"We'd love to pop in. But just for a moment." With that, they put their clipboards back in their car and wandered into the shop for a chat. Esther punched my arm.

"Ow!" I glared at her.

"Good thinking. Bribe them with treats. I've got Shannon ready to serve them the best banoffee pudding they've ever tasted."

"I'm not bribing them. I'm just being friendly."

"Uh-huh. I know a bribe when I see one. Speaking of friendly, Samuel just arrived, and we need to figure out, you know." Esther opened her eyes wide and made exaggerated gestures toward the man who looked at us in confusion from the sidewalk.

"Should I be aware of something?" Samuel asked, and I pasted my customer service smile on, pushing Esther aside with a little more force than necessary. She was older, but she was strong. She could take it.

"Just an interpretive dance move she's been working on. Come in, come in." I ushered Samuel past a glaring Esther and inside. "How was your day today?"

"Och, well enough I suppose. No major dramas among my employees and everything ran fairly smoothly with the customers, so I call that a win." He wore a cheerful smile and was dressed nicely in straight leg jeans and a fitted black sweater.

"I think that's all we can hope for in retail, right? I'm assuming that's what you're in?"

"Och, apologies. Of course you wouldn't know. I'm Samuel and I manage the local Tesco. Just up the road."

"Welcome to Highland Hearts. I appreciate you stopping by. Here, have a seat and I'll grab you a drink."

"Don't mind if I do. Been on my feet since six this morning." Samuel sat down in one of the turquoise velvet chairs tucked in a corner and I went to get him a beer and search for Edina. By the time I'd grabbed the beer, because people stopped me every two seconds for a chat, I hadn't been able to find Edina. Damn it. I hoped she hadn't snuck out.

Returning to Samuel, I gasped as I walked through the crowd just in time to see Esther hip-check Edina so hard the woman went flying onto Samuel's lap. He grabbed Edina, pulling her close so she wouldn't fall, and the two locked eyes.

"Esther," I hissed, my eyebrows at my hairline. "What are you doing?"

"Just helping love along," Esther whispered.

"You can't do that," I gritted out between a forced smile.

"Just did." Esther cooed and waved at Edina. "So sorry, dear. I just don't see as well these days. Samuel, you're so sweet to catch her. Have you two met?"

About as transparent as a shower door.

"Go get Edina a drink." I elbowed her.

"You get her a drink," Esther said.

"If she has a drink, she'll stay longer," I mumbled, still smiling.

Esther finally left and I let out a shaky sigh of relief. This was my first match, and I wasn't letting Esther take it away from me.

"I'm Edina," Edina said and made a move to get off his lap. He held her still.

"Samuel."

The moment drew out and I wasn't sure if I should slowly melt back into the crowd when Samuel jolted and seemed to realize he was holding a strange woman on his lap at a party.

"Och, apologies. I should let you get down. It isn't often a bonnie lass such as yourself lands in my lap."

"Oh, well, aren't you sweet?" A flush of pleasure crossed Edina's face as she eased herself off his lap and into the chair next to him. She glanced up at me and I widened my eyes, giving her a subtle nod in Samuel's direction. Recognition flooded her face, and she gave me a quick nod of understanding back.

"Your drink." I handed Samuel his drink just as Esther returned with a glass of wine for Edina. Blessedly, seeing the two ready for a chat, Esther didn't interrupt other than to hand off the wine, and we both faded silently back into the crowd.

"I did it," Esther crowed, turning to me in delight.

"*We* did it," I pointed out, annoyed.

"Yeah, yeah. If I had waited on you, those two would be walking with a cane before they met."

"He's been in the shop for all of ten seconds, Esther."

"Excuse me, are you Rosie?"

I turned to find the woman who had the two children that Alexander had been playing with earlier. A pretty woman with tired eyes, she glanced around nervously.

"I am. How may I help you?"

The woman wet her lips and then took a deep breath, and then another, before reaching into her pocket and pulling out a twenty-pound note.

Esther shouldered me aside and honestly, the

woman's strength was astounding. I took a step back in order not to fall.

"Is it the Highland Hearts Special you're wanting? Best to talk to me." Esther tapped her chest. "I'm the expert."

"You are not the expert," I said, trying to step in front of Esther. "Ignore her."

"I set them up, didn't I? Look how well that's going." Esther jerked a thumb toward the new couple who were laughing over their drinks.

"Oh, well, yes, that does look nice. It's just—"

"What's your name?" Esther asked.

"Oh, right. I'm Sarah."

"Hi, Sarah. Don't let this one steamroll you. She's an aggressive ambassador of love."

"Hey, I like that. I'm going to put that on a jumper." Esther smacked my arm.

"I don't know if I can find love. Not again." Sarah fingered a slim chain at her throat. "I, uh, lost my husband when I was pregnant with my youngest. Motorcycle accident. That was four years ago. I'm not sure—"

"You can be unsure but still try," Esther said, patting the woman's arm. "Maybe it will stick, maybe it won't. But you won't know unless you give it a go."

"It feels wrong." A shimmer of tears hit her eyes.

"Nobody expects you to live a life without love, Sarah. That's just foolish talk."

"Oh." Sarah blinked at Esther as though she'd just given her a secret code. "Really?"

"Really. Now, let's get the goods. What's your favorite book? What are you looking for?"

I gaped as Esther just drew Sarah away to a corner and grilled her. What the heck? Wasn't I supposed to be the matchmaker here?

"Great place you have here." I turned from glaring after Esther to see Harper's friend, Aiden.

"Thank you. It's new to me, but I'm loving it so far." He had friendly eyes and a nice smile.

"Would you like to get a drink later? Or tomorrow?"

"Oh." Surprised, I did a double take. I hadn't really been expecting to be asked out, particularly by a man here for just a vacation, but then paused to consider. Could he be a no-strings-attached fling that moved me past my last relationship? Maybe. Maybe he could. I knew Jessica would be pushing me out the door with him as we spoke. Thinking of her made me smile. Esther and Jessica had a lot in common.

"Sure, I'd like that." I didn't know if I was feeling impulsive, or just willing myself to go on new adventures, but a drink with a handsome man wouldn't hurt. Plus, it would put the town off the rumors of Alexander and me being a couple.

"Great, I'll give you my number?"

We exchanged numbers and Harper pulled him away to show him something. Looking up, I caught Alexander staring at me across the room, his face a mask. When he turned away, my heart twisted.

Had I done something wrong? I thought we were just meant to be friends. Uncertain now, I blinked as the speaker switched from Christmas music to *Dangerous Game* by Kylie Minogue.

"I'm not playing games," I hissed at the speaker and then realized I was still in a room crowded with people. I honestly wasn't a game player, but it was nice to be asked out. I'd never felt particularly amazing while dating John, so to be kissed by a hot Scotsman and then asked out on a date by a cute American ... well, it was flattering. And I was allowed to have fun. *Right. This is okay, Rosie.* Gathering myself, I scooped up a glass of wine and pasted a customer service smile on my face.

"Cherise. Tell me what your secret is for these shortbread cookies? They're delicious."

Chapter Seventeen

ALEXANDER

Why was she taking that guy's phone number? Had Rosie just said yes to a date? Annoyance flashed through me partnered with another emotion that I wasn't used to feeling.

Jealousy.

And I was *not* a jealous person.

When my ex-wife had cheated on me, it hadn't made me jealous. I'd never cared who her lovers were or what they'd looked like. I'd mainly just felt sad because I knew the relationship was over. I'd later learned that she liked it when men fought over her, as two of her flings had gone to blows over her at a pub. A story she'd told me in gratuitous detail, with a gleeful look in her eye. When I hadn't taken the bait, instead just handed her the divorce papers to sign, she'd been infuriated. *And we'd been married for five years.*

So no, jealousy was not an emotion I was used to.

In fact the last time I think I'd been actually jealous was when BirdKing77 had passed my score on BirdFindr, having seen a critically threatened Bahama oriole when he'd been on holiday in the Caribbean. I'd been holding a silent war with this unknown internet birder for years now, and it had annoyed me that he'd gotten ahead with such a rare find.

But now, as I watched Rosie, in that silky skirt that was driving me more than a little crazy, smile up at some unknown man, I realized that I was, indeed, jealous. Rubbing at the ache in my chest, I looked away.

"Whatcha staring at?" Meredith asked at my side, and I blinked down at her. Tonight she wore a jumper that said she liked them *real thick and sprucy* with a drawing of Christmas trees.

"Nothing," I said. "Just enjoying the party."

"Really? It looked to me like you were watching Rosie get hit on by that cute lad from Boston."

Boston? An American? Even more annoyed now, I grimaced.

"Nope, not at all," I lied through my teeth. "Just happy the windows all came together. When will we know the scores?"

"The judges will post them tonight so we can start preparing for next week. I think Esther wants us to stay after when this wraps up in a bit so we can pick next week's theme."

"No problem." It wasn't like I had anything else to do tonight. Other than to go home and talk to Tattie who was becoming increasingly trusting of me. I'd been able to expand his pen a bit, but I was still working on securing his outdoor enclosure. I hoped he'd be happy with the home I was creating for him. If he could never fly again, at the very least I wanted to give him a good life.

"You could ask her out as well, you know," Meredith said, following my gaze to where I was staring at Rosie again as she laughed with a customer. Damn it. I'd meant to look away.

"We're just friends."

"Uh-huh."

"We are. We agreed on it and everything." And then had the kiss to end all kisses, the taste of her searing a path through to my very soul.

"Och, lad. Why would you go and do that?"

"Because neither of us want to date. I'm happy in my simple life and she just left a relationship. It's better this way."

"Bloody eejit," Meredith muttered.

"Excuse me?"

"Oh, nothing. Well, enjoy your lonely nights not chasing after a good thing. You know that friendships make the best basis for relationships, right?"

"Relationship? Who is in a relationship?" Esther skidded to a stop in front of us and I closed my eyes, wishing I was anywhere else. Except that would mean I wouldn't get to see Rosie in her soft jumper and silky skirt.

"Alexander and Rosie agreed to just be friends, but he just looked like he wanted to belt the handsome lad who just asked her on a date."

"Shite or get off the pot, mate," Esther said, succinctly, giving me a sour look before breezing over to the drinks table.

"There is no pot," I called after her, but she didn't look back. "There's *no* pot. There's no shitting required."

"Keep telling yourself that." Meredith clucked her tongue and wandered away, leaving me to try and put the image of shitting in a pot out of my head.

By the time the party wrapped up, I'd nursed two beers and had used up a month's quota of social interactions—in one night. I was ready to go home to my quiet cottage by the sea and do my best to not think about Rosie and her potential date.

"Right, team, gather round. I just got a text that the scores were up." Esther pulled reading glasses onto her nose and tapped wildly at her phone like people who aren't comfortable with technology do. "Somewhere on here ..."

"Would you like me to look?" Rosie reached out a hand, but Esther elbowed it away.

"I got it, I got it."

Rosie shot me an amused look, sending warmth to my gut. She had a habit of doing that, looking to me, as though we shared our own little private jokes. I supposed it was because we were the youngest of the Winter Windows team, so it was easier to commiserate on some topics than others.

"We won!" Esther crowed, holding the phone up, and Rosie surprised me with an excited hug.

Her jumper was as soft as it looked, the fabric sliding beneath my hands and over her curves. Being this close to her took me back to the kiss from the other night, and how much I wanted another. I'd replayed the moment over and over in my mind, unsure what had made me lean into the kiss other than the desire that clawed for more. More of *her*. And now that I'd had a taste, I was like an addict. I wanted more. More smiles, more shoulder bumps, more kisses. Anything she was willing to give me, I'd take, her smiles like a twenty-pound bill in a beggar's cup.

Realizing I was holding her a touch too long, I released her and caught Meredith's knowing smile. Annoyed, frustrated, and uncertain of what to do next, I stepped back and cleared my throat.

"What was the point difference between St. Andrews?"

"They were only two points below us." Shannon studied the numbers on the screen. "So we've got to step it up next round."

"I found more boxes of decorations in the back storage area, but they are too high for me to reach," Rosie said. She looked up at me. "Want to grab them? They may be of help this week."

"Of course." I'd walk through fire for this woman. Right, okay. *What the hell?* Where had that thought come from? Maybe my three years of abstinence was making me be a bit dramatic.

"Wait, let's decide on a theme first." Esther pulled out the whiteboard from behind the table and propped it back up. "Seeing as how Under the Sea was such a success, I'll make an attempt to be more flexible about some of these other hare-brained ideas."

"I thought you said there were no bad ideas."

"Exactly. I didn't say there were no hare-brained ideas, did I?" Esther scowled and I bit back a grin.

"Don't poke the bear," Rosie whispered to me. "She's running on a high right now, and I don't get the impression she's a benevolent dictator."

"Ahem." Esther smacked her hand on the whiteboard, drawing our attention back.

"My vote is Christmas in Space, since Under the Sea did so well. Though I think we missed a trick." Rosie tapped a finger against those delicious red lips. "We could slip in some books related to the theme. Like if we did outer space, we could put in *The Martian* by Andy Weir."

"*War of the Worlds.*"

"*Contact.* Carl Sagan." Shannon nodded.

"So you want an alien Christmas?" Esther asked, hands on her hips, her scowl deepening.

"Seems to be the vote," I said.

"Aliens it is. But I don't want any talk about alien breasts and if they should be covered."

"But alien smut is one of my favorite genres," Meredith protested, and my eyes widened.

Grabbing Rosie, who was looking more than a little stunned, I tugged her toward the back. "Show me those boxes?"

"Yup. And we'll take as much time as we need until I can erase the image of Meredith reading alien romance from my mind," Rosie grumbled as she took me through a narrow hallway to a back storage room. Flipping the light on, she pointed to several boxes on the top of a bookshelf. The closet was small, with just enough space for two people to walk a few feet into, and dimly lit. I was instantly aware of our closeness as the door swung closed behind us on spring-loaded hinges.

"Maybe it's the extra appendages?"

"The what?" Rosie whirled on me, her mouth dropping open. I grinned down at her.

"The alien stuff." I waved a hand in the air. "You know. More ... options."

"Oh." Rosie tilted her head, thinking it over, and when her cheeks flushed, my body responded. Desire lasered through me and I had to clench my hands together to stop myself from reaching for her. "Oh my. I'd never considered that. I suppose I could see the appeal. Apologies to Meredith for the judgment I suppose."

I'd done this to myself. I had no one else to blame because I was now picturing Rosie in ways that I wasn't supposed to be if we were meant to just be friends. Clearing my throat, I reached blindly up for the box above my head.

And caught it as it fell, spilling its contents everywhere.

"Och, I'm sorry about that." I put the box aside and bent to start picking up the decorations at the same time Rosie did.

Her lips hit my shoulder.

"Oh no!" Rosie gasped, looking down at the red lipstick smudge on my jumper.

I was never washing this jumper again.

"Och, you may need to get help for this shoulder fetish of yours," I said, as Rosie grabbed my arm and tried to rub the stain with her finger.

"Damn it." Rosie stomped a foot, pouting. "I told you I don't have a thing for shoulders."

"There's nothing wrong with admitting it, darling." Please just keep touching me.

"I swear these are all just weird accidents. I've never been so clumsy in my life as I have been since I moved here."

"That's what they all say." I laughed as she smacked my arm and then I held up what I'd picked up from the floor.

"What's that?" Rosie's lips rounded into a perfect O as she saw what I was holding.

"I think you know what it is."

"I do." Her eyes widened, and her throat moved as she swallowed.

"The rules of mistletoe are very clear."

"This is probably a gray area, though, right? Since it was on the floor."

"I'm fairly certain they're ironclad. Do you really want to test the rules? What with our good luck in the competition tonight?" I held the mistletoe up and Rosie considered it for a moment.

"No, best not to tempt fate, is it? I succumb to the rules of long-standing traditions."

Succumb to me, I said silently, as I tossed the mistletoe behind me and wound a hand behind her neck, pulling her face close. Instead of her lips though, I lingered at her ear, nuzzling against her hair, before I softly kissed her neck.

"Alexander," Rosie breathed, and I kissed her soft skin again, the scent of vanilla and cinnamon enticing me.

"Yes?"

"That's not my lips."

"No, I don't think the rules say where to kiss. I want to make sure I'm thorough."

"Oh." Rosie's breath was shaky, and I grinned against her throat. Trailing my lips down her neck, I nibbled at her collarbone, licking lightly and then blowing a soft breath across her skin. When she shivered, my body heated.

I looked up at her under heavy-lidded eyes and saw a face ravaged by desire before she caught me looking and schooled her expression. But I'd seen it. It was all the confirmation I'd needed. Running my hands down her sides, I hitched her up and put her on top of the worktable.

"Eeek." Rosie gaped at me.

"Did I hurt you?" I asked, running my hands lightly along the sides of her thighs in that slippery silky skirt. I eased forward until I stood between her legs.

"No, I just ..." Rosie waved a hand in front of her face. "You lifted me so easily."

"I'll carry you all night long, lass, so long as you let me keep touching you."

"Oh." Rosie's mouth formed that perfect O of shock again and I'd held off long enough. I needed a taste. I needed to know if the feelings from the other night were an anomaly, or if I really wanted her as much as I thought that I did. Cradling her face in my hands, I angled her mouth to mine.

And then I feasted.

My senses were on overload. In this moment, she was everything. The delicious heat of her kiss drew me in, and I dropped one hand to run it along her thigh, the silk of her skirt driving me crazy. Over and over I stroked her thigh until she moaned into my mouth, widening her legs, and arched her hips against me.

"Bloody hell," I gasped against her lips. "I need to touch you."

"Oh, please do," Rosie begged, doing some touching of her own as she ran her hands beneath my jumper until she found skin. I shivered at the trace of her hands against my back, and dipping my head, I took her lips again. Licking inside her mouth, I mirrored her movements and slid my hand over that enticingly soft jumper of hers and underneath the hem. Her skin was warm beneath my touch, and I trailed my hands up her side until I found her breasts.

"Yes," Rosie breathed against my lips.

"Are you sensitive here?" She wore silk here as well, and her breasts hung heavy and lush in my hands. I brushed my hands over them, cupping and kneading, my body begging to be buried deep inside her.

"So much. This is ..." Rosie threw her head back as I tweaked her, thrusting her breasts farther into my hands. "Just like that." Tracing circles, my eyes widened as she bucked against my hips, and I captured her lips once more. Rosie moved rhythmically against me, and I continued to caress her breasts until her movements picked up frequency. Pulling away, Rosie mewled in frustration when I stopped touching her.

"Shh, darling. Just a moment then."

Finding the hem of her skirt, I lifted it slowly up her legs, and her eyes widened as my fingers danced across her inner thigh.

"Should we?" Rosie asked, her eyes heavy with lust, lipstick smeared around her swollen lips.

"Let me take care of you," I said, tracing a finger across her pants. Silk here too. "You're close."

"But ... what about you?"

"Shhh. The rules of mistletoe are very clear," I said as I slipped a finger beneath the silk and found her ready and wanting.

"The rules address this situation?" Rosie arched her hips forward, giving me better access, her wet heat almost undoing me.

"Of course. The lady shall always have her pleasure."

"Oh, I can get on board with those rules." The last word trailed off in a moan as I curled my fingers inside of her, reaching that perfect spot that made her thighs tremble. I stroked leisurely, bending forward to lick my way across her neck, as Rosie bucked her hips against my hand.

"There's a bonnie lass," I breathed at her neck. "I've been wanting to touch you all night."

"You have?" Rosie gasped, squirming as I increased my pace, my mind short-circuiting at how wet and tight she was.

"Aye, lass. This silk skirt and those red lips? I've barely been able to look at you for fear of embarrassing myself." Her legs clenched, another soft moan slipping from her lips, and I kissed her. "Let go, lass."

Rosie licked into my mouth as I took her over the edge, her soft body shaking as she rode the wave of pleasure, her lips hungry on mine. I waited until she'd relaxed against me, and then removed my hand and straightened, beaming down at her. Bringing my fingers up, I licked them, and she gasped. Her eyes fixated on where I lazily tasted her on my hand, and it took everything in my power not to ask her to give more of herself to me.

Never had I seen a sexier woman than Rosie—skin flushed, silky skirt pulled up to reveal soft thighs, lipstick smeared across her lips. Her eyes were sated, her expression loose and happy, and I wanted to pick her up and carry her to the bedroom and dive into all that softness and beauty. It had been over three years since I'd had sex, and before Rosie landed in Kingsbarns, there hadn't been a woman who'd even tempted me to look twice. And it wasn't only because of the demise of my marriage. I'd felt lost, hurt, angry ... all the feelings associated with divorce. And yet, when Rosie arrived, it was as if my eyes had been finally opened again.

What is it about this woman that makes her impossible to resist? But she only wanted to be friends, so I might never find out what she felt like wrapped around me. *And if I don't stop going down that path mentally, we'll never leave this room.*

Shite. There were four crazy women outside that door ... here to talk Christmas windows. *Can't get less sexy than that.*

"We should get back out there." I jerked my thumb toward the door.

"Shit, I totally forgot the Book Bitches. They'll be knocking down this door soon if we don't come out." Fear crossed Rosie's face.

"They absolutely will. You know they're not above stealing a peek."

"Oh, they totally would." Rosie groaned, and then looked up at me, laughter on her face. "You're covered in lipstick. They'll know what we've been doing."

"I think they'll suspect it anyway."

Rosie reached up and rubbed her thumb across my face. Our eyes caught and held, and I turned my face to kiss her hand.

"Oh Alexander, what am I going to do with you? We're supposed to be just friends."

"We are," I promised her. Anything to keep her happy.

"Friends who kiss?"

"That was more than a kiss," I pointed out and her cheeks flushed.

"Friends with benefits?" Rosie asked.

"If that's what you want." I bit the inside of her palm and her mouth dropped open, her thighs clenching around me once more. Bloody hell, it would take all my power to walk out of here without asking for more. As it was, I'd need a few moments to cool down before I could go out in public.

"I think I might. I think I just might."

"We can try it out. See how it goes." I'd never considered suggesting friends with benefits, but maybe Rosie had the right of it. It might fulfill our needs without forcing us into an actual relationship that neither of us wanted to be in. An image of her on a date with the Boston lad brought a scowl to my face. "So long as you don't have this arrangement with others."

"I've been here a week. How many arrangements do you think I have?" Rosie demanded, easing back from me and sliding her skirt down her legs.

"Your friend did suggest you ride a train of men through town."

"Jessica would have destroyed the men of this town by now. I am not her."

"What about the Boston guy?" I couldn't help but ask, but I knew it would drive me crazy if I didn't get an answer. I adjusted my kilt as Rosie slid off the table, a look of confusion on her face.

"Oh, him? I just met him. He's only visiting." Rosie waved it away as she bent to pick up more of the decorations from the floor.

"Things can escalate quickly," I reminded her, picking up the mistletoe I'd tossed behind me.

Rosie glanced at me and rolled her eyes.

"I don't juggle men. I don't share. I don't ... that's not ..." She laughed. "I don't even know how to operate like that."

"Just checking."

"Right, so exclusive friends with benefits?" Rosie arched a brow at me, gathering up the rest of the decorations in her arms.

"Correct."

"Perfect. Thanks for the fun, *mate.*" Rosie left the room with a wink, and I took another moment to catch my breath before I pulled the other boxes down and carried them out to the main room.

"Been drinking cranberry juice?" Esther asked me, looking at my face.

"Red wine," I corrected and put the boxes on the table.

"Funny, that red wine looks the same shade as Rosie's lipstick."

"They must have taken their inspiration from the wine then." And that was fair given she tasted so bloody fantastic. Raising a hand in the air, I waved goodbye, breezing through the shop and leaving Rosie to the wolves. There was no way I was going to stand there and deal with an interrogation from the Book Bitches.

No, the only person I wanted to pick apart every second of that interaction was myself. Whistling, I turned my face to the cold winter rain with a smile. I could still smell Rosie's scent on my skin, and I knew exactly what I'd be pleasuring myself to as soon as I got home.

Chapter Eighteen

ROSIE

"I'm sorry, what was that? Did you just say friends with benefits?" Jessica screeched into the phone. "Yes, *Queen*. I am loving Scottish Rosie. Loving it. *Yes*, this is what I wanted for you."

"Would you stop? It's not a big deal." I shrugged and glanced nervously toward the door. It was around the time when people would start showing up, with complete disregard for any actual posted opening hours at my shop. This did not annoy me as much as it would have if I'd still been working at the discount store.

"It is for you. You never do stuff like this."

"Sure I do." Did I? Maybe I didn't. I kind of just moved seamlessly between relationships. I couldn't quite remember anyone cornering me in a closet before and giving me the best pleasure of my life with just a hand though.

"Please, girl. Lie to yourself all you want. But not to me. Look, I even got you a shirt." Jessica went off screen before returning with a shirt with a fat Santa on it.

"Where's my ho ho ho's at?" I read and glared at Jessica while she threw her head back and laughed. "I am not a ho."

The speaker flipped on next to me and started playing *There's Some Hoes in this House* and Jessica laughed even harder. It's clear Jessica and Moira would have gotten along.

"Oh my God, perfect timing on that song. Told ya."

"Yes, perfect timing." I glared at the speaker, flicking it back off. I hadn't yet told Jessica about the magick here. We hadn't managed to get past my love life.

"But I do hope you're entering your ho era. Every woman needs one."

"Did you really buy that shirt for me?" I asked.

"Nah, I bought it for a Christmas happy hour I'm going to. But it fit." Jessica grinned at me as the door to the shop swung open.

"Bitch," I mouthed and waved at Edina poking her head in the shop. "Gotta run."

"Bye, ho," Jessica whispered, and I clicked off, laughing.

"Edina! How are you?" I asked, pleased to see her. Today she wore a cheerful scarf in rainbow colors and her eyes were bright as she crossed the shop to me.

"I just nipped out to get the messages and wanted to

211

pop by before you opened. Is anyone else here?" Edina looked around the shop.

"Nope, just me." And a cheeky ghost.

"Oh that's grand. Right, so Samuel ..."

"Yes?" I looked at her eagerly.

"Oh, he's a dream, Rosie. Just a dream."

I squealed and rounded the table to give her a hug. Pulling back, I held her arms and beamed at her.

"I'm so happy for you. I was hoping you two would hit it off."

"We really did. Just I don't even know." Edina stepped back to pace. "We've had dinner three nights in a row now. We just can't stop talking. It's incredible. I wasn't expecting to really make a match, and well, so it is then."

"This is great, really, really great. I'm so happy for you both."

"Do I owe you anything else?" Edina looked at me, her lips thinning.

"I don't think so?" Did she?

"Och, I wasn't sure if there was, I don't know, a closing bonus or something. Or a bonus if you made a match."

That would be smart. I waved the idea away. I wasn't in this for money. Well, I was barely in it at all. I was still learning the ropes and toying with magick, so it was best that we just left things the way Moira had run them in that department.

The door opened and an alien poked its head in.

"Um." Edina looked from me to the door.

"Just another day at Highland Hearts," I said, grinning as the inflatable alien blow-up doll waggled its head back and forth.

"Must be another client looking for love." Edina grinned and gave me a quick hug before pausing at the door as Alexander ducked inside holding the alien doll.

"You do you, darling." Edina patted Alexander's arm, giving a pointed look to the doll before she continued to the street.

Alexander blanched and turned to the street. "No. It's not like *that*."

I buckled over, laughing.

"I mean, it could be like that. No judgment, right?" I gasped, wiping my eyes.

"I brought this in for the window." Alexander put the green blow-up alien on the table and crossed his arms over his chest.

"Don't let Meredith steal it." I laughed even harder when Alexander winced.

"Also not an image I want. Listen, what if we just moved on entirely from any alien sex discussions?"

"Did someone say alien smut?" Meredith sang, poking her head in the door, and I collapsed again, holding my hand at my side.

"No. Nobody said that," Alexander rushed to explain.

"Ohhh, is that a blow-up doll?" Meredith's grin spread even wider, and I howled, crossing my legs because I was quite certain I was going to pee my pants at any moment here. "Alexander, I had no idea you were a bad boy."

"I can't." Alexander turned and banged his forehead against a bookshelf.

"I'm dead. I'm dying." I fanned my face, trying to control my giggles.

"Where'd you get this cutie?" Meredith tapped the blow-up doll.

"You'll have to ask Alexander for his source for blow-up dolls."

"It's not a source." Alexander whirled on me. "You make me sound like I'm a dealer."

"Lot of money in sex toys," Meredith commented, unpacking the box of decorations she'd brought with her.

"It's not. I can't." Alexander threw up his hands. "I've exceeded my tolerance for social interactions today and it's not even ten in the morning. Good day, ladies."

With that, he stormed out of the shop while I howled in laughter. Esther came in just then, with Shannon and Cherise on her heels.

"Someone's a bit tetchy today," Esther commented, nodding out the door while she unwound the scarf around her neck.

"I think his social battery is drained."

"Maybe he's just worn out from his blow-up doll." Meredith held up the alien and the Book Bitches crowed with delight.

"Is that his toy?" Cherise looked at me like I would know the answer to Alexander's bedroom contents. I mean, I might, someday, but we hadn't leveled our friendship up quite that far yet. Alexander had been busy with final exams for his students, and I couldn't quite bring myself to call him and ask him to come by. Yet.

"He brought it in for the window, but Meredith derailed the conversation and managed to make it sexual."

"Me? I wasn't the one talking about sex when I walked in the door." Meredith fluffed her hair like she was meant to be minding her own business.

"You two were discussing sex?" Esther scoffed. "What's there to talk about? You either want to have it or you don't. Kids these days. Waste too much time talking."

"Can we focus on the window design please? You all read too many romance novels." Pulling out the diagram for the window, I pursed my lips. "We need to land on a song for the music."

"I think I know," Esther said.

The speaker flipped on, and David Bowie's *Life on Mars* began to play.

"Damn it, Moira. That was my big reveal." Esther snapped her fingers in the air and dropped her tote bag on the table in disgust. "She always loved being the center of attention."

"That's a perfect song," I said.

And it was. If there was one advantage—*and I used that term lightly*—to my mother being absent throughout my life, it was music. Perhaps I used it to drown out my sadness, or maybe it became my friend when I felt so alone otherwise. But it had given me such a good memory for songs, and for song titles. What was weird though was how Moira seemed to know that. I wasn't an encyclopedia of song names by any stretch, but she'd somehow picked easily identifiable songs that I recognized from the introductions. *How is it possible that we're so in sync, even though we never met?*

"Well, let's get to it, ladies," Cherise said. Meredith had disappeared into my kitchen to make tea, something that I was more used to now, and my phone pinged with a text.

> Nice to meet you the other night. Fancy a drink tonight? I leave this weekend.

I paused, my finger hovering over the keyboard, as I thought about it. Did I want to have a drink with a handsome, unattached man? Jessica would be screaming at me to accept. But the thing was, I just wasn't sure what the point was. I didn't want to be careless with Alexander's request for exclusivity, and I also wasn't looking for love.

> Nice to meet you too. I'm sorry, I'm slammed this week. Safe travels back.

Putting my phone down, certain I'd made the right decision, I looked up as the bells jingled at the door.

"Ah, Daniel. Good to see you."

I'd invited him here today because I'd been playing with my magnifying glass, which I'd since learned is also called a quizzing glass. Because I'd had a niggling suspicion that sometimes, maybe it was okay if two people's favorite book was the same. I had to spend some time thinking about what the connection would be, but when it had come to me late last night, I rushed into the shop and wrote their names together along with the word.

Banter.

It had risen off the page in all its shimmering glory. Now, I just had to figure out how to put my plan into action without making my mark suspicious. Because she was a contrary old goat, I knew as soon as she sniffed out my intentions, she'd march the other way just to be difficult.

Daniel looked particularly dapper today with a suit-coat worn over a soft green sweater and tweed pants. A smart newsboy cap was tucked on his head, and frankly, I was surprised one of these women hadn't gone after him yet. He was *very* handsome.

"You as well. How has the window decorating gone?"

"It's coming along." I moved around the table and hooked my arm through his, pulling him past the disco unicorn to where the women huddled by the window. "We're going with an outer space theme this week."

"Christmas in space. Stellar," Daniel said.

Esther raised her head and looked him up and down.

"I'd say interstellar, wouldn't you?" Esther held his look.

"Ah, I stand corrected. I must have spaced out." Daniel grinned as Esther sniffed.

"It's important to pay attention. We take things very Sirius-ly here." Esther's face was a mask as she braided silver twine together.

"I'll make sure to approach the situation with the utmost gravity, of course." Daniel tipped his cap.

The Book Bitches had stopped what they were doing, their heads swiveling between the two like they were watching a tennis match.

"Be sure that you do. We can't have your interruption eclipse our work."

"Of course not, I'd hate to ruin the atmosphere." Daniel's grin widened and it took everything in my power not to jump up and down in excitement.

"Everything will be perfect, because that's how I planet." Esther studied her twine, but I caught her quick glance at Daniel. She was interested. The outer space puns were killing me, and I wanted to jump in with some of my own, but I would never ruin this moment for them.

"Naturally, I am sure everything runs smoothly so long as everyone craters to your every whim."

"It can be a bit of an emotional solar coaster with these three, but we get the job done." Esther's eyes lit with appreciation at her own pun.

"No comet." Daniel's grin widened when Esther flashed him an annoyed look.

I wondered who would back down first. For Daniel's sake, I hope he bowed out and gave Esther the win.

"We have to get back to work. I don't want to get the constellation prize." Esther gave Daniel the side-eye as she pulled out more twine.

"I certainly hope to see you again, lunar than later." With that, Daniel tipped his cap and turned, with what I thought was a perfect exiting line.

"Don't hold your breath, or you'll be all suited up

with no space to go," Esther called after him, and he just chuckled as he left the shop.

"Esther!" I whirled on her. "That was rude."

Esther just shrugged a shoulder. "Just a bit of banter, lass. He'll be fine."

"He was cute," Meredith said, an arm still around the alien blow-up doll.

"He was very handsome, Esther," Shannon agreed.

"You should give him a whirl," Cherise agreed.

"Nah." Esther shook her head. "Didn't fancy him."

"Why not?" I demanded. "That was great. He seems very clever."

"Nope, not for me." Esther turned and began to tack up the silver twine.

Shannon met my eyes behind Esther's back.

"In that case, I might give him a go. Rosie, would you be able to introduce us?"

"Oh, is he not from around town?" For some reason, I just assumed everyone knew each other in this place.

"I haven't seen him before. He must be from one of the neighboring villages."

"I'll be happy to put in a word for you next time he pops in."

"Oh good. He was too cute." Shannon grinned at me as Esther sniffed, and then used a staple gun to loudly drown us out.

"I certainly think so," I continued. *Thwap.*

"I love a newsboy cap on a man," Cherise agreed. *Thwap.*

I grinned, knowing Esther was annoyed. The speaker

219

flipped on, and I bit back a laugh as *Chain of Fools* by Aretha Franklin filled the air.

Thwap.

"Need any help there, Esther?"

"Bloody hell, do any of you ever stop talking?" Esther put the staple gun down and grabbed her pocketbook. "I'm going to Two Sisters for a latte. See if you ladies can stay on track while I'm gone."

With that, Esther sailed from the shop, her head held high.

"Oh, she's bothered by him. I haven't seen her like this in years," Cherise observed.

"She's definitely flustered," Shannon agreed.

"How do you know?" I asked, hope blooming that maybe there was a chance for a match between Esther and Daniel.

"She doesn't drink lattes."

"Ahhhh." My phone pinged with a text, and I glanced down to see a message from Alexander.

> Tattie just told me he misses you and would like you to come see his new enclosure.

Grinning, I wandered back to the front of the shop.

> Well, I certainly can't let Tattie down.

> Perfect. Can you come by this afternoon? That way you can see it before dark. I'll make dinner.

> Tattie and dinner? Even better. What can I bring?

A smile.

I sent him a smile emoji and looked up when a throat cleared.

"Loverboy?" Meredith asked.

"No, my friend Jessica."

Liar by Camila Cabello popped on the speaker and Meredith grinned.

"You said you liked Moira, right?" I pitched my voice over the music, annoyed. "Because I'm having a hard time seeing it."

"Oh yeah, she's the best." Meredith blew a kiss into the air.

Chapter Nineteen

Rosie

I waved to a local woman as I crossed the street, tote bag on my shoulder, humming to myself. It had been less than two weeks since I'd arrived in Scotland and already, I felt part of this community. How had that happened so seamlessly? Was that the nature of small towns everywhere or was it just because the bookshop was a natural hub for people? Was it because of Moira and her wacky legacy? *Was I actually like her?*

Either way, I liked it.

Jessica was right, Scottish Rosie was great.

I liked the Rosie that I was becoming here. At home, I'd been stuck in a routine that it had taken a pretty drastic event to shake me out of. I'd become a complacent, even bland version of myself, and that thought stopped me in my tracks as I crested a small hill on the gravel road to Alexander's house.

Here I'd been putting the blame on others for being boring or bland, when I'd gone right along with it myself, hadn't I? It was easier for me to look to my boyfriends to spice things up or make life interesting than it had been for me to take the reins myself. I'd allowed my fear of taking risks—induced by a childhood of being out of control—to keep me stagnant. It hadn't just been that I'd picked tepid partners, I had also made tepid choices.

It had felt safe to me. Which I am sure many a psychologist would gently point to childhood trauma and give me numerous reasons for why I'd been making the choices I had.

"I don't want to play it safe anymore!" I cried out, the wind ripping my words from my mouth and carrying them across the field. Immediately panic loomed.

"Wait, no, no. I was kidding. I definitely want to play it safe," I called out, just in case the universe got confused on what I'd meant about playing it safe. I'd already done my huge adventurous choice by hopping on that plane and moving my life here. That was enough big adventure for me for a long time. I didn't need to jump into the deep end when I was just learning how to swim. I never understood people who suggested that method of learning. Surely there was a more methodical and incremental approach than shock therapy?

I was a list girl. Organized. Step by step.

And so I would push myself out of my comfort zone, but it would have to be on my terms.

I wanted this to work.

Down to the very marrow of my bones, I could feel how much I wanted this experience to be a fruitful one for me. I didn't just want to dabble in bookselling and grow bored and jaded with it within time. I wanted to constantly improve the store, host events, write books, meet new friends, and become a welcomed member of the little community here. I wanted to explore Scotland and immerse myself in her history, and dream about days past while wandering along crumbling castle walls.

I turned a corner in the road and Alexander's house came into view.

My heart clenched as he rounded the house, not seeing me, a piece of wood on his shoulder.

I wanted him.

There was no explaining it, really, for it seemed too soon. And yet there was also no denying it. Every day he showed up at the shop, even though he worked several jobs and took care of an injured puffin. Still, he made time for a project he'd committed to, he was gentle with the Book Bitches when they were downright overbearing, and he had not been gentle with me in the best ways in that closet the other night. The man was a mass of contradictions. Socially awkward but intensely kind. A computer geek but mind-numbingly sexy. Reserved and shy yet chatty in private.

I was hooked.

Alexander stopped his return around the house and waved when he saw me. Picking up the pace, I laughed as I reached him.

"I've only seen your house when it's dark out. But I get it now, Alexander. I really do. No wonder you're happy to hunker down by yourself out here." Turning, I spread my arms out to encompass the incredible view that stretched behind Alexander's cottage.

Rolling green hills met sand dunes and cliffs, the ocean kissing the shore, birds swooping low to look for a meal. Clouds hung low on the horizon, mere whisps of white in a moody winter sky, and faded winter sunlight speared through, highlighting streaks of light across the slate-blue water. I could look at this endlessly, imagining the mood had to change daily, and wondered if Alexander did just that—sat at his tall windows each morning, staring out over the water.

"Och, it's a grand spot, isn't it?" Alexander grinned down at me. His dark hair was rumpled by the wind. He wore a thick canvas coat over a plaid shirt, and he looked solid and strong and real. I wanted to hug him.

"It really is a great view," I agreed but kept my eyes on him. Appreciation dawned in his eyes, and my heart skipped a beat when he stepped closer, angling me until my back was against the stone wall of his house. Setting the wood against the wall, he pressed himself against me. He slid his hands up the sides of my body, and then pushed my arms over my head, leaning in until his mouth hovered over mine.

A giddy feeling twirled inside me. *See? Small risks. Baby steps.*

When his mouth slanted across mine, it felt like coming home. Everything clicked into place for me, and I gasped against his lips, hooking one arm around his neck. I felt *everything* in this moment. The heat of his mouth, the slap of icy wind against my heated cheeks, the press of his muscular body pushing me back against the stone of the cottage. It was all hot and cold, hard and soft, and the contradictions, much like Alexander himself, were enough to make me mewl in distress at his mouth.

"Shhh, darling." Alexander pulled back and brushed a thumb over my bottom lip. "The light's leaving us. Let me show you what I've built for Tattie and then we can continue this."

I wanted to climb this man like a tree and build a house among his branches and ... never leave. Never had I been so responsive with a partner before, but something about Alexander's touch was driving me straight to the edge. It was so clear that before him—*not that we are a couple*—before Alexander, I had always settled for scraps. I'd never believed I was worthy of someone like this man.

"Can I put your handbag inside?" Alexander asked, bringing me back to the present as I blinked up at him.

"Oh, right. Sure. Well, the tote bag is for Tattie."

"I'm not sure he's much for shopping."

"I meant what is in it." I rolled my eyes at a grinning Alexander. "I looked up some enrichment things for him. They're kind of makeshift, but we can give it a go and see what he thinks."

"I'm sure he'll be delighted." Alexander pulled the tote open and peered inside. "As am I. Even though I'm not sure what your plan is for a baking dish."

"Don't worry. No puffins are on the menu tonight."

"Good, because I'd hate to have to figure out where to bury your body." Alexander laughed as I poked him in the side. I then followed him around the side of the house.

My heart stopped.

"Oh, Alexander. This ... this isn't just an enclosure. This is incredible." I blinked at the sudden press of tears against my eyes. The man was crying out to nurture someone, something, anything.

The enclosure was huge. It took up a massive chunk of his backyard, likely sacrificing a good portion of his beautiful view, and he'd done it without a second thought. The entire structure was enclosed in chicken wire, and one side had a lean-to that sheltered a small boxed-in pen. Alexander stopped by the door and crossed his arms over his chest, watching me as I took it all in.

Tattie stood on top of a rocky outcropping, focused on the pool of water below him. I gasped when he jumped in, but he came out with a minnow in his mouth and I couldn't help myself. I applauded.

"Look at him go." This time I did lean in and hug Alexander. He wrapped an arm around me, and I turned, my face pressed into his chest, and watched as Tattie waddled around his new home. "Truly, this is mind-blowing. Can you walk me through your choices?"

"You want to know why I built it the way that I did?" Alexander's voice was a rumble in his chest at my ear.

"I do."

"Are you deliberately trying to turn me on?"

I laughed.

"I like learning. And knowing you, there are logical choices for the decisions you've made."

"Well, since you asked." Alexander drew back and rubbed his hands together, like a kid about to dive into a year's supply of candy. "Right, so since the vet wasn't entirely sure if Tattie's wing would heal, since sometimes clipped feathers can grow back after a molt, but it depends on the extent of the damage, he didn't seem overly optimistic. He said the wing was quite damaged, but we're still going to hold out hope he can fly again one day. Which meant I wanted to keep his enclosure as natural as possible, but also make it safe for him."

"How on earth is he not going to escape through that pool?" I pointed to the shallow pool of ocean water that Tattie was currently playing in. From my vantage point, it looked like a tidal pool where the ocean water rushed between rocky outcroppings. Tattie wasn't that big. "Surely he could just escape through there if he wanted?"

"Do you want to go in and see?"

"Can we?" I asked, adjusting the tote bag at my shoulder.

"Sure, you can give him his toy."

"Oh, I need fish for it." I'd forgotten that one crucial bit.

"Show me." Alexander took the bag from me and pulled out the baking tray and the small grate I'd found to nestle in it.

"So the idea was to put the fish below the grate, and then add some pebbles and so on. He'll have to dig a bit to pull the fish out. Kind of like a puzzle feeder."

"Ah, sure, sure. Cool idea." Alexander went into the shed and returned with a small bucket of fish, and I watched as he laid them out in the pan, and then covered them with the grate that had beak-sized spaces in it. Then he added some pebbles and sand from a nearby dune.

"Think this will suit?" Alexander asked.

"No idea." I shrugged. "But we can give it a go."

"I hope he knows that we care." Alexander held the door for me, and I ducked through inside the enclosure. Once inside though, I could stand up straight, as could Alexander. He'd installed large posts throughout the enclosure which held up the chicken wire roof, and it was quite spacious, easily forty feet long.

Tattie hid behind a rock and peered out at us.

"Hey, bud, I know it's scary because you're not used to us. Yet. But here, we have a treat." Alexander laid the tray on the sandy shore, close enough so some of the water lapped over it. Easing back, he nudged me to go around the other side.

"So basically you're keeping his environment as natural as possible then?"

"That's the plan. See here?" Alexander pointed to where I'd thought there was an opening in the rocks to head out to the sea. "I put more chicken wire and some smaller pieces of timber down there. It shows him the way is blocked so he doesn't try to swim through, but it is wide enough to allow the tide to come through, along with some schools of minnows."

"Smart," I said, seeing now how he'd cleverly worked with the natural environment.

"Then he's got a little swimming pool. He has dunes, grasses, and I brought more rocks in to create burrowing opportunities for him." Alexander nodded to the various piles of rocks strewn around the sloping grass.

"And this?" I pointed to the box under the lean-to.

"It's also an option for a burrow. It's his choice what he decides, but once he picks his spot, that will be his spot."

"Do they do that in the wild too?"

"Yes." Alexander turned and looked out to the horizon. "Once they pick their burrow, they return to it year after year. It's their spot."

"You say *they*, though."

"Yes, a breeding pair will pick a burrow together. Even if they travel apart, since scientists can't really determine what they do when they go out to sea for so long, they'll return to the same spot and be together. Isn't that nice?" There was a wistful note to Alexander's voice.

He'd built his burrow here. Alexander just needed his mate. His ex had been a fool to let this man go. He was born a nurturer.

"Look!" I grasped Alexander's arm, excitement racing through me as Tattie hopped out from behind his rock to investigate the tray I'd left for him. Tilting his head left and right, he gnashed his orange beak, making an odd little chattering noise as he peered at the baking tray. "Oh, I hope he'll take it."

He pecked at the tray. Bounced back a few steps. Tilted his head a few different times, waiting to see if it was a trap, I guessed. When nothing happened, he bounced forward again, this time dipping his head deeper in and rattling about. When he came up with a fish in his mouth, I gasped.

"He did it. Oh, Alexander. He did it."

"That's my boy. I'm so proud." Alexander mimed wiping a fake tear away, and I grinned, even though I was actually very near tears myself.

"Shall we go inside? It's cold and the light's going."

"But will you just leave him out here?" I didn't want him to be lonely.

"He'll find a spot. Trust me, I've researched this. He easily has fifteen different sheltered spots for a nest, plus plenty of nesting type materials. But I can't pick it for him. He needs to decide where he wants to nest."

"That's fair." We ducked outside the enclosure, and Alexander secured the door. "I'm so proud of you, Alexander. He really looks so happy."

"And he likes his toy." Alexander nodded to where Tattie was growing more confident with digging around in my makeshift puzzle tray. "It's a good idea. They're used to diving for their meals, so it gives him something to do."

Tattie popped his head up and leaned back, giving us that low call that sounded like an old man having a laugh.

"Oh my God, he's happy. You have a happy bird."

"No wankers here," Alexander agreed, nudging me toward the house. "Speaking of, how are your birds?"

"Delightful. And loud."

Alexander laughed as he held the door open for me. "A little too happy for you?"

"A little too happy early in the morning is all," I grumbled.

"Ah yes, they must not have gotten the memo about sleeping in."

"Did you know that I read somewhere that birds sing before dawn to wake the plants up?" I asked, stopping to take my boots off just inside the house. Alexander joined me on the bench, doing the same, and looked over at me.

"Is that right, hen?"

"Supposedly. Some guy on a farm discovered it, then analyzed the pulses of music, figured out classical music hit the same notes, started playing it for his crops and they increased their yield tenfold."

"Truly?" Alexander's eyes widened.

"Maybe. It could be internet legend too. I didn't fact-check in the slightest."

"Naturally."

I skidded to a stop in the main room of the house, caught on the view from his windows. The last of the daylight was lingering, giving me a rough idea of how incredible it would be to sit here, during storms or sunshine, and be a part of nature but sheltered from it all the same.

"I can't get over this room. Somehow, you've

managed to make it both cozy but incredibly airy and open."

"It was a labor of love, that's for sure." Alexander danced his fingers down my arm and then threaded them through mine. Giving me a little tug, he drew me over to a table in the corner by the windows. When I saw what was on it, my eyes widened.

"Wingspan!"

"Ah, yeah. When you mentioned there was a bird board game, I realized I was sadly remiss in adding it to my games stash."

"Are we going to play?" I looked up at him, excited.

"Of course. I just did pizza for dinner, but we can eat while we play if you'd like?"

"Even better." Glancing up at him, I narrowed my eyes. "Watch yourself, MacTavish. I'm ruthless."

"I'd expect nothing less."

"What are we playing for?" I asked.

"Och, the lass wants to heighten the stakes. Fine. If I win, you have to just wear that silk skirt for me again."

My cheeks heated as I thought about his hands on my thighs, the silk slipping across my legs.

"And if I win, you have to wear your kilt for me. With no shirt on."

"Perfect. Either way, one of us will be topless."

My mouth dropped open. "I didn't agree to be topless."

"I said to just wear the skirt."

"I didn't take that to mean ..." I trailed off, my mouth still hanging open.

"You should always ask for clarification before you agree to something."

"You're annoying. But also correct. Fine, MacTavish. Let's get going. I want to watch you squirm."

"You're a bloodthirsty one, aren't you?"

"I hope you cry."

Alexander threw his head back and laughed. Passing me as he went to the kitchen for food, he brushed his lips lightly over my cheek. Despite knowing we were just friends with benefits, I held my hand up to my cheek, my eyes on Tattie, alone in his pen outside. The puffin continued to play in the baking tray, seemingly content, but for how long before he'd grow bored and unhappy?

Turning, I watched Alexander humming in the kitchen, likely unaware he was even singing to himself.

It dawned on me then that Alexander was a mate-for-life person. No wonder he'd been so harmed when his ex-wife had felt otherwise. But did that mean he'd never give it a chance again?

And why was I even thinking this way?

Matchmaking must be making me see life through rose-colored glasses, I realized. I'd come here convinced that I was more than happy to stay single, because I'd truly never had a great love in my life. That had led me to believe that maybe it just wasn't in the cards for me, which in turn made me convince myself that I didn't really believe in true love. And yet, here I was, spending a large chunk of my days looking to help others find it. Everyone except myself, of course.

Heal thyself first, Doctor, and all that.

When Alexander returned, two glasses of wine in hand and a smile on his face, I swallowed against the unexpected emotion caught in my chest.

"Ready to lose?" Alexander asked.

"Not a chance in hell, *mate*." I pointed to the table. "Bring it on."

Chapter Twenty

Rosie

"Let's see the kilt."

"Right now?" Alexander crossed his arms over his chest, annoyed.

The fire crackled behind us, and night had blanketed the back garden, though the moon shone a bright path across the inky surface of the water.

"Aww, are you a sore loser?" I asked, laughing at the disgruntled look on his face.

Not only had Alexander lost, but I'd wiped the table with him.

"I am not." Alexander sniffed.

"Either you can go put your kilt on or I can go into great detail about just how much of a startlingly bad loss it was for you. I mean really just an absolute embarrassment—"

"Och, fine." Alexander trudged away and I laughed. Wandering across the room, I plopped on the couch in front of the fire. Music pulsed low in the background, and I thought once again, just how much I loved this room. I honestly didn't really want to leave. If I had a pile of books with me, I'd curl up right now and read.

Or.

Or ...

Or.

My mouth went dry as Alexander exited his bedroom in only his kilt and nothing else. Walking around the back of the couch, he came to stand in front of me, that scowl still stretched across his face.

My entire body heated.

The man was seriously built. And he wasn't getting those muscles from working on computers all day. Clearly, all the work on his house had paid off because the dips and valleys running down his abs were seriously impressive.

"Like what you see?" Alexander's voice was low, his accent delicious, and his words hung in the air between us. The energy of the room shifted. Desire pooled low inside me, and I wet my lips.

"Um, of course. You're very well formed."

Well formed? I'd just made it sound like he'd hatched from an egg.

Alexander seemed to read my embarrassment because his lips quirked as he moved forward. Surprising me, he dropped to his knees in front of me, nudging my legs open, and I gaped at the incredible image of a hot Scotsman in a kilt kneeling at my feet. The fire danced in the background behind him, casting warmth and shadows across his skin, and he tilted his head at me.

"Would you like to see more of these?" Alexander flexed an arm muscle and twisted to point at his shoulder. "I know you have a thing for them."

I mean, I wasn't going to lie. Based on how ripped he was, I could definitely get on board with having a shoulder fetish.

"Gee, and I left the alien at the shop. I didn't think to bring your blow-up doll with me."

"He is not mine," Alexander hissed, and I laughed as the scowl returned to his face. "Now that you have me like this, what was your plan?"

"Um." Panicking, I tried to straighten up, but he held my legs down with his hands. Hands that I desperately wanted all over my body. Could I just say that? We were meant to be just friends with benefits, weren't we? Wouldn't it be perfectly natural to explore what that meant? Preferably naked and sitting on his lap?

"Rosie?"

"Yes?"

"I'd very much like for you not to be wearing these anymore." Alexander toyed with the button of my jeans, and I blinked at him before lifting my hips so he could unbutton and slide my pants *and* underwear down my legs. Hitching me forward on the couch, Alexander looked down at me sprawled before him.

Before I could start to feel awkward, a look of wolfish desire crossed his face.

"Beautiful," Alexander said. He stroked my thighs lightly, nudging my legs wider. "Do you know one of the things I love about being a software engineer?"

"What?" I bit my lower lip as he stroked higher. "What's that?"

"After we build everything up ..." Alexander stroked higher, running a hand across me, and my hips bucked involuntarily toward him. "We have to make it come undone."

Dear God, he was going to be the death of me, wasn't he? This man was going to ruin me for all others.

"Why ... why would you do that?" I moaned, arching my back and dropping my head against the cushions.

"Because we have to see if we built it right." Alexander leaned forward and blew a hot breath across the skin. "And the only way to do that is to try and ruin it."

I'd been right. He was going to destroy me for all other men. When he dipped his head and took a taste of me, I was already gone, so close to going over the edge that I mewled in distress as he licked and suckled me. A fine tremor worked its way up my body, and I could feel the pleasure radiating across my body, as though it was pulling from every molecule, and centering at my very core where Alexander feasted leisurely like he had all the time in the world to make me forget that any man other than him existed.

When he brought his hand up, touching me, the ball

of lust exploded, and I convulsed around him, digging my hands into the couch and holding on as I bucked against his face, riding the wave of pleasure that vibrated through my entire being. Trembling, I blinked up at Alexander, eyes hazy with lust, and watched as he lifted his kilt and rolled a condom on.

Holy hell, this was happening.

And I wanted it to. I wanted this man inside me, next to me, around me, any which way I could have him.

Holding my arms out to him, I allowed him to turn my body the other way on the couch, so I was lying flat, and he tugged my shirt over my head.

"And then you know what happens next?" Alexander asked, trailing his hands up my sides. I lifted my back a bit so he could unhook my bra and shivered when my breasts sprung free.

"What's that?" I closed my eyes briefly as his hands found my breasts, rubbing and caressing, his touch both gentle and demanding, as he rocked himself softly against my core. I could feel how hard he was for me, and my entire body shivered in anticipation about having him inside me.

"We do it all over again." Alexander's voice was husky at my ear as he nibbled against the delicate lobe.

"Why?" I asked, arching against him as he explored my body like he was memorizing every curve. Realizing I could be doing the same, I reached up and wrapped my arms around his back, loving how hard his muscles were underneath my hands. Tracing the ridges of his shoulders, I lifted my hips against him, needing the pressure of him against me.

"Because we have to see if we can put it back together perfectly. And then we test it again." Alexander's lips were at mine, and he sunk his teeth into my lower lip, just as he angled himself forward and slid inside me.

"Yessss," I breathed against his mouth, my hips jerking as he seated himself deeply, filling me.

"And again." Alexander rocked against me, his motions almost lazy as he took my mouth, dipping his tongue inside to play with mine.

"And again."

"Oh," I gasped against his lips as pleasure rose once more.

"Over and over. We build it up and take it apart. We make it come undone. Over. And over and over again." Alexander increased his pace with his words, and my body fixated on that point of desire that was growing at my core. His words became hypnotic and all I could think about was the building of pleasure and the coming undone, and just how damn good it felt. Dipping his head, he abandoned my mouth briefly, kissing his way across my breasts, leaving slick heat in his wake as he licked and suckled. Every time he pulled out, I hated it, and when he drove back in, my muscles clenched more tightly until I closed my eyes and the only thing I could focus on was this tiny pinpoint of pleasure threatening to claw its way out of me. By the time his mouth found mine again, his lips hot, his breath coming faster, I was ready to explode.

"Come undone for me, sweet Rosie, so I can put you back together again." *Oh God, that sounds good coming out of his mouth ... with that amazing accent.*

At that, pleasure shattered through me and I fell limp, unable to do anything other than experience pure ecstasy, while my muscles convulsed around him and he found his own release.

Wedging himself into the crack between me and the couch, Alexander propped his head up on one hand and looked down at me. The fire reflected in his eyes, and his lips were still damp from my kiss.

"I ..." The word came out as a rasp, and I had to clear my throat. My entire body was buzzing, tingling with awareness, and at the same time I felt so languid and relaxed that I never wanted to move from this space. "I have a newfound respect for software engineers."

"Are you saying that you didn't respect us before?" Alexander pressed a kiss to the side of my breast.

"God no. The worst. Ew." I squealed when he bit me. "Ow! And bitey. I had no idea you all were so bitey."

"Do you want to know something else about us?" Alexander asked, rolling on top of me again. My eyes widened as I felt him against my thigh.

"What's that?"

"We work long hours and we're very thorough."

With that, he dipped his head and captured my lips in a searing kiss.

And I was lost.

Lost to this man.

Lost to this place.

Lost to this new life I'd discovered for myself.

Nothing before or nobody after would ever make me feel the way he did in this moment. Appreciated, admired, lusted after. It was a heady feeling, and I lost myself to the new idea of being with someone who took joy in bringing me pleasure.

Merry Christmas to me. And then I could think no more.

Chapter Twenty-One

ALEXANDER

"You're sure you want to do this?" I asked, handing Rosie a pair of binoculars.

"Get up early and walk in the cold when your bed is so much warmer?" Rosie raised an eyebrow at me, and I laughed.

I'd been laughing a lot the last few days.

Good, no, *great*, sex was bound to boost anyone's mood. But it was more than that. It was just well, hell, Rosie was just plain fun to be around. She had a cheerful approach to life, so long as she could follow all her lists, which I very much appreciated. The way she went about tasks made sense to me, and we often found ourselves comparing our daily schedules and making notes on where one could improve. Efficiency was a turn-on it appeared, because every time she added *me* as a to-do on her list, I'd bend her over a table.

Just to cross off an item on the list, naturally.

"It is, but just think how much warmer it will feel when we get back."

"Plus, you're carrying my shopping home." Rosie patted her coat pockets, looking around. "Where is my grocery list?"

"Pocketbook?" I asked, pointing to where it had been left on my kitchen counter.

"Sure, have a look." Rosie unzipped her coat and dug in an interior pocket while I unzipped her handbag and pulled out a folded piece of paper. Seeing the neat title at the top, I blinked up at her in amusement.

"I'm not sure that Tesco sells what you're looking for here." I waved the paper in the air and confusion crossed Rosie's face.

"What's that?"

"What I want in a man," I read out loud and her cheeks paled.

"Give that to me." Rosie lunged, but I stiff-armed her and held it closer to read.

"Since we like to share lists so much." I laughed as she tried to wrangle closer and squinted at the page. "Let's see. Tall. Broad-shouldered. Ah, there's that shoulder kink I knew about."

"Damn it!" Rosie laughed, trying to duck under my arm.

"Trustworthy." At that, I paused and looked down at her. As much as I wanted to read the rest of the list, it was hers to share or not. If I wanted to respect her, I had to hand it over. "Here you go."

"Thank you." Rosie snatched the paper from my hand, blushing.

"But if you want to share it with me, I won't mind. We could compare lists."

"You have a similar list?" Curiosity popped into Rosie's eyes.

"Not written down, but I have it here." I tapped my head.

That was a lie.

I didn't have a list.

Not really.

And if I did, it would just have one word on it.

Rosie.

But it was too soon for all that, and I needed some time to get comfortable with how seamlessly she'd fit herself into my life.

"Well, in the nature of transparency then." Rosie walked to the kitchen counter and smoothed the paper out, and I leaned over to have a look.

"Interesting hobbies." I looked up at her. "Does bird-watching and board games count?"

"Absolutely. I guess I should have clarified that they might be hobbies I also enjoy." Rosie gave me a shy look.

"Ex-boyfriend had boring hobbies?"

"He gambled. On sports. It was sort of all-consuming for him and deeply uninteresting for me. Do you gamble?"

"Nah, maybe a cheeky bet among friends here and there. Not a proper wager or anything of the sort."

"Good to know." Rosie sniffed. She tapped a finger on the paper. "Likes to read."

"A good thing for a bookshop owner," I agreed. Thank goodness I loved to read. "I also like a partner that enjoys books."

"Enjoys travel."

"Naturally, exploring is always good." So long as she didn't want to travel every weekend. I liked some consistency in my life. But travel meant I could possibly up my score on BirdFindr.

"Sense of humor. Intelligence. A kind heart. Won't leave me." At the last one, Rosie's fingers clenched, wrinkling the paper, and I reached out and traced a finger across the back of her hand, wanting to ease her obvious tension.

"Because your mum left a lot?" She'd told me about her chaotic upbringing, and I could understand why she craved stability in her life. I was much the same, but that was because I'd grown up in a stable environment that I'd really enjoyed. After the chaos of Tara, I was happy to be finally back to my baseline of a consistent and reliable routine.

"I just want someone to choose me, I guess, and to put me first. I don't want to be an afterthought anymore."

"I understand." I did, but for different reasons. My ex-wife had made so many decisions without me, that being kept in the dark had torn us apart—and that was long before she'd started cheating on me. She'd wanted

247

the excitement of doing whatever she wanted, whenever she wanted, and I'd hated feeling like I never had all the information. That I was inconsequential in her life because she didn't share even the most basic of things with me like wanting to book a trip to Wales for the weekend. Simple things, but it had eroded our foundation of trust. So, yes, I understood wanting to be put first in someone's life. It should be a priority. "My ex-wife made a game out of hiding things from me. She seemed to find it fun, this keeping me on my toes, but I just realized after a while that I wasn't really her person. It would be nice to be an actual partner with someone someday."

My breath left me. It was the first time I'd articulated that I actually wanted to take a chance on a partner again. Hope bloomed. Maybe this Christmas season wouldn't be so lonely after all.

"It's tough, isn't it? Feeling out of control in someone else's choices?" Rosie shook her head. "I think that's why I settled into a tepid life for a while. In some respects, the blandness soothed me."

I wondered if Kingsbarns would do the same, and then one day she'd wake up and realize that it was too boring for her and on she'd go. Off to another big adventure.

A shaft of sunlight speared through the window, and I shook my head. Those were heavy thoughts for a morning of birdwatching with my friends-with-benefits friend.

"Och, well you're in for a treat this morning. Because

there is nothing bland about birdwatching." I leered at her and Rosie laughed.

"Oh, I can imagine. I mean, it must be riveting," Rosie teased, and I held up my phone.

"Here's the main one we're looking for. A cedar waxwing. Quite rare to the area, but we'll luck out if we see one."

"And then you'll advance in your ranks on Bird-Findr?" Rosie squinted at the photo.

"That's the plan." I zipped up my coat and hung the binoculars around my neck.

"Let's do this. I'm ready to kick some birdfinding ass."

Two hours later, and Rosie was still enthusiastic. I couldn't believe it.

Not once did she complain as we trudged across frozen fields, bitter winter wind making our cheeks ruddy with the cold. Moody clouds hung low over the slate-gray ocean, white caps marring the choppy surface. We'd wandered along the beach for a while before we'd tucked ourselves away in a forest near Cambo Gardens, the ancient trees a canopy over our heads.

Never once had she moaned about the bitter cold or scrolled her phone mindlessly.

Instead, she'd alternated between chatter and silence, patiently waiting when I posted up at a spot, scanning the horizon with my binoculars. She never pressed me to head home early, instead happy as can be, clutching a thermos of coffee in her hands. My ex would have been bored out of her mind, but instead, Rosie was genuinely enhancing my birdwatching experience. She was so genuine. *Trustworthy.*

"Alexander. Look," Rosie hissed, her binoculars trained on a tall tree spearing up from a ravine. "Is that it?"

I raised my binoculars, excitement flowing through me when I saw the cedar waxwing perched in the tree. Quietly, I lifted my camera and took a few photos before turning to beam down at Rosie.

"You've just advanced to a new level, Rosie," I whispered. Helpless not to, I leaned down and kissed her gently, her lips cold against mine.

"What's the level?" Rosie whispered back.

"Official bird nerd. Welcome to the club. We're pretty friendly over here."

"I want a badge." Rosie grinned at me.

"I'll make you one. Along with the no wankers allowed for your bird feeder," I promised her. Happiness ballooned inside me. It was grand, this sharing of small moments together.

Maybe, just maybe, Rosie's list might have led her to me for a reason.

"Come on. Let's upload these photos and make the other birders jealous." Grabbing her hand, I tugged her back home, my heart full.

Chapter Twenty-Two

Rosie

We won the next two windows.

Riding a high, the group met to discuss our final window, which would be put up this weekend. It also landed just two days before Christmas.

"I liked the enchanted forest more than the outer space one," Cherise said. Today she wore a puffin shirt that read *Here Goes Puffin*. "But I'm partial to unicorns."

"And the Highland coos with dragon's wings were inspired," I agreed. Both the windows had been so well-received that we had garnered more coverage in local media and the bookshop had been hopping. Between that and spending almost every night at Alexander's, the days had flown by.

And, yes, I was spending almost every night at Alexander's. I made sure I slept at the shop one night a week, just to make sure I was keeping some independence, but it was scary how quickly friends with benefits had evolved into whatever this was.

A situation-ship?

Neither of us spoke about it. It was like if we carefully avoided the topic then nothing would change, and we could just casually keep pretending that we were just friends who occasionally scratched an itch for each other.

Except it wasn't occasional.

And it was starting to feel like a lot more than just friends. I'd never had a boyfriend that I'd wanted to spend every night with, not that we were boyfriend and girlfriend. But I thoroughly enjoyed his company. He was quiet, reserved, but incredibly attentive. *A bonus from his career choice, according to him.* Dinners were fun together. We talked as we cooked, and I felt as though I was learning just as much about Scotland as I was him. He was fascinating. Looking after Tattie was enlightening. My life just felt so ... full.

Jessica was beside herself, threatening to fly over herself if we didn't own up to the fact that we were, in fact, dating. I threatened to disown her if she did. I wasn't ready to admit the depth of my feelings for Alexander, even to myself, and the last thing I needed was Jessica to be a wrecking ball in my carefully constructed fantasy world I was living in.

But, oh my, was Alexander an incredible human being.

I think my favorite was watching him with Tattie. Every morning he'd go out and take his coffee with Tattie, no matter the weather, and soon the puffin was coming to hang out by his side, taking the fish he offered. He talked to him the entire time, too, telling Tattie about the window competition or random current events. The puffin listened, I swear he did, and the two made an oddball pair that pulled at all my heartstrings.

But it wasn't just his care with Tattie that made him so amazing, it was his care with everyone. The man was a natural-born nurturer, and even though he professed to have social awkwardness, he still managed to show up for the people in his life.

He started buying lemons when he discovered I liked to drink lemon water first thing in the morning. He moved my bookshelves for me whenever I wanted and was slowly helping me recategorize the shelves so they weren't such a disorganized mess. He bought me bright pink gloves when he realized I didn't have any. He complimented me constantly and basically had me convinced that my body was his own personal nirvana.

He bought Meredith an alien key ring.

He drove Esther two towns over to check out a bookshop that catered to romance-only books.

He helped Cherise when her computer broke.

Whether he knew it or not, Alexander was an integral part of this community, and the Book Bitches had even managed to bully him into letting them meet Tattie. Much to his horror, they were now threatening to hold their book club meeting at his house every Thursday night, just so they could check on the little puffin.

But he had made a fresh loaf of bread and homemade soup when they'd come by.

How any woman could have hurt this poor man's heart was beyond me.

"What's it going to be for the last one?" Esther demanded, referring back to her whiteboard. "Narnia might be fun."

"I really like the *Alice in Wonderland* idea. It could be fun to dress all the characters in Christmas outfits instead of their usual. Think of the Cheshire cat with a Christmas bow tie," I said. I could identify a bit with Alice, I supposed, going down the rabbit hole into an entirely new existence. Alexander gave me an approving smile, and I warmed inside. That happened pretty much every time I looked at him.

"I think it would be a lot of fun," Meredith agreed.

"I don't hate it," Esther admitted, which was high praise from her.

"All in?" I looked around and everyone nodded. "Esther, will you draw this one up?"

"Of course, I'll get on it right now."

The rest of the ladies cleared out and Alexander helped me take the cups to the kitchen. I had to open soon, and I knew he had some end of term paperwork to deal with for work.

"Hey," Alexander said, wrapping his hands around me from behind at the sink, nuzzling his face into my neck. "What are you doing for Christmas?"

"Oh. I don't have any plans. Probably just watching Christmas movies here." I couldn't believe that I hadn't given much thought to how I would spend Christmas, but I never had been one to make a big deal of the holiday. With a non-traditional mother who barely remembered my birthday, it wasn't like I'd grown up with the usual Christmas routine of presents under the tree.

"Would you like to do that at my place? Tattie mentioned he has a gift for you."

Wiping my hands on a cloth, I turned in his arms.

"Is that right? Tattie has a gift for me?"

"He does."

"Not his father?"

"Me? I mean ..." Alexander bit his lower lip, holding back a laugh, and I grinned.

"You didn't have to get me anything."

"I know. I just ..." He looked around to make sure Esther wasn't going to pop her head in and interrupt us. "I've been thinking a lot about us."

"Is that right?" A thrill of excitement tugged at my heart. "And what have you been thinking?"

"That I like you."

A smile split my face. "Well, I like you too, Alexander."

"I mean more than that. More than our arrangement." His look grew serious, and I stilled, tilting my head in question.

"I didn't think I'd ever be here again, Rosie. Truly. And I know it seems a little fast, but I'm just ... I don't know." Alexander shook his head and laughed. "I feel good, you ken? About us. I feel like this is right. I don't want to dance around and pretend like I don't or keep it to just friends with benefits."

"What are you saying?" I asked, my heart thumping in my chest.

"It's wild to me, that I've been so resistant to even the possibility of dating. And then suddenly, poof! There you are and now you're all I can think about. I want this to be real. Boyfriend and girlfriend. Partners. A couple. However you want to say it." Alexander looked at me hopefully.

"Well, sir," I said, surprised to find I was equally as thrilled at his words. "As an early Christmas gift to you, I will say yes. Yes, I will be your partner."

Alexander sealed it with a kiss so hot that I almost forgot Esther was there until she called out.

"Do you need me to leave? I'm getting all heated just from the fumes off you two."

We jumped apart, guilty.

"I've gotta run. Catch you later?" Alexander gave me another lingering kiss and I shoved him off me.

"See you later."

Alexander pretended to tip a fake cap to me and then disappeared. Grinning, I gave a big sigh of relief. He'd articulated what I'd been thinking. What a breath of fresh air it was to be dating an actual adult who was direct with his feelings toward me.

Humming, I wandered back out into the shop and found Esther sitting at my front table, sketching out the window design, a fancy box of markers at her side. And by fancy, I meant an actual wooden box with flowers burned into the outside, and the markers laid out neatly inside.

"That's pretty," I said, running a finger over the box. "Where did you get that?"

"Get what?" Esther stayed focused on her drawing, steadfastly not looking up from her paper.

"This." I tapped the floral box and waited.

"Nowhere." Esther's face was a mask. I gave her a curious look. That was odd.

"This pretty box? That happens to look handmade? You just got from nowhere? It just showed up one day?" I wasn't sure why I was pressing this issue, but Esther was acting weird, and something niggled in my brain.

"So you and Alexander?" Esther began, still not looking up at me.

Grabbing the box off the table, even as Esther made a soft sound of protest, I lifted it above me.

"'Create beautiful art. Love, Daniel,'" I read out loud, my mouth dropping open. "You little sneak."

"I am not a sneak," Esther declared, rising from the chair and grabbing the box back from me.

"You told us you weren't interested in him."

"I wasn't."

"Clearly he's interested in you."

"Of course he is. Who wouldn't be?" Esther looked at me like I was out of my mind.

"And you like him," I said, not answering her question.

In response, Esther shrugged.

"Oh, come on," I groaned. "He seems really great. And he's handsome too."

"I suppose."

"Esther." I widened my eyes at her. "What gives? Are you embarrassed of him?"

Esther rose and walked to the other side of the room where the tea tray and biscuits had been set up by the statement wall I'd been working on. She picked up a biscuit, dropping onto a chair, so I joined her.

"I'm not ready to share it with everyone yet," Esther admitted in a rare moment of vulnerability. "Right now, it's this perfect thing that's just mine. Nobody can pick it apart or tell me why it wouldn't work out."

"Oh, Esther." My heart twinged. "I *so* understand that." It was what I had been doing with Alexander really. Keeping it just mine for a little longer, existing in this precious space of the unknown where if there were no expectations to be made, none had to be met.

"I figured as much, what with all the sneaking around you've been doing with Alexander."

"I do not sneak," I said, tapping a finger at my chest. "I walk confidently, like the strong woman that I am."

"Speaking of strong women, have you found a match for Sarah yet?" Esther asked, diverting the conversation.

"No, I'm working on it, but the magick is failing me. I've gone through every past customer that I think could be a match, but when I use the quizzing glass, no linking word appears." I worried my bottom lip as I thought it over.

"Matchmaking isn't an easy business. Moira wouldn't

have trusted you with it if she didn't think you could do it."

"But isn't the magick supposed to help? I should be able to make matches left and right so long as I keep using the magick. I should be able to match even the most difficult of cases."

"Like fixing your own love life?" Esther asked, teasing.

"Oh, please. I haven't done that."

"You haven't? You have the tools at your disposal. I'm not going to deny that Alexander was smitten with you quickly, but I did wonder if you'd helped it along a wee bit," Esther said.

"I—"

"Aye, Rosie." Alexander's voice cut across the shop, and I jumped as I realized he was standing across the room, his eyes burning a hole through me. "Did you fix yours then?"

"I never ..." I said, standing, worry coursing through me at the ravaged look in Alexander's eyes. He looked like a wounded animal ready to flee.

"Esther, can you give us a moment?" Alexander asked, his voice low. Tension filled me, and I felt like I was a tightrope walker balancing on a very narrow rope.

"Fine." Esther gathered her coat and her tote, tucking her box of markers and notebook inside it. "Don't be stupid, boy."

Alexander didn't answer her, just continued to stare at me like he'd never seen me before.

"Alexander, please, let me explain."

"You're a matchmaker?" Alexander looked around the bookshop. "This is all a front?"

"It's not a front. It's really a bookstore, but it seems Moira was running a small matchmaking business out of it. One that I inherited."

"And you didn't think to tell me this?"

"I haven't gotten there yet, no."

"Because of the magick?" Alexander raised an eyebrow at me, and I tried to think of how to explain magick to my logical, pragmatic, software engineer boyfriend.

"I guess so. It's something I'm still learning. I had no idea, you see? People kept coming in and handing me twenty pounds, asking for the Highland Hearts Special. I had no idea what was going on. Until I found a letter from Moira that told me about the history of the shop and the magick that came with it." I stepped nearer, wanting to touch him, hug him, to lean into all his warmth and have him tell me it would be okay. But he stayed back, closed off to me.

"The Highland Hearts Special?"

"Yes. The magick allows you to pair people based on their favorite book."

Alexander closed his eyes, his face falling, and he nodded once to himself, as though confirming his worst fears.

"Which is why you asked me what my favorite book was."

"What? No, *no*. I was just making conversation." I

remembered now, asking him about his favorite book, but not for those reasons. I had just been interested.

"You know, it took me by surprise, I'll admit." Alexander shook his head and looked away, and the tone of his voice sent chills down the back of my neck. "Here I'd been more than happy to be alone. I was happy. Content in the life I'd built for myself. Happy with my peace, you ken?"

I nodded, my heart filling with dread.

"And then boom! There you are and, all of a sudden, I'm feeling things I haven't felt in years. In years. Just out of nowhere. Bam! And you're like an addiction. I think about you constantly and can't get you out of my head. I was genuinely starting to fall for you."

Tears pricked my eyes as I began to understand where he was going with this.

"Alexander, I didn't—"

"But it makes sense now. If what you say is real about this magick of yours, I was an easy enough mark, wasn't I?"

My heart shattered.

The pain in his eyes was almost unbearable and I stepped forward to reach out to him, to make him understand that I'd never do that, but he moved out of my reach. Again.

"I promise you, it wasn't like that at all. This was all a surprise to me as well." I pointed between the two of us.

"I think it's best if we stop seeing each other," Alexander's voice rasped in the silence of the bookshop. "I refuse to be a plaything in your toybox."

"Excuse me?" Shock had my mouth dropping open. I brought my hand to my chest. "Plaything? You seemed just fine with friends with benefits, didn't you? Weren't you the one who also didn't want something serious?"

"And I'm also the one who admitted my feelings first, wasn't I? How long would you have carried on with the friends with benefits ruse when we were clearly falling into an actual relationship with each other?" Alexander demanded.

"I ... I don't know. I'm sure I would have brought it up at some point?" Of course I would have. We wouldn't have continued calling each other just friends but basically living together.

"Like you did with your ex-boyfriends? The ones who you moved quietly into your life and never made a change until they did?"

Ouch. Wounded, I glared at him. "It wasn't like that. *This* is not like that."

"Isn't it though? You keep letting everyone else make the choices for you, but when are you going to make your own?"

I gasped. "Wait, so you're accusing me of not making choices yet at the same time using magick to influence our ... whatever this is?" I waved between us.

"Even now you can't say it, can you?" Alexander looked at me in disbelief. "Unbelievable. This is a relationship, Rosie. Or it was."

"Don't act all high and mighty because you just changed the nature of things like, ten minutes ago," I seethed.

"I'm upset." Alexander's hand was on the doorknob. "Trust is important to me. And this ... well, it just feels wrong. All of the magick and matchmaking. You had an entire life, a business, that you were running underground that you never breathed a word of to me. And on top of that, you used this supposed magick to influence me."

"Alexander, I swear to you that's not how it went down. I never—"

"You can say what you want, Rosie, but don't you see? Once trust is broken, it's hard to get it back. I don't want to be a part of your big life. Your *big* new adventure. I don't want big adventures, Rosie. I want a simple and satisfying life. A small life. But a good one. One that doesn't make me worry if I can trust my partner. I ... I have to go."

With that, Alexander left the shop, an icy blast of wind slapping my face before he firmly closed the door. I'd taken the bells down from the door earlier this week to fix them, and now I berated myself for not having them up. If they had been, I would have heard him enter the building and none of this would have happened.

You still wouldn't have told him about the magick. Yet.

Berating myself, I locked the door and flipped the sign to closed, not caring if the women were coming back to decorate. I needed a moment, just one moment, to myself to lick my wounds in private. Flipping the lights off, I crawled into bed and buried my face in a pillow, the tears coming fast and hot.

"And I'm also the one who admitted my feelings first, wasn't I? How long would you have carried on with the friends with benefits ruse when we were clearly falling into an actual relationship with each other?"

Was he right? Would I have let things go on as they were? *Yes.* But also no. Because Alexander was a truly good guy. He'd stopped my "pattern" in its tracks and took our relationship to the next level as soon as he realized what was happening. The man was validating me, and I'd been just quietly floating along on this river that was taking me directly toward love.

And on top of it, I'd hidden something very important from him. He was wrong about me using magick on him, but he was right about me not being honest. I didn't even know that it had been an intentional choice, so much as instinctive. The world wasn't always kind to those who practiced magick, and so I'd hidden it.

From someone I cared deeply about.

Hell, someone *I* was even falling in love with.

The tears fell harder, and I started when a hand fell on my back. Turning, I saw Esther with a worried look on her face.

"I screwed up," I said. "Also, how did you get in here?"

"Moira gave me a key years ago."

I waited for Esther to say something snarky, to tell me to put my big girl pants on and move on, but instead she did something surprising.

She hugged me.

"Don't worry, Rosie. We'll fix this. I promise we'll fix this."

"I don't know that it can be fixed."

"Och, you kids are so dramatic. Everything can be fixed. If you want it badly enough. Do you?"

"I think that I do," I cried into her shoulder, realizing that for once, I wasn't ambivalent about my life at all. I wanted all of this. The shop. The magick. The new friends. The man.

"Then we'll make it work."

It was a promise I'd have to hold on to, because in the moment, I just couldn't see how it would. Alexander already had a wounded heart, and I'd just inadvertently stomped all over it due to my carelessness.

"I don't know if we can."

"Och, lass. Do you want this?" Esther pulled back and gave me a stern look. "Really think about it. Is Alexander the one you want?"

Is he? Yes. The answer came immediately. *We just ... fit.* He nurtured when I needed it, gave me space to breathe when I craved it, and matched my quirkiness perfectly. And I'd probably shared more with him about my mom than I had anyone else. I felt like our souls completed each other. I'd found my place—*and my person*—to put down roots. I'd found ... home.

So, yes, Esther, Alexander is the one that I want.

"He is."

Chapter Twenty-Three

I t hurt to see her.

Despite our breakup, I had still gone to the shop twice that week to finalize the lighting and the music for the windows. I'd worked in silence, headphones on, ignoring even the Book Bitches' attempts at getting me to chat. I had agreed to help, and I wasn't going back on my word, but I couldn't handle anything more.

I had to force myself not to drink in the sight of her, like a hungry man craving a meal, and did my best to focus on the task at hand. It was our last window, and after that I wouldn't have any reason to go to the shop at all.

I could buy my books elsewhere. It wasn't a big deal.

The final judging was today.

And I was home, with Tattie, sitting under the lean-to in his pen, while icy wind prickled my skin. I enjoyed the sting of it, because at the very least it made me feel something. I'd been existing in a cocoon of numbness since my argument with Rosie, focusing so narrowly on every task I needed to accomplish for end-of-year projects and grading at work, that I'd kept myself from feeling anything at all.

Now, as I knew everyone would be at the shop for the final window judging, and I sat here alone with Tattie, I couldn't help but feel it all.

I was lonely.

Tattie hopped over and pecked at my shoelace, a new favorite activity of his. I never tried to approach him, but let him come to me as he was comfortable, and I realized that he was likely quite lonely too. Puffins were social animals, they mated for life, and they returned each year to not just their partners, but to where their parents lived. I wondered if Tattie's family missed him. I had no way of knowing where his burrow was or where he'd come from, so all I could do was give him the best life possible.

I wondered if he missed Rosie too.

Because I absolutely miss the light and laughter and joy she brought to my life.

I hadn't expected these feelings to arise, and I put the blame squarely on Rosie's shoulders.

Whether it was fair or not.

But I'd been happy before she'd come along. I'd liked my peaceful life and then she'd barreled into my world, all laughter and snark, and my world had gone from black and white to full color.

Tattie tugged at my lace.

"It's not food," I said and opened a packet of fresh herring for him that I'd brought out with me. Tattie hopped over, watching me as I filled his little toy tray that he loved, and then I handed it over to him. Delighted, he dove in, digging among the sand and pebbles for the fish. It was Tattie's favorite enrichment exercise, and Rosie had given that to him.

Rosie might be my favorite enrichment exercise.

Groaning, I buried my face in my hands. I had been right to not start dating again. It wasn't worth these complicated feelings.

My phone buzzed in my pocket and reaching in, I pulled it out, surprised to see my ex-wife calling. I almost didn't answer, but since she rarely contacted me anymore, I figured it might be something important. I also knew she'd keep calling until she got what she wanted, so best to just get it out of the way.

"Aye?" I answered, letting my head drop back against the wood, my eyes trained on the line where the slate-blue water met the misty gray sky.

"Alexander. Hello, how are you?" Tara asked.

I felt nothing when I heard her voice now. This woman, who I used to spend hours agonizing over pleasing, now elicited very little response from me. It was a good confirmation, even if it was a small win in the big scheme of things, but the last time we'd spoken over a year ago, I'd still held anger toward her.

Now I was just disinterested.

"I'm just fine. What do you need, Tara?"

"You don't have to be so short with me," Tara grumbled into the phone.

I sighed, rolling my eyes, and Tattie, seeming to understand I was frustrated, abandoned his toy to hop over to me. This time he pecked at my trousers, and I grinned at him, amused at his antics.

"You don't get my time anymore," I said, knowing that simple and direct was always best with her.

"Ugh, why do you make this so difficult? I was calling to apologize and I'm not sure I even want to anymore."

At one time, I'd wanted an apology from her, but now it didn't seem to much matter. It was amazing how time and some good self-help books had changed my perspective on things.

"Okay," I said.

Tara let out a wee keening note of frustration.

"You make things so hard. You don't have to be so black and white all the time," Tara seethed.

Was I black and white all the time? I guess I was. That was just how my brain worked. It was what made me a good engineer.

But maybe the rest of the world didn't work that way.

It would explain why I often bumped up against miscommunications or awkwardness in social situations.

"Fine, whatever." Tara blew out a breath, continuing on. "I'm in therapy now. And my therapist suggested that maybe I needed to apologize to you before I moved forward. So, I'm sorry."

269

"For what, specifically?" I asked, wondering if she really understood how outlandish her behavior had been.

"For lying to you. For cheating on you. For not appreciating what I had."

She'd appreciated me? That was new information.

"Thank you," I said, not sure what else to say. None of this mattered anymore.

"Don't you want to see me?"

"I thought you were dating someone else." Ah, it was making more sense why she'd called now. Tara had never been good with being alone. She was looking for a quick fix, someone to get her off, before she moved on to her next target.

"We broke up." Tara waited and when I didn't say anything else, because frankly, I didn't really care, she sighed heavily into the speaker.

"Don't you have something to say to me?" Tara demanded.

"You want an apology from me?" I asked, incredulous. Tattie pecked extra hard at my leg as though he agreed with me.

"Or forgiveness would work too, you know." Tara huffed on the other end of the line.

"Tara. I don't owe you anything anymore. Not an apology, not forgiveness, nor frankly, even my time." With that, I hung up and pocketed my phone, ignoring when it buzzed in my pocket again. Tattie looked up at me, and I smiled down at him and held my hand flat on the ground.

When he hopped in it, my heart lifted.

270

"It's just us, mate. But I'll take care of you. I promise."

Tattie tilted his head back and forth at my words and then seeming to come to whatever conclusion he needed to in his head, he hopped off and bounced back to his toy, digging for more fish.

Tara's call hadn't upset me, but she had given me something to think about.

Was I really too black and white when it came to relationships? Maybe I was trying to slot emotions into neat little boxes like computer code, assuming that all things would line up correctly and make sense.

But what made sense in my head, didn't feel so good in my heart.

I knew that Rosie had hidden something important from me.

But I also knew that I missed her. Desperately.

What I didn't know was how to align the two things in my mind. I had no code for this, no roadmap, no way of knowing how to resolve the fracture point. And I think, that was the crux of it for me. Without a clear path forward, my brain just kind of shut down, leaving me in this endless loop of uncertainty, my thoughts spinning into nothingness.

There had to be a way forward, but the only way I knew was the one I'd tried last time my heart had been hurting.

Bury myself in work and a new project.

I had Tattie now, and more excuses to build a bigger enrichment area for him. Maybe I would just use that as my project to dive into in order to avoid the discomfort of having no straightforward way through my feelings.

A shimmer of white against the murky gray sky caught my eye and I straightened, my eyes widening.

Gently, so as not to startle Tattie, I eased myself to standing and out of the enclosure, walking across my yard until I stood at the top of a grassy dune overlooking the sea.

The snow buntings had arrived.

A sharp pang of longing hit me, and I blinked at the sky as the birds circled, their song like Christmas bells, a sharp reminder of a woman who had also once brought color and joy to my life. My mother wouldn't want to see me like this, lonely with an aching heart, especially this close to Christmas. If ever there was a way to honor her, it would be by trying to find a path forward even if I couldn't see it yet.

I never wanted to feel like a pawn in someone's relationship game again. Tara had used me as a foil for her exploits, loving the highs and lows and the drama of it all. I hated feeling powerless, like someone was throwing firecrackers at my feet, when all I craved was predictability and a stable foundation with my partner. With Rosie, discovering she had actual magick and was using it to matchmake, well, it had thrown me back into feeling like I was constantly dodging explosions. Though the two women were night and day different, the surprise had led me to withdraw and do the one thing I'd finally prioritized in my life—protecting myself.

When my phone buzzed in my pocket again, I took it out to see a two-word text message from Esther.

She'd gotten my number from someone and had been pestering me incessantly all week, most of which I'd ignored. But I couldn't ignore this message.

> We won!

> Tell everyone I said congratulations.

> Tell them yourself. We'll be at the pub later.

But the pub wasn't where I wanted to see Rosie. I needed to get things straight in my head and have a conversation with her, and I wasn't about to do it in front of prying eyes.

> I can't tonight. Give everyone my best.

And then I turned off my phone.

Chapter Twenty-Four

Rosie

Our win had been overshadowed by Alexander's absence. Even though I'd gone to celebrate at the pub, my heart hadn't been in it, and I'd gone home early the night before.

You keep letting everyone else make the choices for you, but when are you going to make your own?

Alexander's words rang in my head. I'd repeated them to myself over and over the last few nights, agonizing over his words, little truth bombs that I hadn't been prepared to acknowledge. The fact of the matter was he was right.

I'd grown up allowing my mother to drag me every-where, accepting when she'd forgotten about me half the time, waiting for her to come back and take me somewhere else. Granted, I'd been a child, so the parent was in control, but it had established a pattern of accepting what life threw at you. Which wasn't a bad mentality to have in the grander scheme of things, but when it came to being in charge of my own life, it clearly wasn't working for me. I'd been so desperate for stability that I'd put the burden of building a foundation on my relationships instead of on myself. I needed to create my own life and my own safe space for myself. Nobody else could do that for me.

Certain that I'd found it here, in this bookshop and in the lovely little community of Kingsbarns, I knew I had to make a change. *I* could be my own stable base and provide the comfort that I'd craved my whole life by providing myself with a career that I loved and friends that made me laugh.

And love would only complement it, if I let it. I realized that I needed to be the one in the driver's seat, which sounded silly when I thought it, but I'd been in the passenger seat for too long. Now I knew what I wanted, which was a future here as a bookseller and matchmaker, and I wanted Alexander as a part of my life.

Now I just had to convince him that my actions hadn't been calculating when it had come to not sharing the matchmaking with him, more so that I was still getting my feet under me when it came to this new life. I absolutely should have shared it with him, and I would have, but I hadn't gotten a chance to before he'd discovered it.

But I had a plan. A loose one, which involved some groveling and presents for Tattie, but it was still a plan.

Zipping up my coat, and checking my face in the mirror once more, I took a deep breath.

"You can do this. Go get your man, Rosie."

Eye of the Tiger boomed from the speaker, and I laughed, giving it a thumbs-up.

"Thanks for the confidence, Moira."

With that, I snagged a card I'd written for Alexander and slipped it inside the gift bag for Tattie. Now I just had to work up the nerve to knock on Alexander's door and give it to him.

Kingsbarns had received the smallest dusting of snow that morning, enough that people were hopeful for a white Christmas, and I huddled deeper into my coat as the icy wind barreled across the fields. Still, a few people were out and about, and most gave a friendly wave as I passed. It was weird, this cheerful acceptance of newcomers in a small town, and I realized now that maybe this community was part of what my heart had been craving all along. I didn't need a big adventure, at least not how Alexander had phrased it. What I needed was consistency and stability. A small life full of simple joys was the key to my happiness, and there was nothing wrong with that. It was something my mother had never understood, or it hadn't resonated with her, and I had to accept that her path was her own. She shouldn't have dragged her daughter along on it, but that no longer mattered. What did matter was the decisions I made for myself moving forward.

I wanted to sip tea while I read books by the fire and watch the moody winter light over the ocean. I wanted to stop in the supermarket and chat with my neighbors and make friends over our shared love of books. I wanted to build a future with Alexander, if he would have me, and settle in, right here, and find our peace. Together.

Even though I talked myself up the whole way to Alexander's house, by the time it came into view, nerves derailed me. Immediately abandoning my plan to knock on his door, I veered right instead and stumbled my way over the dunes toward the beach. Maybe I needed just a few more minutes to gather my courage before I knocked.

Annoyed with myself for delaying, yet at the same time trying to give myself grace, I came out over the edge of a small cliff.

And saw a puffin struggling on the rocks.

"Oh no," I gasped, as it tried to hop about, one leg dangling at an awkward angle. Unsure of what to do, I unwrapped my scarf and crept forward hoping to catch it.

The puffin paused, tilting its head at me.

"I promise I'm just trying to help," I said, whispering softly, crooning to the little one as I crept closer. Ever so gently, I draped the scarf over the bird and scooped it up. To my surprise, it didn't even struggle. I wondered if the poor thing was simply exhausted. Bundling it inside my coat, to keep it secure, I turned on the rocks to head for Alexander's house when I caught my toe.

"Shit!" I gasped, turning to protect the puffin as I went down.

Hard.

Pain speared up my ankle and I winced as my back hit the sharp rocks. Somehow, I managed to twist my body so the puffin didn't hit the rocks. I lay there for a moment, the puffin wiggling in my arms, tears spiking my eyes as I gasped for breath. For a moment, nothing came, and panic seized my throat.

You've just had the wind knocked out of you.

I repeated it over and over to myself until I could finally drag in a shaky breath, and then another, before I shifted on the rocks and sat up. The puffin was starting to freak out in my coat, and I was worried it would hurt itself more. Easing myself forward, glaring at the deep crater in the rock that I'd missed, I tried stand.

And sat back down with a sharp cry of pain, my ankle unable to support my weight.

"No, no, no. Shh," I whispered into my coat, tears streaking down my face. Murderous dark clouds had gathered on the horizon, a winter storm rolling in fast, and I had no other option than to call for help. Fumbling about, I reached into my pocket and called Alexander.

When he didn't answer the first time, I called again.

"Please pick up, please pick up."

This time, when his voice sounded over the line, I cried even harder.

"Rosie?"

"Help me. I need help. I'm hurt."

"Where are you?" Alexander's tone sharpened and I cried harder, choking on the words.

"At your beach. I rescued a puffin and I think I broke

my ankle. I can't move." Just saying it out loud made the pain worse, and the reality of my dire situation set in. How was I going to get off this beach and save the puffin at the same time?

"Don't move."

Like I could. Alexander had already clicked off, so I just did my best to soothe the puffin, wrapping the scarf a touch tighter around its wings so it didn't flap about so much, and waited. It wasn't long before I spotted Alexander coming at a dead run over the dunes, in just gray sweatpants and a hoodie. He must have been relaxing at home in front of his fire, a spot I desperately wished I could be in right now.

"I'm here," Alexander said as he skidded to a stop by me, crouching.

I cried even harder. I couldn't seem to stop.

He'd come for me.

Without a second thought.

I loved him. Oh, God, but I loved him. The truth slammed into me, and I gasped, not from pain this time. No, from the understanding that this man had irrevocably changed my life.

"Are you hurt anywhere else? Is it just the ankle?" Alexander ran his hands across my head, checking for blood.

"Bruised, I think. But just the ankle." Angling my coat, I looked up at him through the blur of tears. "I have a puffin in here. Also with a broken leg."

"Of course you do." Alexander shifted and put his arms around me.

"What are you doing?" I gaped at him.

"Just hold tight to the puffin. I'm going to lift you."

"You can't lift me from a squat, Alexander! I'm too heavy!"

"Wheesht. Just let me carry you."

I squeaked as he did just that, lifted me from the rocks and cradled me in his arms as I held tight to the puffin, crooning into my coat. He strode across the beach, as the first drops of rain stung my face, and I burrowed deeper into his arms, my emotions an absolute mess inside me.

By the time we reached his house, an ambulance had arrived.

"You called the ambulance?"

"I didn't know how bad it was and I wanted to be sure I had proper medical help available."

A paramedic with a stretcher moved toward us and Alexander placed me gently on the stretcher.

"Here. You have to help her," I said, motioning to the puffin. The paramedic looked down at the bird and shook his head.

"I don't do birds, lass."

"I'll take her." Alexander reached for the puffin, and I handed her over, trusting that he knew what to do.

"Right to the vet? You'll make sure she's okay?" I was worried.

A brief smile crossed Alexander's face and his eyes softened when he looked down at me.

"Aye, lass. I'll take care of her."

"And this, give this to Tattie." I handed the gift bag,

which was still hanging off my shoulder, to Alexander who took it with a bemused smile.

"I will. I'll call Esther and make sure she knows where you are," Alexander said. He tapped the paramedic's shoulder, who was already urging me to lie down so he could take my boot off. "Take care of her. She's important to me."

My heart swelled.

And then he walked away.

There was nothing else to do.

Nothing else to be said.

It had happened so fast and now we both had bigger problems on our hands than our miscommunication. Alexander had to save another puffin and I had to see if my ankle was broken.

This was not how I'd planned my apology tour.

"Come on, lass, lie down. The rain's coming on something fierce."

Lying back, I blinked at the storm clouds as the rain sheeted over me and I was loaded into the ambulance.

"Do you have someone we can call, lass? An emergency contact? Or will your husband meet us?"

"He's not my husband," I said, weakly, as they slipped my boot off and stabilized my ankle. "And no, there's nobody to call."

I couldn't help but feel so wildly alone as I was driven to the hospital, realizing I didn't even have an emergency contacts list. I'd been alone so much of my life, but this was the first time I felt so bereft. I might be *important to Alexander*, but I wasn't his to claim.

I was still a stranger in a strange land. I desperately wished that Jessica would be here, my one person I could rely upon, giving the comfort I so desperately wanted.

Instead, I'd just have to figure this one out on my own.

Chapter Twenty-Five

ALEXANDER

They decided to amputate her leg.

Niall assured me that the puffin was otherwise in good health, but because of the nature of the break and how infection was setting in, losing the leg was the best choice.

I'd also decided to keep her. Niall had gently asked if I wanted to put her down, but once I explained that I'd already built a large enclosure for Tattie and was prepared to give this puffin a new home if she survived, we'd agreed that euthanasia was out of the picture. The vet would be keeping her for the next few days after the surgery, and then she'd be on limited movement for the two weeks following that. All told, she should be fully mobile and functioning within six weeks, if everything went smoothly.

I'd just returned home from the vet and was making myself a cup of tea before I showered to warm up, and then I could check on Rosie. I'd made sure the Book Bitches knew where she was and what was happening, but I wasn't sure she even wanted me around her. I'd said some pretty harsh things to her in our argument, and maybe she wouldn't be all that forgiving of me.

Spying the gift bag she'd thrust at me, I plopped down at my kitchen counter and opened it while I waited for the water to boil.

Inside was a card and another mini puzzle tray for Tattie. Handmade, with an even more intricate puzzle system, the tray would present new challenges to keep Tattie busy.

The card was addressed to me.

Slotting the envelope open, I pulled out a card with a puffin wearing a Santa hat on it. Inside, I found Rosie's loopy handwriting.

Alexander,

I want to start off by saying just how sorry I am for not telling you about the matchmaking and the magick. It was all very new to me, and I was trying to learn more about the magick, while also trying to help these random strangers who kept walking in the door and ordering a

Highland Hearts Special. I think I also wanted to keep it to myself for a bit, just to see how I felt about it, before I shared this with more people. I hadn't thought about how it would make you feel to be on the outside of this, and for that, I'm very sorry. I truly never wanted to hurt you or give you any reason not to trust me.

As for what you said about big adventures and allowing others to make choices for me, again, you weren't entirely wrong there either. And that's okay. I don't mind when someone calls me out for something that I do need to work on. Because you're right, I have sort of drifted along and allowed others to dictate my future. Coming to Scotland was the first time in a long time that I've made a significant decision for myself. And to me, this is my big adventure. Being here, meeting new people, and running my own shop—that is the adventure that I've been craving. So, no, I won't be running off and looking for more. I found what I've wanted here, in the bookshop, in this community, and with you—if you'll have me.

Love,
Rosie

My stomach twisted and my heart dropped, but at

the same time that hope bloomed. *I had been too black and white about this situation.* What Rosie said made sense to me. Of course if I'd just taken a huge leap on a new life and then discovered that magick existed on top of all that, I'd probably be cautious with whom I shared that with as well. At least until I understood it better. And I was still withholding judgment on whether magick actually existed or not, but I was Scottish, so I believed that there was often more than meets the eye.

A knock sounded on the door, and I stood, flipping the boiling kettle to off.

"Esther," I said, opening the door to the bedraggled woman. She stepped inside, shook off her rain jacket, and hung it up on the coat hook.

"I'd really hoped that the snow would stick but seems rain it is," Esther said without preamble and wandered inside.

"Ah, yes, I suppose that would have been nice." Esther stood by the window, hands behind her back, and looked out at where Tattie huddled in his wee house in the enclosure. "How's the wee lad doing?"

"He's good. Seems fairly happy."

"And you rescued another today?"

I closed my eyes. So she *had* spoken with Rosie. "How's Rosie? Is she okay?"

"Pretty bruised up. She landed hard because she was protecting the puffin from her fall, so her back took the brunt of it."

I winced, pressing my lips together.

"And her ankle?"

"Not broken, thankfully. But a nasty sprain. Which is sometimes worse than a break. We got her back home and she's on crutches."

"You were there for her?"

"Aye, lad. We all went to the hospital to make sure she didn't have to get home alone. Where were you?"

"The puffin was getting her leg amputated."

Esther sniffed, glancing at me over her shoulder, a look of derision on her face. "And were you doing the surgery?"

"What? No, of course not."

"And were you doing the follow-up care?"

"No, I'm not. But I will be when she gets out."

"I'll be needing a better excuse for why you couldn't be at the hospital for Rosie then."

"I ..." I didn't have one. She was right, I should have gone to her.

"The lass was looking for you. She's had the wind knocked out of her sails. I have to imagine it feels pretty lonely to ride in an ambulance by yourself in a new country."

I grimaced.

"I did make sure she had people who would help her," I pointed out, my last-ditch effort.

"Yes, her friends. And whatever your arrangement was, from my understanding it started as friends. Has that changed?"

"No." I dropped my head, feeling like shite about the whole situation. "In fairness, I did rescue her from the beach."

"A small point in your favor."

"Jeez, tough crowd." I went into the kitchen. "Tea?"

"Of course." Esther followed me and plopped down at my counter, twisting her hands together as she studied me. "I came here to tell you that you're a bloody eejit."

"Gee, thanks," I muttered. *Like I didn't already know it?*

"But I can tell by your face that you're hurting just as much as she is. And it's not in my nature to kick people when they're down."

"Kind of you." I poured her hot water into a mug and added a tea bag. "Milk?"

"Just a bit." Esther accepted the mug and held it in front of her hands. "Lad, do you want to be with Rosie?"

"I—"

"As in really be with her? Date her seriously? Not this sneaking around friends with benefits malarkey you two were doing."

"I do." The truth settled over me and some of the tension knotting my shoulders released. "I really do."

Esther held my eyes and whatever she found there seemed to make her happy.

"In that case, I won't be kicking your sorry arse. Instead, I have a plan."

"I'll take all the help I can get."

"Good. Now is the time for groveling. I've spoken to her best friend, Jessica, and I have some ideas."

"I'm all ears. Let's do this."

Chapter Twenty-Six

ROSIE

It was Christmas Day, and everything hurt.

I'd slept poorly through the night, wanting to curl onto my side, but the dull ache from my ankle made it awkward to do so. I'd taken one look at my back in the bathroom mirror yesterday and winced at the bruises that had bloomed across my skin. Even worse was trying to navigate around the tiny flat on my crutches. There wasn't much room between furniture for me to maneuver, so I'd largely just stayed in bed, feeling sorry for myself.

Yes, I'm aware that's dumb. I was lucky, the puffin was saved, and I had a cool new job and a new life in Scotland. But I hadn't heard a word from Alexander, had no idea if he'd even read my note, and I was in pain. So, yes, I was allowed to pout. And today was Christmas, everyone was with their families, and I'd lied to the Book Bitches about having plans. I was going to hole up under the covers and watch a movie marathon depending on what I could stream on my laptop. I'd just managed to make my way back from the bathroom and had pulled myself back under the covers. Propping myself up on the pillows, I let my head fall back and closed my eyes.

This was just a bad day. It wasn't a bad life.

My ankle would heal, the Christmas season would pass, and I would have better days.

But today? Today everything hurt. Including my heart.

The speaker in the shop flipped on and began to play *All I Want for Christmas is You* by Mariah Carey. I sighed. Moira had been good about not playing that song too much, but it did feel like a punch to the gut now that I was sitting here, single and lonely, on Christmas Day.

"Rosie?"

My eyes flipped open. Alexander.

Damn it, I was in a stained oversized Sponge Bob T-shirt and my hair was likely greasy and matted to my head. I tried to wipe the sleep from my eyes.

"In here."

Alexander appeared in the doorway, looking warm and wonderful and so sexy he took my breath away. His dark hair gleamed with a few droplets of rain, and he wore a chunky sweater and dark jeans. I wanted to hug him.

"Hey." I waved. "Sorry, but I just got back in here. I'm not getting up."

"That's all right, hen. I'll come to you." Alexander disappeared and returned with one of the velvet chairs, carrying it to my bedside. Dropping it next to the bed, he sat and simply looked at me.

The silence drew out until I wanted to squirm and just when I was going to break it with awkward conversation instead of asking the real things I wanted to know—like, do you still want to be with me?—he spoke.

"Your face is bruised."

"Oh yeah, caught a rock on the side of my face. You should see my back."

"Bad?" Alexander winced.

"Let's just say the rocks won."

"And the ankle?"

"It's nasty. It's going to take a while to heal, I'm told."

"I'm sorry. What were you doing down on the beach?" Alexander's eyes never left mine, as though every word mattered.

"I ... I, well, I was coming to drop a gift off for you and then I lost my nerve. So I decided to stroll the beach for a moment to work up the courage to come back and that's when I saw the puffin. How is she? Did she ..." I couldn't bring myself to ask if she'd made it. She had to have made it. I would have hated to go through all this for her not to survive.

"She's doing remarkably well for a bird that just lost a leg."

"Oh no," I breathed, sympathy filling me. "Will she survive an amputation?"

"Aye, lass. She will. I'll introduce her to Tattie once she's stable. By the way, the vet confirms what you already seemed to know. It's a girl."

"I *knew* it. Oh, I hope Tattie likes her." I didn't want him to be lonely forever. *I* didn't want to be lonely forever. Emotion clogged my throat, and tears pricked my eyes.

"I hope he does too. They look to be around the same age, so maybe it will work out. If he gives her a chance."

"Do you think he will?" I blinked at him, realizing we were no longer talking about puffins.

Alexander reached inside his pocket and unfolded a crisp twenty-pound note, which he handed to me.

"I'd like to order the Highland Hearts Special."

Tears flooded my eyes and I had to wipe them away with the back of my hand. Hope filled me, and I took a shaky breath.

"Of course, sir. If you could do me a favor and get my supplies?"

"No problem. Where would they be?" Alexander kept his voice very polite as though he was a paying customer and not someone who had brought me so much pleasure that I'd almost fainted from it once.

"Top drawer behind the table. Notebook, pen, magnifying glass."

When he disappeared from the room, I reached for a tissue and wiped my face, forcing myself to try and stay composed.

"Here we are." Alexander sat and handed me the supplies. Flipping to a new page in the notebook, I cleared my throat.

"Name."

"Alexander Theodore MacTavish."

I wrote it down, realizing that I hadn't known his middle name.

"All right, Mr. MacTavish, can you tell me your favorite book?"

"Yes, of course. It's *The Hobbit*. Have you heard of it?"

I grinned as the pen scratched across the paper.

"I have indeed."

"Can you tell me how this works?"

"Well, now that I know your favorite book, I'll start looking through my database of possible suitors. Once I pick a select few, I'll pair their book choices with yours and try to determine whether there are any commonalities that will result in a good pairing."

"I believe that I can narrow that database down for you," Alexander said, and my heart stood up and cheered.

"Is that so? I wouldn't want you to miss out on the full experience of my professional services."

"I'm certain you can make it up to me in other ways." His voice had grown husky, and heat flooded my body. I ached for his touch, for his nearness, and had to force myself not to throw this notebook across the room and beg him to crawl into bed next to me.

"Of course, sir. How would you like to narrow the

database? Did you have a particular candidate in mind?" I stared carefully at the paper.

"You." His voice drifted across my skin, as soft as a gentle touch, and the tension I was holding in my shoulders released.

"Yes, sir." I wrote Rosie Withers on the page and beneath it, *The Hobbit*.

"Now what?"

"Now I like to see if I can pick out the common theme in the book that resonates with both of us and we use the quizzing glass to guide us to the correct choice."

"Show me," Alexander whispered, and I took another shaky breath. He was willing to trust me, to give this magick thing a try, and I wanted him so much in this moment I could barely speak.

"I would say that there are many big themes to this book, adventure among them, but I think the commonality here likely comes down to the traits that Frodo himself embodies."

"Resilience," Alexander said, his eyes on mine. I nodded.

"I was going to say courage."

"Try it," Alexander urged.

I wrote courage carefully on the notebook and then held the quizzing glass over the page. Holding my breath, I waited.

When the word courage drifted off the page, shimmering in golden light, I half-laughed, half-sobbed.

"Would you look at that?" Alexander breathed, caught on the word dancing in the air. "Incredible."

"Isn't it?" I whispered.

"In your professional opinion, does this mean that you're my match?" Alexander asked.

"Based on my short, but highly professional career as a matchmaker, yes, I would say so."

"Good, because I was going to throw this notebook out the window if it wasn't."

I let out a laugh as Alexander leaned over and brushed the softest of kisses against me, as though I was a delicate porcelain figurine, ready to shatter at the smallest touch. I sighed into his mouth, wanting more, but he pulled back. Cupping my chin with his hand, he bent his forehead to me.

"I'm sorry I hurt you, Rosie. I'll be more careful with your heart in the future."

"I'm sorry that I didn't tell you about this. I'll be more open in the future."

Alexander pressed a tiny kiss to my forehead, and then we breathed each other's air for a moment, our future recalibrating to include each other in it. He drew back.

"I have something for you."

"You do?"

"Aye. Permission to enter?" Alexander pointed at the bed, and I patted the spot next to me.

"All aboard."

"Perfect, I'll be right back." A minute later, Alexander was back with his backpack, and he eased carefully into the bed next to me. Reaching in, he pulled out a Tupperware container and handed it to me.

"What's this? Cookies?" I popped the lid and then gaped at him as the smell hit me. "Are they cinnamon oatmeal chocolate chip cookies?"

"They are."

"These are my absolute favorite." I beamed at him. "How did you know?"

"Jessica is quite helpful."

"You called her?" At his nod, my heart leapt. The only other person who had done something like this for me had been Jessica, and that was because she was my best friend. *No, it's because she loves you and shows up when you need her.*

Like Alexander had done today.

He cared. He really cared. He'd called my friend and found out what I liked, and ... he hadn't left me alone on Christmas Day.

Alexander had showed up.

My heart fell off the ledge and completely in love with him. "Did you make these?"

"I did."

I took a bite and moaned around them. "I love you."

"Are you saying that to the cookie or me?"

I grinned around a mouthful of deliciousness. As soon as I'd said it, everything had clicked into place for me.

"I love *you* and I love these cookies," I amended.

"I love you too," Alexander said, leaning over to slant his lips across mine. I heard rustling and broke the kiss to see his hand in the Tupperware.

"Are you stealing a cookie during our *I love you* kiss?" I demanded, my mouth dropping open.

"Guilty." He shot me a cheeky grin, took a bite, and then opened the laptop he'd pulled from the bag. Settling back against the pillows, he flipped it open. "Ready for a *Lord of the Rings* marathon?"

Yup, this man had my heart. Through and through. Grinning, I snuggled down, the pain and aches forgotten.

"Hey," I said, drawing his eyes back to mine.

"Aye, lass?"

Damn it, that got me every time. Desire pooled low, even though there wasn't much to be done about it in this moment. Snuggling closer, I grinned up at him.

"I puffin love you."

Alexander threw his head back and laughed.

"I should find that annoying, yet I don't. I don't at all. I puffin love you too, Rosie."

Epilogue

ALEXANDER

The puffin puns had taken on a life of their own.

"You realize you're all out of control, right?" I said, hands on hips, scanning the group in my living room.

I was having a party of sorts.

Which surprised even me, to be honest, but once word had gotten out that I was getting close to introducing the rescued puffin to Tattie, everyone wanted to come see. I allowed it on one condition, that they stayed inside and watched from the living room windows so as not to frighten the birds on their first meeting.

It had been several weeks since Rosie's fall and she was limping along, albeit slowly. The sprain had been a particularly bad one, and she'd spent the last few weeks sitting on a chair in the shop with her foot up while the Book Bitches had free rein with running the place. Even though she complained about it at times, I think Rosie secretly loved the company.

"Feeling left out?" Esther handed me a bag and I closed my eyes briefly.

I had to open my fat mouth, hadn't I?

Sighing, I dug in the bag and pulled out a black jumper with two puffins frolicking on the front.

"Double or puffin." Damn it, but it was perfect. Sighing, I shook my head but then shot the Book Bitches a grin. "I hate how much I like this. It's perfect for the occasion."

"See, Cherise? Told ya he'd love it." Esther held out her hand and Cherise slapped some money into it, shooting me a glare.

Whoops. Grinning, I pulled the jumper over my head and turned to the room. It was more than just the Book Bitches who had joined us. Gregory, an honorary Book Bitch, was there, as were Harper, Reed, and Esther's flame, Daniel. Sarah, one of Rosie's recent successful matches, was here with her two children, though her new boyfriend was at work today.

And everyone wore a puffin-themed jumper.

Rosie wore an *I Puffin Love You* shirt, which was a particular favorite of mine for sentimental reasons. But the rest of the shirts were varied.

Puffin around the Christmas Tree.

Much Ado about Puffin.

It's all or puffin.

299

Here goes puffin.
Merry Christmas, stud puffin.
Happy Puffin New Year.
Just puffin around.
Keep calm and puffin.

It was madness. And secretly, I loved every moment of this. I was getting much better about not being such a hermit these days, and even my students had claimed to notice a difference in me.

"Shall we crack on?" I asked. Rosie would come outside with me while the rest of the group stayed inside.

"What's the new puffin's name?" Gregory asked.

I opened my mouth, but Cherise turned, wine glass in hand.

"Neeps," Cherise declared, and the room cheered.

I sighed.

"Hoping for something more prestigious?" Rosie wrapped her arms around my waist and grinned up at me.

"I was, but it was only ever going to be this, wasn't it?" I grumbled down at her.

"To Neeps and Tattie, the two cutest puffins in all the land." Esther held her glass up and the room cheered once more.

"Come on, Alexander. Time to make your first match." Rosie nudged me and, leaning on her cane, she followed me through the kitchen and to the mudroom where I'd kept, well, Neeps, in her recovery. She'd grown accepting of us quite quickly, with a particular fondness for Rosie, and my heart warmed as she bounced across the pen on one leg to greet us.

"Ready to meet a new friend?" I asked her. Crooning softly, I scooped her up and held her close, and Rosie limped to the door and held it for me as I walked outside.

It was a windy day, but remarkably, we had a bright blast of winter sunshine. Tattie poked his head out from his burrow as we approached, making his welcoming chuckle call that he liked to do when he saw us coming. Stopping by the door, I waited as Rosie unhooked it and then ducked inside.

"You okay to get in with the cane?" I asked.

"Not a problem at all." Sunlight pulled out red streaks in her hair, and it curled wildly around her head as her eyes lit with excitement. She was just the prettiest of pictures and I didn't want to be without her. Ever.

"Hey, Rosie?" I asked, still cradling Neeps as Tattie sidled closer.

"Aye, stag?" Rosie grinned up at me. She'd taken to calling me stag even when I'd explained that we didn't call the lads that here in Scotland. Something about fair is fair and all that.

"Want to move in with me?"

"Really?" Rosie beamed up at me. "I mean I guess I pretty much live here anyway."

"No, but I want you to, officially. Your own side of he wardrobe, all your stuff here, toothbrush next to mine. don't want the back and forth. I miss you on the nights ou're not here."

"Well, how can a girl say no to that?" Tilting her head up, she accepted my kiss.

Neeps chuckled in my arms and Tattie lost it.

"Oh shit, put her down. Let's see what happens." Tattie was bouncing in circles, racing around the enclosure, looking for the puffin who had called out. Gently, I bent over and put Neeps on the ground.

Rosie and I drew back slowly until we were tucked under the lean-to and not blocking the view for everyone inside the house.

Neeps looked around, tilting her head this way and that, and she fluttered her wings. Bouncing in a circle, she saw the water and headed toward the little pond.

And then Tattie saw her.

He let out a call, unlike any I'd heard before, and her head whipped up. She stayed still as Tattie raced over and the two circled each other, keeping a few inches apart.

And then ... then it happened.

Tattie moved forward and rubbed his beak against Neeps.

And she did it back.

"Oh," Rosie gasped, reaching for my hand. "They're bonding."

"They are." Wrapping my arm around her shoulder, I watched as Neeps and Tattie performed a complicated beak-rubbing courtship ritual, and joy flooded me.

He wouldn't be lonely anymore.

And neither would I.

Leaning down, I rubbed my nose softly against Rosie's.

"I puffin love you."

Cheers sounded from inside and we both laughed as Neeps and Tattie took off around the enclosure, Tattie racing on his feet and Neeps occasionally kicking off into flight to keep up with him.

"Look how happy they are."

"I am." Rosie looked up to see me looking down at her, not at the puffins. A grin split her beautiful face.

"Congrats, sir, it looks like your first match is a success."

* * *

Want to see if love blooms with Esther?
Download the bonus scene today!
www.triciaomalley.com/free

Did you love the puffin puns in Highland Hearts? Get exclusive puffin merchandise in time for the holidays! https://triciaomalley.myshopify.com/collections/the-christmas-collection

Author's Note

This year, I'll be spending Christmas in Scotland. I've been dearly missing cozying up by a fire, snow falling outside, and bundling into my winter coat to stay warm. Yes, I know that having to deal with winter constantly can be soul-sucking for many as I used to live somewhere with brutal winters. However, since I've given up my snow shovel and absconded to the Caribbean, I can't help but miss some of the good things that come with those frigid temperatures.

Writing this book in one of the hottest months of the year on a Caribbean island was a bit of a challenge, and I hope my love for all things cozy and winter still managed to shine through.

A huge thank you to my editing team who help to make my books shine: Marion Archer, Julia Griffis, and Dave Burness. Thank you for all of your help and feedback in bringing my stories to the world.

Thank you to the Scotsman for his unending support,

even when he finds me buried in blankets with the AC blasting in the middle of July while I try to write Christmas stories. The man was even so good as to host a Christmas-in-July date night for me and decorated the whole living room and put the tree out. He's a keeper!

Lastly, thank you to my incredible readers who bring me such joy with their enthusiasm for the worlds I create. Sending you all so many sparkles this holiday season!

Sparkle on!

Tricia O'Malley

Wild Scottish Knight

Book 1 in the Enchanted Highlands series

Opposites attract in this modern-day fairytale when American, Sophie MacKnight, inherits a Scottish castle along with a hot grumpy Scotsman who is tasked with training her to be a magickal knight to save the people of Loren Brae.

Read on for a sneak peek!

Sophie

What was it about death that brought out the worst in people? Most of those at the celebration of life today hadn't spoken to my uncle in years, and now I was being showered with rabid curiosity dressed up as forced condolences. Let's be honest. Uncle Arthur had been filthy rich, and everybody was here for the READING OF THE WILL. Yes, I heard it like that in all-caps whenever someone asked me about the READING OF THE WILL. I barely suppressed a hysterical giggle as I envisioned a small man with a heralding trumpet, standing on the balcony and unfurling a long roll of paper, reading off the terms of THE WILL like Oprah during her Christmas specials. *And you get a car...and you get a boat...*

I was currently winning the bet on how many times my uncle's ex-wives would try to console me, a fact which simultaneously cheered and annoyed me. There were seven wives in total, having multiplied like Gremlins being exposed to water, before his last, and my favorite, had cured my uncle of his marrying hastily habit.

Bagpipes sounded behind me, and though I wasn't usually a nervous sort, my drink went flying. Turning, I glared at the bagpiper who had the gall to wink at me. Cheeky bastard, I thought, narrowing my eyes as he confidently strode past, parting the crowd like a hot knife through butter. Suitably impressed, because the bagpipe was the type of instrument that demanded attention, my eyes followed the man as he crossed the lawn, kilt billowing in the wind.

"Damn it, Sophie." Wife Number Two glared at me and dabbed at her tweed jacket in sharp motions. "This is Chanel." The only thing tighter than the woman's severe bun was her grasp on my uncle's alimony. Before I could apologize, Number Two strode off, snapping her finger at a caterer, her lips no doubt pursed in disapproval. Only my uncle would plan and cater his own funeral. I grabbed another glass of champagne from the tray of a passing waiter.

Arthur MacKnight, of Knight's Protective Services, leader in home and commercial security systems worldwide, did not leave anything to chance. His attention-to-detail, pragmatic attitude, and strong code of ethics had rocketed his company to the top of the list. On the personal side? Arthur had been a known eccentric, disgustingly wealthy, and one of my favorite people. With a ten-figure company on the line, I guess I couldn't blame people for wanting to know the contents of THE WILL. But not me. I didn't care about the money. I just wanted my uncle back.

"Prissy old scarecrow," Lottie MacKnight whispered in my ear. As the proud owner of the title of Wife Number Seven, Lottie had withstood the test of time and had made Arthur very happy in his later years. She was creative, quirky, and the most down to earth of all the wives, and I had bonded with her instantly over our shared hatred of fancy restaurants. I still remembered giggling over a plate that had been delivered with much finesse but carried little more than a sliver of carrot with a puff of foam. Arthur had looked on, amusement dancing in his eyes, as his new wife and only niece had tried to maintain their composure in front of the stuffy maître d'.

When I was twelve, I had come home one day to the contents of my bedroom being placed in boxes by our very apologetic housekeeper. Much to my horror, my parents had informed me—via a note on the kitchen counter, mind you—that I was leaving for boarding school that same evening. Somehow, Lottie had caught wind of it and rescued me, bringing me back home to live with her and Arthur. I'd happily settled into a life of contradictions—business lessons at breakfast, fencing lessons at lunch, and magick studies after dinner. Well, not magick per se, but Arthur had nourished an insatiable love for myths, legends, and the unexplainable.

Once a year, I dutifully endured a phone call with my parents from whatever far-flung destination they were visiting. As an afterthought, I would occasionally receive inappropriate birthday gifts that would leave me blinking in confusion. A few we kept, for the sheer madness of it all, like the gold-plated two-foot penguin statue. Lottie had promptly named it Mooshy, set him in the front hall, and put little hats or bows on him depending on the occasion. Because of them, my tender teenage years had gone from stilted and awkward to vibrant and fulfilled, and I would forever be grateful.

Arthur's loss numbed me, like someone had cut out the part of me where my feelings were supposed to reside, and now I was just shambling about making awkward small talk with people who were suddenly very interested in speaking with me. Even the Old Wives Club, as Lottie and I referred to the other six wives, had made weak attempts at mothering me. Hence the bet I'd made with Lottie. Upon arrival at the funeral, the wives had besieged me, like a murder of crows dressed in couture, angry in the way of perpetually hungry people. Lottie, being Lottie, had swooped forward in her colorful caftan and flower fascinator, rescuing me from the wives by cheerfully suggesting they look for the attorney who carried THE WILL. The Old Wives Club had pivoted as one, like a squadron of fighter planes, and narrowed in on the beleaguered attorney with ruthless efficiency.

The funeral was being held on the back lawn of Arthur's estate in California, his castle towering over the proceedings. Yes, *castle*. Arthur had built his house to remind him of the castles in Scotland, much to the chagrin of the neighborhood. His neighbors, their houses all sleek lines and modern angles, had hated Arthur's castle. I *loved* it. What was the point of earning all that money if you couldn't have fun with it? Arthur had nourished a deep affection for his Scottish roots, often traveling there several times a year, and had spent many a night trying to convince me to enjoy what he claimed were the finest of Scottish whiskies. As far as I was concerned, if that was the best Scotland could do, then I was not impressed.

It was one of those perpetually cheerful California days, and the sun threatened to burn my fair skin. Arthur had always joked that he could get a sunburn walking to the mailbox and back. He wasn't far off. I'd already wished I had brought a hat with me. Instead, I slid my bargain-bin sunglasses on my nose to dull the light. Designer sunglasses were a no-go for me. At the rate I sat on my sunglasses and broke them, it was far more economical for me to grab some from the rack on the way out of the gas station.

"Nice glasses. Dior?" Wife Number Three drifted up, her knuckles tight on the martini glass she held.

"No, um, BP," I nodded. I pronounced it as Bay-Pay, skewing the name of the gas station.

"Hmm, I haven't heard of them. I'll be sure to look for their show this spring in Paris. Darlings!" Number Three fluttered her fingers at a fancy couple and left to air-kiss her way into an invitation to a yacht party.

"Break another pair of sunglasses?" Lottie asked, biting into a cube of cheese. There was cheese? I looked around for the waiter who carried that coveted tray and grinned.

"Third this week."

"That's a lot for you." Lottie turned to me, her eyes searching my face. "You okay, sweetie? This is a tough time for us. I loved Arthur, and I'll miss him like crazy, but it's different for you. He was like..."

"My father," I whispered, spying across the lawn my parents who had arrived over an hour ago and still hadn't bothered to greet their only daughter. Their indifference to my existence still shouldn't sting...and *yet*. Here we were. I tried to frame it in my head like they were just people that I used to room with back in the day.

"And as your mother"—Lottie waved a jewel-encrusted hand at my parents—"I don't care that those two idiots are here. *I'm* claiming Mama rights. So, as your mother, I want to make sure you'll be able to grieve properly. I'm here for you, you know."

"I know, I know." I pressed a kiss to Lottie's cheek, catching the faint scent of soap and turpentine. Lottie must have been painting her moods again. She was a world-renowned painter in her own right and worked through her emotions on her canvasses. All of Arthur's and my spreadsheets and business talk had made her eyes glaze over with boredom. "I don't really know yet how to think or feel. I'm numb, if I'm being honest."

"Numb is just fine. As Pink Floyd would attest to... it's a comfortable place to be. Just live in that space for a little bit and we'll handle what comes. What about Chad? Or is it Chet?" Lottie affected a confused expression, though I knew very well she knew my boyfriend's name.

My boyfriend, Chad, was good-looking in a polished private school kind of way, and at first I'd just been drawn to someone who'd paid careful attention to me. Now, as I watched him schmooze my parents—*not that he knew they were my parents*—I felt an odd sort of detachment from him. Perhaps that was grief numbing my feelings. Or maybe I liked the idea of a Chad more than an actual Chad himself.

"He's been very supportive," I told Lottie. Which was true. Chad had doted on me constantly since Arthur had died, but so had all my new besties that had crawled out of the woodwork upon the news of Arthur's death. Lottie patted my arm and turned as the celebrant began speaking.

The words flowed over me, intertwining and blurring together, as my own memories of Arthur flashed through my mind. Our heated fencing battles—a sport Arthur had insisted I learn—his quirky obsession with all things Scottish, his willingness to always listen to any new ideas I had for the company, and the way he'd always called me his wee lassie. No, I wasn't ready to say goodbye.

"Oh, shit." Lottie gripped my arm, her fingers digging into the soft flesh, and I pulled myself from my thoughts to see what had distracted Lottie.

The bagpiper had returned to the back of the crowd, having circled the lawn, and now stood waiting for the celebrant's signal. Behind him, Arthur's five Scottish Terriers tumbled about.

"Did you let the dogs out?" I whispered, horror filling me. Arthur's Scotty dogs, while decidedly adorable, were quite simply put—terrors.

"No, I didn't. But the lawyer had asked where they were..." Understanding dawned and we turned to each other.

"Arthur," I said, shaking my head.

"That *crazy* man. God, I loved him." Lottie brushed at a tear as the wail of bagpipes began again and the kilted man once more strode forward.

Amazing Grace. For one haunting moment, the music transported me to another time where I could just imagine a Scottish warrior crossing the land in search of his love. Romantic thoughts which had no place here, I reminded myself, fixated on the bagpiper. The dogs bounced after the man like he was a Scottish Pied Piper, and only then did I see that one of them carried a large stuffed Highland cow. *Coo*, I automatically corrected myself. A heiland coo had been one of Arthur's favorite things to photograph on his travels to Scotland, and he'd even talked of developing a Coo-finder App so that the tourists could more easily get their own photographs.

"You don't think..." A thought occurred to me, but it was so ridiculous I couldn't bring myself to say it.

"Nothing that man did surprised me." Lottie chuckled. We watched with horrified fascination as the dogs reached the front of the funeral gathering. The Old Wives Club shifted in unison, likely due to the possibility of getting dog hair on their Chanel, and I couldn't look away from the impending doom. It was like watching a couple fight in public—I knew it was bad to eavesdrop, but I always wanted to listen and pick whose side I was on. Spoiler alert. I usually sided with the woman.

"Tavish and Bruce always fight over toys," I hissed as two of the dogs separated themselves from the pack, their ears flattening.

"Arthur knows...*knew* that," Lottie said, her hand still gripping my arm. I winced as it tightened. A gasp escaped me when the dogs leapt at each other. Houston, we have a problem.

A flurry of barking exploded as the last notes of *Amazing Grace* faded into the sun and the bagpiper strolled away seemingly unconcerned with the chaos he left in his wake. Maybe he was used to it, for the Scots *could* be unruly at times, and this was just another day's work for him. I grimaced as Tavish and Bruce got ahold of the coo, each gripping a leg, and pulled with all their might. The celebrant, uncertain of what to do, walked forward and made shooing gestures with his hands.

The dogs ignored him, turning in a manic circle, whipping their heads back and forth as they enjoyed a fabulous game of tug. Growls and playful barks carried over the stunned silence of the gathering, with everyone at a loss of how to proceed.

With one giant rip, Bruce won the toy from Tavish and streaked through the horrified crowd. A fine white powder exploded from the coo, coating the Old Wives Club, and spraying the front line.

"His ashes," I breathed. My heart skipped a beat.

"Indeed," Lottie murmured.

Bruce broke from the crowd and tore across the lawn toward the cliffs, the rest of the dogs in hot pursuit, a doggy version of Braveheart. Tavish threw his head back and howled, and I was certain I could just make out the cry for "freeeeedom" on the wind.

The wind that now carried a cloud of ashes back to the funeral gathering.

Pandemonium broke out as the crowd raced for the castle, trying to beat the ash cloud, while Lottie and I stood upwind to observe the chaos from afar. A muffled snort had me turning my head.

"You can't possibly be..." I trailed off as Lottie pressed her lips together in vain, another snort escaping. To my deep surprise, the numb space inside of me unlocked long enough for amusement to trickle in. In moments, we were bent at the waist, howling with laughter, while the Old Wives Club shot us death glares from across the lawn.

"Oh." Lottie straightened and wiped tears from her eyes. "Arthur would've loved that."

I wrapped an arm around Lottie and watched Wife Number Three vomit into a bush.

"It's almost like he planned it." As soon as I said the words, I *knew* he had. Raising my champagne glass to the sky in acknowledgement, I felt the first bands of grief unknot inside me. He'd wanted us to laugh, as his last parting gift, to remember that in the face of it all...the ridiculous was worth celebrating.

Wild Scottish Knight
Book 1 in the Enchanted Highlands series

Also by Tricia O'Malley

The Isle of Destiny Series

Stone Song

Sword Song

Spear Song

Sphere Song

* * *

A completed series in Kindle Unlimited.

Available in audio, e-book & paperback!

"Love this series. I will read this multiple times. Keeps you on the edge of your seat. It has action, excitement and romance all in one series."

- Amazon Review

The Enchanted Highlands

Wild Scottish Knight

Wild Scottish Love

A Kilt for Christmas

Wild Scottish Rose

Wild Scottish Beauty

Wild Scottish Fortune

Wild Scottish Gold

* * *

"I love everything Tricia O'Malley has ever written and Wild Scottish Knight is no exception. The new setting for this magical journey is Scotland, the home of her new husband and soulmate. Tricia's love for her husband's country shows in every word she writes. I have always wanted to visit Scotland but have never had the time and money. Having read Wild Scottish Knight I feel I have begun to to experience Scotland in a way few see it."

-Amazon Review

Available in audio, e-book, hardback, paperback and Kindle Unlimited.

The Wildsong Series

Song of the Fae

Melody of Flame

Chorus of Ashes

Lyric of Wind

* * *

"The magic of Fae is so believable. I read these books in one sitting and can't wait for the next one. These are books you will reread many times."

- Amazon Review

A completed series in Kindle Unlimited.

Available in audio, e-book & paperback!

The Siren Island Series

Good Girl

Up to No Good

A Good Chance

Good Moon Rising

Too Good to Be True

A Good Soul

In Good Time

* * *

A completed series in Kindle Unlimited.

Available in audio, e-book & paperback!

"Love her books and was excited for a totally new and different one! Once again, she did NOT disappoint! Magical in multiple ways and on multiple levels. Her writing style, while similar to that of Nora Roberts, kicks it up a notch!! I want to visit that island, stay in the B&B and meet the gals who run it! The characters are THAT real!!!" - Amazon Review

The Althea Rose Series

One Tequila

Tequila for Two

Tequila Will Kill Ya (Novella)

Three Tequilas

Tequila Shots & Valentine Knots (Novella)

Tequila Four

A Fifth of Tequila

A Sixer of Tequila

Seven Deadly Tequilas

Eight Ways to Tequila

Tequila for Christmas (Novella)

* * *

"Not my usual genre but couldn't resist the Florida Keys setting. I was hooked from the first page. A fun read with just the right amount of crazy! Will definitely follow this series."- Amazon Review

A completed series in Kindle Unlimited.

Available in audio, e-book & paperback!

The Mystic Cove Series

Wild Irish Heart

Wild Irish Eyes

Wild Irish Soul

Wild Irish Rebel

Wild Irish Roots: Margaret & Sean

Wild Irish Witch

Wild Irish Grace

Wild Irish Dreamer

Wild Irish Christmas (Novella)

Wild Irish Sage

Wild Irish Renegade

Wild Irish Moon

* * *

"I have read thousands of books and a fair percentage have been romances. Until I read Wild Irish Heart, I never had a book actually make me believe in love."- Amazon Review

A completed series in Kindle Unlimited.

Available in audio, e-book & paperback!

Stand Alone Novels

Highland Hearts Holiday Bookshop

As Christmas looms, and lonely hearts beg for love, I'm tossed into the world of magic and romance, aided by a meddling book club who seems more interested in romance than reading.

Ms. Bitch

"Ms. Bitch is sunshine in a book! An uplifting story of fighting your way through heartbreak and making your own version of happily-ever-after."

~Ann Charles, USA Today Bestselling Author

Starting Over Scottish

Grumpy. Meet Sunshine.

She's American. He's Scottish. She's looking for a fresh start. He's returning to rediscover his roots.

One Way Ticket

A funny and captivating beach read where booking a one-way ticket to paradise means starting over, letting go, and taking a chance on love...one more time

10 out of 10 - The BookLife Prize

Contact Me

I hope my books have added a little magick into your life. If you have a moment to add some to my day, you can help by telling your friends and leaving a review. Word-of-mouth is the most powerful way to share my stories. Thank you.

Love books? What about fun giveaways? Nope? Okay, can I entice you with underwater photos and cute dogs? Let's stay friends, receive my emails and contact me by signing up at my website

www.triciaomalley.com

Or find me on Facebook and Instagram.
@triciaomalleyauthor

Made in the USA
Las Vegas, NV
10 December 2024

13754179R00198